slim
to
none

Cedar Tree series #1

FREYA BARKER

SLIM TO NONE
(Cedar Tree, Book One)

Copyright © 2014 Margreet Asselbergs as Freya Barker
All rights reserved.

This book is a work of fiction and any resemblance to any person or persons, living or dead, any event, occurrence, or incident is purely coincidental. The characters and story lines are created and thought up from the author's imagination or are used fictitiously.

Cover Design:

RE&D - Margreet Asselbergs

Editing: Dana Hook/Karen Hrdlicka

DEDICATION

To Linda, my 'twin',
who made me fall in love with Colorado,
and reminds me to appreciate the 'smaller' things
in life.
Who cares for many,
but allows only few to care for her.
Who is the strictest of taskmasters
but encourages everything I undertake.
Who is one of the smartest women I know
and still remains the salt of the earth.
Who is my best friend...

TABLE OF CONTENTS

DEDICATION 5

TABLE OF CONTENTS 7

PROLOGUE 9

CHAPTER ONE 14

CHAPTER TWO 22

CHAPTER THREE 29

CHAPTER FOUR 42

CHAPTER FIVE 52

CHAPTER SIX 68

CHAPTER SEVEN 79

CHAPTER EIGHT 87

CHAPTER NINE 98

CHAPTER TEN 107

CHAPTER ELEVEN 115

CHAPTER TWELVE 123

CHAPTER THIRTEEN 131

CHAPTER FOURTEEN 137

CHAPTER FIFTEEN 143

CHAPTER SIXTEEN 154

CHAPTER SEVENTEEN 161

CHAPTER EIGHTEEN 167

CHAPTER NINETEEN 174

CHAPTER TWENTY 183

CHAPTER TWENTY-ONE   190

CHAPTER TWENTY-TWO   197

CHAPTER TWENTY-THREE   203

CHAPTER TWENTY-FOUR   207

CHAPTER TWENTY-FIVE   217

CHAPTER TWENTY-SIX   225

CHAPTER TWENTY-SEVEN   229

CHAPTER TWENTY-EIGHT   238

CHAPTER TWENTY-NINE   242

CHAPTER THIRTY   250

CHAPTER THIRTY-ONE   255

EPILOGUE   260

ABOUT THE AUTHOR   262

ACKNOWLEDGEMENTS   263

Also by Freya Barker   265

PROLOGUE

"Hello?"

"Hey, you…" She heard a deep sleepy man's voice.

"Uhm…hi? Do I know you?" she asked.

No clue who this person was, Emma's mind was frantically going through its databanks, trying to sort through files to find a matching sexy, dark sounding voice, but…nothing. She had no clue as to who she was talking to, but he sure sounded good, even from those two raspy words.

"Sure you know me, babe…"

"Erm, nooo…actually, I really don't. I think you may have a wrong number… Who are you trying to call?"

"My friend, Katie," he said, sounding a little more awake now, "but now I think I'd rather talk to you…"

She couldn't help the snort that escaped her. Seriously? Maybe fifteen years ago, but now? Being middle-aged, probably wearing the same damn thing she wore yesterday–she couldn't even remember. Barely able to get one foot in front of the other, having a body that long ago had given up on her; fighting an ongoing battle with gravity, and proudly hosting the battle scars of pregnancy, surgeries, illness…yeah right! It wasn't pretty, so she needed to set him straight.

"You don't want to talk to me, trust me."

"Oh, but I do. You sound so fucking sexy…"

OMG. He is delusional! And he just growled that out…in her ear, over the phone. She didn't even know this guy, but he still he had her all flustered. Emma was starting to have a little freak out. Should she hang up? Play along? No, she should definitely hang up…shouldn't she? More than a small part of her was intrigued. Shit like this didn't happen to someone like her, to anyone, really, ever.

She tried, "Listen…what's your name?"

"Why is that important right now? Don't you enjoy the mystery of this little chat?" He chuckled. A nice deep vibration rumbled over the line.

"Okay, fine. Listen, you truly don't want to talk to me; believe me. If you knew who you were talking to, you'd be off the phone in a heartbeat. I'm forty-seven years old, have an adult daughter, and by the sounds of you, you..."

"I'm what? I don't care how old you are; you have an amazing voice. Besides, you have no idea what I like or don't like. Your voice is sexy as hell, and you already have me hard has a rock here."

A puff of air left her mouth as it fell open, and a hot flush reached up to her hairline. It was unbelievable that this guy was actually turning her on. Knowing that continuing a conversation like this with a total stranger, she was playing with fire. It had Emma's imagination going in all kinds of kinky directions, thanks to her well-hidden addiction to those deliciously smutty romance books.

His deep voice cut in, "Let me tell you what I want to do to you. I want to slide my hand down your body, feel your soft skin, and dip my fingertips inside your panties…Are you wearing panties?"

She swallowed, starting to breathe a little harder now. She couldn't help but clench her thighs; not quite sure whether it is was to stop the tingling or increase the friction.

Finally, she answered him, "…um…yeah?"

"Do you shave?"

Fuck…seriously? Was she seriously going to do this? Talk dirty on the phone with…well, whoever the hell he was? She was wet already. Damn. However, it could be worth it, "…yes, bare."

He groaned out, "Fuuuck, that's so sexy. I want to lick your bare pussy, trace your lips until I find your clit, and rub my face between your legs. Then I'm going to sink my tongue deep inside you, to really taste you. Christ, I want to devour you; have your juices all over my face."

His irregular breathing was obvious over the phone…Christ, was he…

"Are you jacking off?" Leave it to her to state the obvious.

"Sooo good, baby. I bet you taste so good. I'm sliding two fingers in your pussy, pumping you while my lips and tongue play with your clit. Jesus, you are so wet for me. I want you to touch yourself for me."

Beet-red and panting, both mortified and hungry for release, Emma couldn't recall ever being this turned on. This man's dirty-talk was doing a number on her; had her primed and ready with just the sound of his voice…she had already been close to coming.

With a quick peek around, just making sure that no one could see her, she let her free hand slide down between her slick labia, and then, just like that, with barely a need to touch herself, an embarrassing squeal escaped as Emma experienced the first real intense orgasm she'd had in decades.

On the other side of the line, the voice could be heard groaning loudly…then nothing: just two people breathing heavy over the phone.

Suddenly, intensely mortified at the decidedly unconventional situation, and how she completely let herself go with a stranger, Emma quickly mumbled,

"Sorry, I…I've gotta go," and finally hung up the phone. Flushed, and more than a little shaky, she grabbed her cane to make her way to the kitchen. She desperately needed a cup of coffee for fortification, and some semblance of normalcy, while trying to make sense of what the fuck just happened…Holy hell.

Fuck me! Talk about intense. That had to be the strangest, and hottest, telephone conversation he'd ever had. He sank back on to the rickety motel bed where he was staying for the night. He needed to take five minutes to catch his breath after that surprising, mind-blowing orgasm. He had to be up and out soon to meet with Joe Morris, his contact at the Montezuma County Sheriff's Department.

What the hell number had he just called? It just dawned on him that he got the relief he was looking for, but it sure as hell hadn't been Katie on the other end. Katie was always convenient in a pinch, but neither of them had any expectations: never had, never would; just friends with benefits who would scratch each other's itch every now and then. His work didn't really allow for anything more involved, and even if it did, Katie wouldn't really be in the running. She liked playing things loose, but she served his needs...for now.

Just as he was about to roll out of bed and hop in the shower, the phone rang.

"Flemming."

"Hey, Gus, it's Joe. Did you get any hits yet?"

"Joe, I was just about to have a shower and then call you. Yes, one of my guys were able to pull an IP address off Corbin's server yesterday, and traced it to an account in Cedar Tree. Just got the number last night." That's when it hits him. The number he had accidentally dialed this morning...it was the number he wrote down last night, the one his computer guy, Neil, called in. Shit, that was not smart. Still groggy this morning, he must have dialed the last number he memorized by mistake–his lead. Damn, it was a woman, a sexy one at that, if her voice was anything to go by. He knew he'd better tread carefully, or he could blow this case.

"Hey, buddy, you still there?"

"Shit, sorry, Joe, yeah...just thinking over some details. I think I'm going to move very carefully with this lead. Corbin has kept a step ahead of us since skipping bail, and so he's probably waiting for us to pick up on this lead. They're either working with him, or they could be in danger if he thinks we are close. Either way, we can't just barge in."

"Which is your job, Gus. You know we don't have the manpower, the resources, or the patience to finesse a case like this, but we need our hands on Corbin before he ties up all his loose ends and disappears completely on us."

CHAPTER ONE

"Em, you in here?" The door slammed open as Arlene made her usual noisy entrance.

"Kitchen!" she hollered back, neither one of them skimping on their volume. No need, since Emma lived a little off the beaten path, just outside Cedar Tree, Colorado. A mere blip on the map as it was, and she still found a dead end dirt road to live on. She liked her privacy, that was to say, as long as there were pretty views to look at, and boy, they didn't come much prettier than the ones here. The back of the house–cottage probably was more appropriate since it was definitely a one-person deal–looked in the direction of Mesa Verde. There were mountains in the distance all the way around. Fragrant sagebrush and yucca dotted the front of the house with a wrap-around porch to enjoy it all from. Everything was on one level, with a hallway from the front, all the way to the kitchen in the back. Down the middle were the bedroom, a tiny storage closet, and bathroom on the right. To the left of the hallway was the living space. It included a sitting room, a workspace, and a dining area, opening up to the kitchen with a counter and stools; all was easily accessible.

Two months ago, Emma moved to Cedar Tree to finally get away from the big city, where the speed of life had finally gotten to her, along with the stench, bricks, and steel that were everywhere you looked. With her daughter, Kara, grown-up and settled, there really wasn't much holding her back. It had been a long time since she had made a choice, based on what it was she wanted, after a lifetime of putting other people's needs first. What Emma wanted was to move closer to her best friend in the whole world, Arlene Bowers.

Arlene owned and ran the diner in Cedar Tree. They met in an online support group a few years back, and they just clicked. When Emma received a settlement a few years ago, she managed to visit Arlene, and got her first taste of the Four Corners area of Colorado…She was sold. She absolutely loved the area, and Arlene instantly, and vowed that if ever given the chance, she'd pack up and move there.

So there she was, a trailer load and a week's worth of driving. After about two months of settling in, she had her bestie hollering down the hallway.

"Em, I picked up your mail for you since I was in town."

"Thanks, hon, put it down on the counter, I'll get to it in a bit. You want some coffee? Just made it fresh."

"Yeah, I have time for a cup, but remind me to haul the groceries in that I have in the back of the truck for you. Went into Cortez for supplies and picked up some good deals; I thought you could use a few things."

"Wish you would have told me, Arlene, I would have gone with you. I wanted to head in to send a package through FedEx to Kara, so it would get there in time for her birthday."

"Why don't you let me bring it into the post office here?" Arlene asked.

Emma snorted, "Seriously? You do remember how long it took for your packages to get to me whenever you sent something, right? Wasn't it you who told me, your post office was like the Bermuda Triangle? Some things were never seen again? No thanks, I'll play it safe."

Arlene shrugged. "Fine, I'll be going again in a few days, so

I'll give you a heads up. You don't want to go in by yourself?"

Emma hesitated, not sure if she should tell her or not.

"Well, it's just…the last few weeks, the few times I've gone into Cortez for my appointments, I got this uncomfortable feeling."

Arlene's eyebrows shot up. "What do you mean, uncomfortable? You don't feel safe driving anymore? Do you need to see a neurologist again?"

"God, no, nothing like that, woman. What I mean is that I keep seeing the same truck every time I pull out onto the 160, into Cortez. At least, I think I do. It just seems to be sitting in that emergency stop area, just at the junction where County Road G hits the highway, and I always see it again when I get into Cortez."

"Are you serious?" Arlene looked over, slightly concerned. "That's just creepy. How are you so sure it's the same truck? Never mind, that's a stupid question; forgot for a minute, I'm asking Miss Hawkeye here, the only person I know who can spot wildlife three miles away with the naked eye."

"Oh, haha, very funny, Arlene. Just because you're blind as a bat and can't spot a bear unless you trip over it…" She took a moment to recall its description. "It's a pretty new, expensive looking truck, nothing like the kind of rust buckets you usually see on the road here, and eh…." She shrugged her shoulders, not really wanting to go into the bizarre phone conversation she had a few weeks ago.

"Spill," Arlene barked out. "I can tell you're sitting on something; you're squirming in your seat, so just spit it the hell out. You know you can tell me anything. For shit's sake, you know more about me than is healthy."

16

Emma couldn't help but burst out laughing. Arlene could be funny when she tried to be firm; one of the reasons they got along so well. She tried to be all badass, and Emma seemed to be the only one who laughed instead of cowered. Arlene pretended to be pissed off when Emma was not impressed, but secretly, she probably loved that Emma wouldn't intimidate so easily.

"Fine, I'll tell you…Geeze, woman, chill." Emma took a deep breath.

"About two weeks ago, I answered the phone to, what I know now, was a wrong number dialed, except the guy on the line didn't hang up."

"What do you mean, he didn't hang up?" Arlene piped up.

"Well, we kind of started talking and ended up…well, he started…I mean…Okay. The deal is, I had phone sex with a complete stranger," she blurted out. With eyes shut tight, Emma couldn't look at Arlene. She was fully expecting a good scolding, but she was met with silence.

Peeking over her shoulder, she saw Arlene bent over the counter, her face a dark shade of purple.

"Jesus, girl. Are you okay?'"

"Fuck me!" Arlene exploded. "Finally! You get some action, and it had to be from a stranger on the phone? I'm dying here…shit's too funny!"

"You know what? Kiss my ass, Arlene." Emma chuckled along with her.

It didn't take Arlene long to turn serious, and with her infamous evil eye on Emma, she returned to the topic.

"Are you saying you think this truck has something to do with the phone call?"

"I have no idea. It just seemed like a bit of a coincidence that the truck appeared for the first time the day after the call."

After Emma recounted as much of the conversation as she was comfortable sharing, Arlene assured her she was happy Emma got her "rocks off"–her words. Arlene told her they would drive to Cortez together next time in Emma's car, to see if one of them could get a tag number, or something, to try and at least get a better description if the truck was there again. Emma agreed. If that was the case, she'd mention something about it to the sheriff.

Not long after, Arlene brought in the groceries she picked up for her. They discussed the order for the next day, and then she took off with a wave and a yell, "Later, Em!"

She didn't seem overly concerned.

A little while after Arlene left, Emma finally got a chance to look through the mail Arlene had brought in. She was hoping to find the paycheck from one of her freelance bookkeeping jobs. Great little gigs she had managed to pick up through an online professional posting site, at least great when they paid on time. One guy had not answered any of her emails in weeks, and she hadn't received his check yet. It had only been the second invoice on that contract. Unfortunately, that was one of the risks you took with everything being done digitally and online. All they had was a post office box number in Cortez, and both she and Arlene had a key, so whoever was in town would check to see if anything was there. That way, Emma's privacy was secured, as well.

Ticked about the still missing check, Emma hauled her stool into the kitchen to get some baking done; something she had started doing since coming to town, anything to make an extra buck, so she would bake fresh pies and pastries for Arlene's diner. Since her husband left her five years ago, Arlene had been working like a dog to keep that place going. Even though she had some help, a waitress, and since recently, a short-order cook, she didn't really have time to do much baking anymore. The requests were still there though, so Emma offered to do it for her. She loved baking, but unfortunately, loved eating too.

While she was elbow deep in butter, eggs, and flour, Emma let her thoughts slip back to her anonymous caller. He'd been on her mind quite a bit over the last few weeks, getting her all hot and bothered at the most inopportune moments, but leaving her with a smile on her face every time. Dammit. It was stupid that after so many years of feeling more and more unappealing, as her body had gone into a slow breakdown, one phone call could make her feel so…desired. Ridiculous, especially since she knew damn well that whoever it was would probably be turned off if he ever saw her in person. If that didn't do it, her list of health issues would surely scare him away; but she couldn't complain, she had an amazing daughter, wonderful friends, and had chosen a gorgeous spot to live. Other than that, she didn't need much; she'd make do with the romance she got from her Kindle.

Four hours later, and feeling moderately better; her favorite black yoga pants and hoodie were covered in flour. Why couldn't she ever remember to wear an apron? With already wild enough hair buzzing around her head, now even wilder, Emma had three pies, two dozen muffins, and a couple of trays of homemade granola ready. The kitchen looked like a war zone. If only she could put the kitchen, and herself through a high-powered car wash, but the deep cleaning of the kitchen would have to wait. A simple rinse and go would have to do for Emma, since everything needed to get to the diner. The dinner crowd wanted their pies and the rest of the food was for breakfast tomorrow. It was the weekend, so it was always a little busier with families coming in.

Quickly popping pans and utensils into the dishwasher and hand-washing her beloved KitchenAid Pro, she shoved the stool back under the counter and grabbed her walker.

Thank God Arlene had known this little one-level house was up for rent. An added bonus was that the owner had renovated the bathroom two years ago for his elderly mother, who had been living here at the time, which meant an accessible shower for Emma. No climbing and clambering over and into slippery bathtubs anymore, which was a good thing, because if she ever fell out here, it could take a while for someone to find her. On a day like today, when she'd already been upright for a few hours, Emma's legs were even wobblier than normal.

Sitting on the bench in the shower, she stripped off her clothes and tossed everything into the laundry basket. Turning on the hot water, she couldn't help the pained grunt that left her mouth. Shit, her body was sore! A quick soap and rinse, and then after a perfunctory towel-dry, she was ready to get dressed for the outside world. *Not her favorite thing.* Give her yoga pants and a hoodie, comfort clothing, any day of the week and she would be a happy girl, but feeling self-conscious enough as it was, she tried to make a little bit of an effort when she stepped outside the door;

so jeans and top it was. Ugh. At least she didn't have to wear dainty shoes. She liked bare feet at home, clogs outside in the summer, and Uggs in the winter…Easy. Snorting at herself, as she got dressed, she yelled out to no one, "Out of the way, hot momma coming through."

Making two trips, with the boxes of pies and muffins stacked on the walker, to her trusty Ford Escape, and she was ready for town…well, sort of…her hair was still wet. Oh well, she'd just stick her head out the window.

CHAPTER TWO

"What can I get ya?" The tall blonde waitress, with a friendly smile and a face sprinkled with freckles, shook Gus out of his thoughts.

"Coffee, black please, and if you have it, a slice of pie."

"Coffee'll be right up, and fresh pie should be here in a few. Expecting a delivery any minute, and I'll be able to tell you your choices then."

"Sounds good," he said with a nod.

Gus turned back to the window, contemplating his next move now that he was finally in Cedar Tree. After getting a number off Corbin's hard drive two weeks ago, a hot lead had come in from Albuquerque on the case, and he had spent his time chasing down a bunch of dead ends there. Liaising with the local police department, he worked to see if anything additional could be stirred up from any of their street sources. If Corbin had been there, he had long since left. He was a step behind again. It was getting frustrating, being on this bastard's tail, but never quite getting quite close enough. Ernst Corbin was the lynchpin in the case against crime boss Bruno Silva. He had agreed to collect some additional, specific information to solidify the joint departmental task force case against Silva, in return for a reduced charge for himself. Corbin had been picked up a few months ago on fraud charges and was let go on bail, after agreeing to the deal with the DA's office. Just a few weeks later, he had vanished without a trace, and that was when Gus had been called in. After retiring from the police force, he had started his own business, running down bail jumpers and doing investigative work. His many contacts within the police force kept him pretty busy, and his great tracking record and knowledge of the area was what got him asked in on this case.

There wasn't much to go on. The only thing left was the evidence the police still held in the original fraud case against Corbin, which included his hard drive. On that hard drive, they discovered the email and attached IP address for an online bookkeeping service he had contacted, under a fake corporate name, shortly before his arrest. Gus's techie wunderkind, Neil, had been able to trace that email, and address, back to a PO box number in Cortez, which in turn, provided them with the phone number here in Cedar Tree.

So here he was, sipping on the strong black coffee the friendly waitress had slid before him moments ago, trying to come up with a good plan of approach; one that would get him in the door without raising any suspicion.

He watched as a small older Ford SUV, with a disabled tag, pulled into the parking lot, and someone with a wild riot of auburn curls peeking over the steering wheel. With the driver's door on the opposite side of him, he didn't have a good view of the driver. When he saw a deliciously ripe-looking woman, topped with a vivacious head of hair, come from around the car pushing a contraption loaded with cake boxes, it took him a minute to realize she was actually pushing a walker. Obviously disabled, she was balancing the cake boxes on the seat of the walker, while trying to get to the door. With a quick look in the direction of the counter to find no one aware of her approach, he quickly slid out of the booth, and with a few large strides of his long legs, made it to the door before her. Just as he pulled it open, he spotted the stack of boxes starting a sideways slide, and heard a loud yell, "Oh, shit, no!"

"I've got 'em," he said, startling the woman whose bright blue eyes shot up to meet his over the pile of what, he assumed, were the pies. Momentarily stunned by the fiery look she threw him, a slow grin spread over his face when he recognized it as defiance.

"Thanks, but I can handle it." She all but snapped at him. "I may look decrepit, but I think I can still handle a door. I'm not that old." Followed by a mumbled, "Not yet, anyway," as she tried to wiggle past him through the entryway.

Now full out grinning at her bluster, Gus couldn't help himself.

"Wasn't you I was worried about. I've been waiting for my pie, and figured that's what you got in those boxes. Just hungry, I guess…"

Throwing him another killer look, before making her way to the end of the counter, she yelled, "Arlene! Pies!"

"Hand them over, darlin', have someone waiting for a slice already." The tall blonde coming out of the kitchen motioned to where he sat back down, with a good view of the "pie-lady." Well, her nicely fleshed-out backside, anyway.

He never had any particular preferences, one way or another, when it came to women, or what appealed to him. Some women just did, as did whatever attributes they came with. Her ass was luscious, getting a welcome rise out of him. He better stop looking at her *attributes* right this minute, before his well-worn jeans showed the evidence of his *appreciation*. Somehow, he figured the pie-lady wouldn't take too kindly to his dick pointing in her direction...at least not yet.

"Holy crap, Arlene. Who the hell is that big hunk of man flesh?"

"Dunno. He came in, sat down for coffee, and been staring out the window." She shrugged. "You know I'm not much for small-talk. I leave that to Beth, but she called in sick earlier, so the customers have to put up with me today. Good thing it hasn't been that busy yet."

Darlene started opening up the boxes Emma brought in with her.

"Do you have any more in the car?"

"No, I brought everything in, that's why I almost didn't get through the door, and our hero, over there, had to come run and rescue the cripple." Emma chuckled. She knew damn well that she had made a bit of an ass of herself, but she hated getting caught unprepared. Not only was the guy hot, he was massive; at least six three or so, with the shoulders of a linebacker. His dark, mussed up hair was a little on the long side and greying at the temples, and his squared jaw was deliciously scruffy. The entire package was so very far out of the range of possibilities for her, she couldn't help but get self-conscious. That, of course, pissed her off, at herself mainly, and at him for making her feel like that. Poor guy didn't have a clue, but it all seemed very amusing to him, since he was still sporting that snarky grin on his face. She would love to know what that was all about.

-

"With Beth out for the day, you need any help around here with the dinner crowd coming in? I can man the register and keep the coffee fresh for ya."

"Seb's in the kitchen, and he can manage the grills on his own. I can probably handle the front end, but stay for a bit anyway…I'd welcome the company. As an added bonus, we can both enjoy the improved view we have here today." Emma rolled her eyes at Arlene when she tilted her head toward the hunk sipping his coffee, blatantly staring at them from his booth.

"Okay, let me get these boxes folded and give this the man a slice of my humble pie…I'm starting to feel bad."

"That's one of the things I love about you," Arlene snorted, as she slid a slice on a plate, "your flammable temper…such a short fuse for such a wise old lady."

"Bite me," Emma spat back at Arlene, as she carefully managed to walk the pie over to the booth.

"Was that an invitation?" He smiled at her.

Gah! Immediately flustered again, she'd forgotten what she was going to say and felt her white pasty face turn a blotchy shade of red…great, just great.

"Umm, no, that is, I was just talking to Arlene. She accused me of a short temper, and she's right," Emma said, offering him the pie. "I'm sorry for snapping at you. It was a knee-jerk reaction, I'm afraid, coupled with a long day, and erm…yeah, well…I'm sorry."

Head down, unable to look at his amused eyes for fear she would get all pissy again, Emma turned around, heading back to the counter.

"Hey!"

She heard from behind her and turned to face him.

"No problem, but...what kind of pie did you give me?"

"Oh, sorry, it's a peach pie with almonds." Emma watched as he forked a big bite into his mouth.

She stared at him a little too long, watching the movement of his full lips and generous jaw, until finally his tongue gave his lips a swipe, getting rid of any lingering crumbs. She felt a slight tingle in her rusty 'nether-regions,' seeing his mouth curve back up in that amused grin. She caught herself and turned back around when she heard him say, "Great damn pie."

Yup. That put a smile on her face.

"Ems...Frank's on the phone!"

Emma had spent the dinner hours greeting and seating whenever needed, but mostly she stayed behind the counter, manning the coffeepot and the register. Mr. Hot Guy had left with a smirk and a nod, after finishing up his pie. Although Emma felt a bit disappointed her eye candy had left, she was a lot less self-conscious moving around the diner without wondering if he was looking. Shaking her head at herself, she had to smile, *what an idiot.* What was she thinking? As if he would give her a second, or even a first look. He wasn't necessarily a 'baby,' but she was pretty sure she had at least a few years on him, and besides, he was pretty gorgeous, and she was...well...not.

Her legs and back killing her from spending way too much time on her feet for one day, Emma was about ready to go home when Arlene called her to the phone.

"Yeah, hey, Frank…what's up?"

"Problem at your house, Emma. Need you to come here," Sheriff Frank Cooper said gruffly over the phone.

"What do you mean, problem at my house? What kind of problem? What's going on?" Her eyebrows shot up as she turned to Arlene, who had walked up beside her. Emma had a feeling her quiet life in Cedar Tree might have just come to an end.

CHAPTER THREE

He had thought about starting a conversation with her, but figured it was probably not the smartest idea to make himself stand out any more than he already had; especially given that he hadn't even had a chance to get a proper lay of the land, so to speak…job first. That prick, Corbin, had been on the loose for too long already, and since he hadn't been able to run him down in Albuquerque, he would need to pick up his game to try and get ahead of him. First course of action was to find the person behind the online bookkeeping service. He had wondered over the past few weeks what the woman he had accidentally called would look like. He'd assumed the business was hers, but who was to know. He'd find out soon enough, since he was on his way to the address now.

Driving down the dirt road toward the small bungalow at the end, he was surprised when a big, new model, black Ford F150 went peeling around the far side of the house and almost sideswiped him on the narrow road. Trying to get a tag number proved to be difficult, since the license plate was covered in mud; pretty odd, since the region hadn't seen rain in a few days. Pulling up in front, Gus got out and walked up to knock on the door, noting that there seemed to be no other vehicles around; pretty secluded here. After waiting a minute or two, he tried knocking again, but when no one answered, he got down off the porch and decided to walk around to the back. That's when he spotted the open window with the torn blinds dangling out. Sliding his hand to the small of his back, where he kept his gun safely tucked, he edged up to the window, trying to get a look inside. All he could see was what looked like an office area that had been completely turned inside out: drawers pulled out, furniture upended, files and papers everywhere. Someone obviously had been looking for something, and he had a nasty feeling about it. Afraid he might have been too late once again, he was worried about what else he might find inside. Pulling his cell, he quickly dialed Joe.

"Do me a favor? I'm outside the bookkeeper's house in Cedar Tree, and it looks like someone may have broken in. I may have just passed the guy on the road coming in, so alert the locals. Tell them I'm on scene so they don't shoot me by accident."

"Stay outside, Gus. Don't go messing around with a potential crime scene!" Joe snapped.

"Easy for you to say. What if someone is in there bleeding? I'm just gonna have a peek, so make sure you tell the locals." He hung up and carefully lifted himself through the open window, moving carefully, trying to not to disturb any evidence. After checking the entire house, there didn't seem to be anyone there, but the thief had done a thorough job; the place was a mess. With most of the damage done in the office, the intruder had done a bang up job of the single bedroom, as well. They went as far as to dump out stuff from under the sink, and the medicine cabinet. Yup. Obviously not a random burglary, they were looking for something specific, and by the looks of things, the woman he talked to lived here alone. There was no evidence of anyone else here.

Hearing a car coming down the drive, Gus figured it was the sheriff's men, and decided he'd rather meet them out front than in the close quarters of the small house. So he made his way out front, and to be on the safe side, he walked out with his hands out and up.

It didn't take long after checking him for the officers to clear him and validate his credentials with the Montezuma County Sheriff's Office.

"Sheriff Frank Cooper," the burly, gray haired man introduced himself. "Good thing Joe Morris called and gave me the heads up, or things could've been mighty uncomfortable. Although, I'm none too happy that you went inside," he grumbled.

"Couldn't wait, not on the off chance that someone inside might be hurt. I didn't want to take that chance, but I took care not to stomp all over your crime scene…and I may have seen your perp, too."

"Oh yeah? How's that?"

"Black, new model F150 came tearing up the road from behind the house, just as I was turning in. Tag was all dirtied up, so I couldn't get that, but the rest of the car was clean as a whistle. Looked brand new to me, or it could be a rental."

"Did you get a look at the driver?"

"Nah. Tinted windows, and I was pretty busy trying not to get sideswiped. All I can tell you is it was a good-sized man, head close to the roof of the car. No hat, no glasses, and that's about it."

The sheriff shot him a glance from under the brim of his hat. "You think it has something to do with the case ya'll are working on?"

His eyebrows rose as he answered, "Possibly. Did Joe fill you in?"

"Some. You and I will talk some after we're done here. Anything goes on in my county, I'd like to know about it." He leveled a stern look at Gus, who met his eyes straight on.

"Fair enough. We'll talk, but let me check in with Joe first."

Frank nodded once and finally looked back toward the house.

"Well, I called the tenant; she's on her way in. Once my deputy's done clearing the house, I guess we'll go in with her and have a look around."

Okay, so she was freaking out a little. Who'd want to break into her house? Here in Cedar Tree, for Christ's sake! Arlene offered to drive her, and Seb was going to close up the diner.

"I think you should tell Frank about the truck you keep seeing," Arlene urged.

Emma's head whipped around to look at her friend with wide eyes.

"Shit. You think this has something to do with that? Great, now I'm officially freaking the fuck out. It's not like I can run away or anything, Arlene. Jesus."

Trying to calm herself down by breathing deep, she knew better than to start panicking before she got all the facts. She'd had enough bad experiences to know that much. Calm, cool, and collected–come on, Ems…get it together.

Moderately calmer when they pulled into the drive leading up to her bungalow, she could see all the lights on in her house and three cars out front; two sheriff's vehicles and one big-ass, black SUV she had seen parked outside the diner just a few hours ago!

"Frank!" Emma almost tumbled out of the car as Arlene grumbled at her.

"Hold your friggin' horses, woman! Let me get your walker before you land flat on your face, will ya?"

Pulling the walker from the back and rolling it over, Emma barely had her hands on it before she started moving toward the two men, who had turned around to face the women. It almost stopped Emma in her tracks to see the pie-eating hot guy from the diner, standing right there, next to the sheriff. What the hell?

"You that taken with her pies?" Arlene, with her smart mouth, had obviously spotted him too. His mouth pulled into a smirk.

"Is that a trick question?" he said. "Loved the pie, no denying that, but I was simply passing by here."

"What's going on, Frank?" Emma interrupted, while looking between the sheriff and the stranger.

"Seems someone broke into your house, Emma. Need you to come in with us and have a look around to see what's missing."

Slowly shaking her head, Emma was trying to make sense of what he was saying.

"Wait, I don't get it. I don't own a thing worth anything. Break in? How? And what are you doing here?" She turned to Mr. Hot Stuff, taking him in properly for the first time. Tall...so very, very tall. Of course, against her short stature, everyone pretty much seemed tall, but this guy towered over everyone there; even Arlene, who was taller than a lot of guys. He was wearing an old, brown cord jacket over a white Henley shirt. His jeans were worn, and he had on light brown boots that'd seen

33

better days. As her eyes traveled back up–way up to meet his–she noticed his dark lashes first. The dark, long fringe framed his deep brown eyes, and right now, they were surprisingly warm. Damn. Those eyes made her squirmy in an inappropriate way, given the circumstances. Holy hell…was that a hot flash? She quickly turned her attention back to Frank, before she completely embarrassed herself and started drooling on him, or humping his leg.

"Who is this, Frank?"

"Name's Gus Flemming," he rumbled from behind her. "I was the one who called in the sheriff."

"Oh yeah?" Emma whipped her head back to him. "And how did you come to find out my house was broken into? What brought you out here, anyway? Who are you?"

"Now settle down, Emma." Frank tried to calm the obviously agitated situation down a bit, especially with the overprotective–and highly vocal–Arlene, who was not too far behind in putting her two cents in. "Gus here is working with Montezuma County on a case and happened to see a truck tearing out of your drive, so he came out to check. When he found the blinds to your office dangling outside of the window, he suspected something amiss, so he put two and two together, and gave us a call. Now, Ralph is almost done in there, and then we can get on in and find out what is what. Why don't we sit down on the porch for a spot, you look ready to drop."

Arlene grabbed her arm and almost hoisted her onto the porch.

"When the heck are you gonna get that ramp installed, Ems? Thought you said you had some contractor lined up to come look and quote you?"

Emma slowly turned her head to Arlene and gave her an incredulous look.

"Seriously? You're picking now to scold me over a ramp I haven't had installed yet? Need I knock something over your head to clear the obvious fog that resides there, so you might realize, I have other priorities right now? I can't even think straight."

Dropping her head in her hands, her fingers scratched her curls into an even bigger frenzy. She lifted her head and speared Gus with a glare.

"Wait a minute! Gus, right? Are you a cop? What case? I'm the only one who lives here, so does this have to do with me? Were you looking for..."

Throwing his hands up, Gus interrupted, "Whoa. Hold on with the fifty questions. I'll explain as best as I can, but let's do things in order, okay? Let's deal with this break-in first."

"Were you spying on me?" Emma narrowed her eyes at him. "At the diner? Were you there because of me?"

"Can't say I won't be next time I show up, but today, no. I was simply having a coffee after a long drive."

"Hey there, Emma, Arlene." Ralph appeared on the porch carrying some bags and a case. "Sheriff! All done in there, so it's all yours."

"Thanks, Ralph. Come on folks, let's see what we have."

Not a very pleasant experience, to say the least, knowing that someone has gone through your stuff; been in your house, in your space…your sanctuary. It feels like a violation of some kind.

Emma left the walker outside and took her cane out of the clip as she followed the sheriff into the hallway. At the far end, she could already see the disaster that had been her relatively neat kitchen. Groaning, she turned toward the living area, which was just as big of a mess. She was so, so tired already, and trying hard to tough it out through her pain, but she finally lost it when she turned into her bedroom, where everything–absolutely everything–was upended, torn, and thrown around. Even the photos she had hanging on her wall were flung through the room. Unable to hold back anymore, she sagged against the wall, her knees buckling as the tears started running down her face.

"Ahh, geeze, honey." Arlene hurried over, trying to keep Emma upright in a hug. "That's all you need, right? Like you don't have enough on your plate already. Come here."

Emma could feel someone move in behind her, holding her up as she heard Gus's voice say to Arlene, "Why don't you make some room on the couch? I'll get her over there." No longer caring, she let herself be held up by two strong arms as her cane clattered to the floor. One arm hooked around her waist, the other behind her knees, and before she knew it, she was lifted off the ground. Turning her face into his body, she managed to mumble, "Your back may not survive this little breakdown of mine…"

"Nah. I like my hands full," his deep voice rumbled from his chest.

After settling Emma on the couch with a cup of tea, Arlene offered to do a quick walk through to see if there was anything obvious missing, even though it seemed pretty obvious this wasn't a regular burglary. The sheriff suggested they close off the house for now, and for Arlene to pack Emma a bag and take her home for the night–leaving the follow up for tomorrow morning at the sheriff's office.

"You staying around here?" Frank asked as he turned to Gus.

"I was going to drive back to Cortez, but I'm thinking I'd better stick around town."

"There's a motel you would've passed coming into town, right off County Road G. They should have room; I can call 'em for you, if you want?"

Gus turned to look at Emma sitting on the couch, watching them.

"No thanks, I'll be okay. Think maybe I'll make sure the ladies get home okay, while you close up here, and I'll head straight to the motel after. I'll meet you at your office in the morning. Nine okay?"

Frank looked him over with one eyebrow raised, and finally shrugged his shoulders.

"Fine by me, tomorrow at nine it is."

Helping Emma into Arlene's truck, he filled them in on the plans for the next day. Arlene grudgingly agreed to let him follow them back to her place, for safety purposes only. Once he had seen them home, he let them know he'd be at the diner for breakfast the next morning. He was off to find the motel for a good night's sleep.

He noticed that Emma seemed to have perked up a little after her meltdown, but when he left, she was still quiet, looking pensive and a bit worried. She had felt pretty good in his arms, even though he didn't want to think about the effect she seemed to have on his body too much; at least not with an audience, and not under those circumstances. If he was honest with himself, he had to admit that he liked having his hands full of curves—especially knowing the curves belonged to the incredibly hot woman he had phone sex with not too long ago. Who'd have thought it?

When Emma cracked an eye and found the early morning sun coming in through the opening of the curtains, the smell of coffee hit her nostrils as a slight hung-over feeling settled in her body. Arlene must be up already. Last night when they got in, Arlene hustled her right up to the spare bedroom, hoisting her up the narrow stairway without exchanging more than a couple of words; not normal for the two of them to be so uncommunicative. They had already been exhausted from the long day yesterday, and last night's events must have taken all the stuffing right out of them.

Emma couldn't remember the last time she had such a complete meltdown. Damn, and right in front of him too…embarrassing as shit. Not to mention being picked up, as if she didn't weigh a ton. Ugh. Oh well, c'est la vie…can't be helped now. Better get her ass out of bed and have a pow wow with Arlene before they had to meet up with Gus and deal with the sheriff. Emma was curious to find out what the hell Gus's story was.

-

Rolling herself out of bed, Emma made her way over to the guest bathroom and freshened up. Arlene had left out the toiletries she had grabbed from Emma's bathroom and some towels. Emma pulled out some yoga pants and a hoodie for comfort—screw dressing for the public eye. She was sore and wanted to be comfortable, so lounging wear it would be, everyone could just deal with it.

Emma gingerly sat down at the top of the stairs and slid down on her ass, not willing to complicate things by falling on her face too. Arlene must've heard her, because she was waiting at the bottom.

"You could've hollered, woman."

"Yeah, I know. I managed so no biggie. I smelled the coffee and I need some. STAT."

"Here's your cane." Arlene handed it over. "I have your cup ready for ya. You sleep okay?"

"I did, surprisingly." Emma walked over to the kitchen and sat at the counter. "I was out like a light, but I feel like I partied like an animal last night. We both know that ain't true. I still can't believe someone broke into my place, Arlene…here, in Cedar Tree. What would they want from me of all people? And what do you think that big hunk of a man was doing there?" She glanced at Arlene while taking a sip of her coffee.

Arlene smirked.

"Other than eyeballing you? Not a clue, although, he seemed to be there in some kind of official capacity, or Frank wouldn't have been so friendly with him, I figure."

"He was not eyeballing me. You're delusional, Arlene. Have you seen the guy? He's gorgeous and way out of my league. Besides, he picked me up last night, which would instantly cure him of any fleeting interest he might have thought he had."

Ignoring Emma, Arlene popped some bread into the toaster.

"Toast okay, for now? We can have breakfast at the diner, or do you want breakfast now?" She turned to Emma. "And knock it off with the dumb talk before I slap you. You're beautiful, and any guy is lucky to have you. I don't want to hear any more out of you on that!"

Emma stuck her tongue out and said with a smile, "You have to say that because you love me."

"Whatever. You want butter on your toast?"

"Please."

Arlene slid a plate in front of Emma. "Eat up. We're supposed to meet up with Gus in fifteen minutes, and I want grab some cleaning supplies so we can clean up at your house later–if we can get in."

"You think we might not be able to. Why?"

"Well, let's just find out what is going on and see, but if the sheriff, or someone from their office still has to get in, they may want to preserve things as they are for now. I don't know how these things work, but Frank will tell us."

"Jesus, I hope I can at least get my laptop or something."

"Ems, your laptop is missing."

"What?"

"Your laptop was not in the office area or anywhere else in the house when I went around with Frank last night. I was kinda hoping you had it in your car."

"Shit! All my contacts are in there! My work…how am I going to do my work? Emma dropped her head in her hands. "I am so fucked"

Arlene walked over and rubbed her shoulders. "Now hang

on. You have all your accounts on an online server, right?"

"Yea, I can access them remotely from anywhere. My files are stored on a server too…Okay. I guess I'm less fucked than I thought, but I'll still need something to work on."

"Well, we'll have time to figure that out, as long as your files and contact lists aren't lost, you should be alright." Arlene grabbed the dishes and the cups and set them in the sink. "Come on, girl, we have a hunk to meet!"

CHAPTER FOUR

Pulling into the parking lot of the diner, Emma could see Gus's big body leaning against the driver's side door of his SUV. With his legs crossed, he was clad in jeans and a loose plaid shirt, over a grey Henley. His hair looked wet, like he just stepped out of the shower–and that thought sent her mind spinning in all kinds of inappropriate directions. The same directions her hands and tongue wanted to wander on that imaginary hard, wet chest and abdomen…

"Coming out?" The object of her momentary slide into la la land was standing with the passenger side door open, waiting to help her out. *Busted.* She felt a blush creeping up her chest–of all places–and tried to turn around to get her walker from the back. Beating her to it, Gus had it pulled out of the truck bed and set up in front her before she managed to finish her turn.

"You move on ahead, I'll be right behind you," Emma said, hoping to avoid having to feel self-conscious with him walking behind her.

"Why?" he asked, one side of his mouth lifting, "Wanna check out my ass?"

Stopped dead in her tracks, Emma just stared at him with her mouth hanging open, then coughed out a laugh.

"You just said that. I can't believe you just actually said that!"

"Well, I was planning on walking behind you and checking out your ass, but if you insist, I guess I can let you check out mine, just this once." Smiling broadly now, Gus turned on his heels and slowly made his way to the diner's entrance, leaving Emma shaking her head in amused disbelief.

"Cocky bastard," she mumbled. So she followed him in, making sure to get a good look at his *assets*, and they were mighty fine *assets* indeed, she thought as she slipped through the door he held open for her.

Arlene had the coffee going already, and Seb, who had come in the back entrance, was heating up the grills.

"Grab a booth, guys." She called out, "I'll be right there with the menus, and we'll talk over breakfast, but wait for me! I want to hear everything."

Gus stood by the booth he'd been sitting in the day before, motioning for Emma to sit down, then he slid in across from her, bending his head down to try and catch her eye. Emma couldn't help the smile that snuck out, no matter how hard she tried to keep a straight face.

"What?" She wanted to know, tilting her head to the side, irked with the mildly arrogant grin on his face.

"Don't feel bad. I snuck a peek in," he said with a wink.

"Good Lord! You are something else."

"What's funny?" Arlene piped up, as she slid three mugs of coffee and a few menus on the table. "Move over, Toots," she said to Emma, as she settled in beside her. "Seb's serving this morning, and I'm planning to enjoy being on the receiving end for a change. So, what did I miss?"

"Oh, not much," Emma informed her. "Gus was just saying how much he enjoyed the view from where he was sitting." Not even trying to contain her snicker, Emma glanced at him across the table, noticing his eyes quietly fixed on her. A little unnerved now by his silence, she quickly averted her eyes, focusing on the menu.

"I'll just have a mushroom omelet, and you guys, better get some breakfast down too. We don't have a lot of time before we're due at the sheriff's office, and I still really want some kind of explanation as to what you were doing at my house yesterday, Gus, if you don't mind?" She stared straight at him, willing him to answer. He met her eyes without blinking.

"Yes, I guess it's time for me to lay my cards on the table. I am actually working together with a task force in an ongoing investigation, and although I am no longer a police officer, I am sometimes hired to try and find people who have gone off the grid."

"Cool!" Arlene smiled, "You're like Dog!"

Emma snorted as she watched a puzzled look come over Gus's face.

"Dog?"

"Yeah…the Bounty Hunter. Big dude, long blond hair, buxom wife, and he has that hot, scrumptious son…Damn. What's his name again, Ems?"

Arlene turned to her. By this time, Gus was shaking his head and Emma was chuckling. They had gone through a phase where they watched that show all the time and would chat about it online. That was before Emma had moved out to Colorado.

"Hmm," Gus muttered. "Sorry to disappoint, even though I guess I am licensed as a bounty hunter in a few states, I can promise you, it's a pretty boring job."

Wanting to get things back on track, Emma prompted him,

Freya Barker   SLIM TO NONE

"So, you were saying you are working with some task force? What does that have to do with my house being broken into, or you being there? I'm still really confused."

"The person I am looking for is instrumental in a big case. He made a deal with law enforcement and disappeared. We think he may be trying to clean up some loose ends before he hops a border somewhere, and we'd like to nip that in the bud"

"Okay, and you think he's in Cedar Tree?"

"Actually, we discovered some of his so-called loose ends, and one of them was a post office box in Cortez, where I happen to have a buddy working for the county sheriff's office. With his help, I found out the renter of that box lived here in Cedar Tree."

Emma slowly felt the blood draining from her face when Gus mentioned the post office box in Cortez, and she felt Gus's eyes on her the whole time. Slowly lifting her eyes, she saw the confirmation in his face.

"Are you saying…? Do you…Am I? Me?" she stuttered out.

Arlene, who was slow to clue in, suddenly slammed her fist on the table, rattling the coffee cups. "Damn, Ems–that truck!"

Gus whipped his head around to face her. "What truck is that?"

"Ems was telling me yesterday that she was freaking out over it…"

"I did not say I was freaking out," Emma cut in. "I said I didn't feel safe because that truck followed me into Cortez a few times, and I would feel safer going with someone, but that's not freaking out; that's being safe!" She glared at Arlene, willing her to stop bringing up the damn truck, because the next thing would be the anonymous phone call. She had no intention of discussing

45

that with a man who made her feel all kinds of niggly, little persistent things she hadn't felt in forever, no thank you.

"What.Truck.Is.That?" Gus bit out, making both Emma and Arlene snap to attention.

"Well then," Arlene huffed. "Ems here would drive into town to check her mail and found this truck sitting at the intersection at the highway into Cortez. Once getting to Cortez, it would be there at the same time."

"Excuse me, but what does all of this have to do with me? I'm still not understanding any of this. I just moved here two months ago, and all I do is bake pies and do bookkeeping online. Fine, and I also go to doctor's appointments. Other than that, I don't do a damn thing." She was getting a little impatient now, and more than a little anxious. She was not liking where this was going.

"Alright," Gus said. "I'll tell you what I know, and then you can maybe fill in some blanks before we head over to the sheriff's office." That earned a nod from her.

"My guess is that the person we are after, Ernst Corbin…Is that name familiar by the way?" He looked at her with his eyebrows raised.

Emma shook her head. "No, never heard it. However, I mostly deal with business names or business emails. To be honest, I rarely look closely at signatures on checks."

"Yeah, I figured that would probably be too easy, but like I said, I assume he must have called in for your bookkeeping services at some point. He may have inadvertently given you some sensitive information, and now wants to make sure that information disappears, and never sees the light of day."

"So I guess that's what he was looking for? But I never

actually print off much at all. Only time I might is if there are discrepancies, because sometimes it is easier to find errors on paper than it is on a computer, but then I destroy the paper in my shredder right away when I'm done. I just can't see how there is anything incriminating that I could have. I would remember if something was off, wouldn't I? It just doesn't make any sense to me." Emma dropped her head in her hands, massaging her scalp where a nice juicy headache was forming. Recognizing the signs, Arlene moved in to try and loosen the muscles in her neck, but Emma couldn't stop thinking of the mess her house was in. What in God's name would someone want with her, and how the hell had she gotten herself into this mess in the first place?

"One more thing," Gus broke through her depressing thoughts. "I went ahead last night and called a security company I've worked with before. I noticed you don't have a security system on your house, and you don't have any direct neighbors…"

"Wait a minute." Holding up her hand, Emma interrupted Gus. "Let me get this straight. You called someone to put an alarm on my house?"

Regarding her calmly, Gus simply said, "Yes, I did, and I also told them to be on standby and wait for my call to confirm." Leaning across the table, he pinned her with his gaze. "I wasn't going to have them come in without your say so, darlin'; no need to get all worked up. The guys are good and they owe me one. Seemed like a good opportunity to call it in, but it's entirely up to you, of course."

"Great idea, right, Ems?" Arlene turned to her with a big smile on her face. "It'll sure make me feel a shitload better having you a bit safer in your home."

With that, all of her resistance disappeared. Last thing she wanted was to have Arlene worry about her even more than she already did. Dammit, the woman already helped her out so much. So what if it had been a bit presumptuous of Gus to make the arrangements? It was also kind of nice, if she was being entirely honest, for someone other than Arlene, to actually consider her well-being.

With a stern look at Gus, Arlene said. "Well, if we're done discussing stressful stuff, I'm going to give Seb a hand bringing out the food. We are going to eat, have another coffee, and then we'll be off and get the sheriff done with. Giving yourself a migraine is not gonna help any...you got your meds on you?"

Flicking her eyes up at Arlene, who was getting up out of the booth, Emma replied snidely, "Yes, Mother."

"Don't be a bitch, Ems. The day is long yet, so let's eat."

"Fine."

Gus looked at Arlene giving him the evil eye, and then glanced over at Emma, who didn't look so good, across the table from him. He reached over, grabbing her hand. Startled, she looked up, but didn't pull back.

"Don't worry, we'll figure it out; I'm not gonna leave until we do. I won't let you deal with any of this on your own–trust me on that." A very slight hint of a smile flicked over her lips as she mouthed the word, "*Thanks.*"

Moments later, when Arlene and Seb brought plates of food to the table, Gus found himself still holding her small hand, rubbing the palm with his thumb and staring into those incredibly blue eyes, set in a strong, gorgeous open face. He was totally losing track of time and place...Christ, get a grip already.

Standing outside the sheriff's office after giving his statement, Gus was waiting for Arlene and Emma. He was pretty sure Arlene would need to go back to the diner, and he really wanted the opportunity to get Emma alone for a bit; there were things they needed to talk about. He just dodged a bullet in Frank's office when Arlene was urging Emma to say something about "that phone call." He had a feeling it wouldn't be long before that little minor lapse in judgment would turn into a big clusterfuck. Luckily, Emma told Arlene to hush up before she could go any further, and Frank had been distracted by one of his deputies, otherwise, it would have been quite embarrassing for them both. Crap. Just thinking back on it made his cock come to life. He couldn't quite put his finger on what it was about her that got under his skin. Perhaps it was the contradictions she seemed to embody, the vulnerability she already hinted at on the phone through her self-deprecating comments, countered by her quick wit and courage to dive off the deep end. They were a heady mix of nice and naughty. Those first short impressions had only been further confirmed in the time he'd spent with her so far. She was very addictive, the self-conscious, but fierce Emma.

Deliberately stopping his train of thought, he quickly adjusted himself before the girls made their way back out. No need to show Emma what a pervert he was before he had a chance to tell her first. This could be interesting.

"Hey, you waiting on us?" Arlene called at him, as she and Emma made their way over to Arlene's truck, catching him daydreaming.

"Yeah, actually," he said, sauntering over. "I was going to suggest that maybe I could take Emma back to her house to have another look around in the daylight. I assume you need to go back to the diner?" He looked at Arlene, but saw Emma throw a furtive look his way from the corner of his eye.

"Sure, fine by me. Emma? Okay with you?"

"Ehh, sure–I guess?" Raising an eyebrow, Emma turned to face him full on. "What exactly are you hoping to find there?"

"I just want to have a quick look, and maybe we can make a start in cleaning up a little."

"Oh, I'll worry about that later, there's no need." With a dismissive shake of her head, Emma turned to Arlene. "I'll call you later then?"

"Sure, Toots. Later." Arlene waved as she pulled her old truck out of the parking lot.

"I, umm…may have a bit of trouble getting up in that massive vehicle of yours," Emma admitted with a grin.

"Won't be any trouble at all, it just means I can get my hands on you." Smirking, he opened the passenger door of his big Yukon. Although he was not looking forward to coming clean about the telephone call, he couldn't deny he wouldn't mind spending some alone time with the luscious Emma–without Arlene's eagle eyes picking up on every nuance. He'd bet his truck that woman had already picked up on his attraction to her friend, and he was trying so hard to focus on the job…Well, he was.

"You just spit out anything that comes to mind, don't you? Is it me, or does it just seem to occur when Arlene happens to not be around?" Emma squinted her eyes at him, making him chuckle.

Ignoring what she said, he grabbed her arm, put her walker to the side and swiftly lifted her up into the passenger seat, while Emma clutched at his shoulders for dear life.

"Holy crap! You keep doing that–picking me up like I don't weigh 170 pounds or more. Do you lift cows for fun or something?"

Gus threw back his head and let out a hearty laugh as he folded the walker, tossing it on the backseat.

"Woman, first of all, don't mention yourself and cows in the same breath; and secondly, I don't think I've ever met any female who willingly informed me of her weight. You are something else…" Shaking his head, he made his way to the driver's side, amused to find her staring out the window mumbling something about *idiot* and *dimwitted female* under her breath.

Yeah, she sure was something.

CHAPTER FIVE

Walking into her house, Emma took a few deep breaths, willing herself not to freak out again like she did last night. That was so not her style. Wilting flowers were reserved for others; Steel Magnolia was more her speed, or she'd like to think so, anyway. There was no way in hell she was going to let that big, hulking behemoth of a…fuck! He is gorgeous…No, not going there. She wasn't going to let him distract her, especially now that the reality of the shitpile she somehow found herself floating in was so evident around her. Dammit, what a mess!

Gus walked in and around her; slowly making his way through her living room and kitchen, then back through the hallway to stand in front of her.

"So, I was thinking, we need to talk. If you wanna take a seat in the living room, we'll start there. I'll start and just pick up and you can tell me where it goes. We'll talk about what we find, and what's missing, as we go."

Emma snorted. "Well, that's gonna take forever. I may not be as able-bodied as you are, but I'm not bloody helpless! Let's just start somewhere."

Gus threw his hands up. "Okay, no problem. Didn't mean any offence." Leaning into her space, he looked her straight in the eyes, "But no bloody heroics. If you get tired or sore, you sit. No damn excuses, okay?"

"Fine. Bossy much?" But she couldn't hide a smile. That made her feel pretty nice.

A few hours, and half a dozen breaks later, the living room, dining area, and the kitchen were back to normal, and Emma was about to fall over from hunger.

"Hey, you hungry?" she called out, not quite sure where Gus went off to.

"Gettin' there." Was the response coming from the vicinity of the other end of the hall.

"Gonna make us some sandwiches and a quick soup, that okay?"

"Sounds good to me." Seeing Gus sticking his head around the door of her bedroom had her drawing in a sharp breath. Her bedroom. Fuck. He was in her bedroom!

"Erm…need any help in there?" She quickly made her way over to see how deep his investigative powers went, hoping to God her little bedside buddies were still in their protective pouches and tucked away nicely.

"Nope, finding everything just fine, thanks."

Oh no. She could hear it. She couldn't see it yet, but she could hear the contained laughter in his voice. Cocky bastard had found something to smile about. She began a deep breathing exercise to fight off the blasted perimenopausal flush that was creeping up her chest again. She made her way around the doorway to find him sitting on the bed, with the contents of all her drawers spread out around him.

53

"What are you doing?" She managed to get out.

Eyes sparkling with amusement, the bastard looked at her with the edges of his mouth twitching, like he was fighting a losing battle not to burst out laughing. He'd better win that battle, or he might find a cane up his arse!

"Picked up everything that was tossed from the drawers onto the floor and put it on your bed. I was just trying to sort through it to see if I could put some stuff back for ya."

"Uh huh…and, eh…were you successful?" she ground out, now trying to hold back on her own grin that was trying to make its way out.

"Sorta…" Gus said, bringing his hands up from beside his legs, where they seemed to be resting on the bedspread, but instead, were apparently covering her best little buddies…

"I rescued these from the floor. Is there any particular spot you would like these?" With that, Gus let go, bending over laughing, while clutching her pink rabbit and her sparkly G-spot stimulator to his stomach, which, in turn, made Emma lose it. Nothing she could do now, her secret was out…she liked her toys.

"Again, I'm really sorry." Gus said over lunch. "I probably should've just stayed out of your bedroom, but I wanted to get a head start there, so we'd have more time for the office."

"Don't sweat it. Other than it being a tad embarrassing to have you find my mechanical companions," Emma blushed, "it is what it is. I'm too old to really give a shit, so there. If you have any lasting issues, well, I guess that'll be your problem." She looked at him from under her eyebrows, giving him a little smartass smile.

"Oh, I don't have any issues, but thank you very much for your concern. While we are on the topic, I think there is something you should know."

Straightening her shoulders, Emma prepared herself for some bad news, always expecting the worst.

"I heard Arlene mention something about a phone call at the sheriff's…"

"Oh, that's nothing. It's nothing to worry about because it was just a wrong number. She shouldn't have even mentioned it. It was just once, and it was nothing. Really," she nervously interrupted Gus, not wanting to go there at all.

"Yeah, but Emma, I need to tell you something about that phone call. You deserve to know now too."

Finding him tilting his head so he could look her in the eye, she was starting to feel an odd little tingle of premonition in her stomach. Oh God. Don't tell me…

"See, you know me better than you think, Emma. That was me on the phone."

Slapping her hands in front of her face, she dropped her head down on the counter.

"How? Oh my God…O.M.G! I'm gonna be sick."

Gus started chuckling. "Well, darlin', that's not the first thing that comes to my mind when I remember the phone call—at all. I have very fond memories of that phone call, in fact; I can't seem to get it out of my mind, but it was a mistake. I did dial a wrong number, and I ended up having one of the shortest, yet hottest, conversations that I can remember. It was with a very sexy woman, who ended up being you. I didn't know at the time, and didn't put two and two together until after I saw you here at your house when I had called in the burglary."

Barely able to contain what he was telling her, Emma's mind was still reeling with the fact that the person she shared a very private, and what she thought was, a very anonymous moment with, was sitting right in front of her in her kitchen. Holy fuck. She would never be able to look him in the eye again. Never. Oh God, he knows she shaves. She frickin' told him she shaves. How crazy was that? She would never do spontaneous shit again…never! She was absolutely mortified.

"Emma, darlin', look at me." Lifting her chin, he tried to catch her eyes, but she stubbornly kept them downcast. "Don't be a brat, Emma. Look at me—I still have more to tell you."

"I can't look at you. I am so, so embarrassed right now. You must be disgusted. I…I just…whatever. I don't want to bawl all over you again." Fighting to keep her tears in check, Emma was swallowing like crazy, but Gus grabbed her jaw, forcing her to face him.

"Listen." The rumble of his deep voice gave her goose bumps. "Did you hear me when I said I had no idea it was you until you showed up on the burglary call? And do you remember what took place before that?"

Tentatively she lifted her eyes to meet his. His warm, deep chocolate brown eyes, that carried laugh lines at the outer edges, were soft and kind, so she nodded, an indication for him to go on.

"When you came to the diner to drop off your pies, I had no idea who you were; not one. All I saw was a gorgeous, ripe and vivacious woman, who obviously took life by the balls, no matter what. I saw all that in the two minutes it took you to get out of your car and to the door of the diner, and I hadn't even talked to you yet. When you opened your smart mouth, and that rich, full-bodied sound came out, it rippled down my back. You gave me attitude then joked around a bit. Darlin', phone call or not, I was attracted to you already. Finding out that was you on the phone? I'll admit; that was a very welcome surprise."

Slowly stroking his thumbs down her cheeks, he could feel Emma's face relax in his hands.

"You okay, darlin'?" He needed to know.

Looking up at him with her head tilted, Emma frowned a little. "Who is Katie? Is she your wife, your girlfriend? I would feel pretty shitty if knew I had been stepping all over someone else's territory."

What the fuck? That was what she comes back with? Amazing. He just about spewed his guts all over her kitchen counter, and she wanted to know who Katie was. Fine. Letting go of her face, he straightened up, schooling his features for this disclosure. This should be fun.

"Katie is just a friend I call from time to time."

"Ahh. So she's a booty call then?" Glancing up at him, she looked to be enjoying making him squirm a little.

"Booty call? Umm…well, she…we've known each other for a long time, but it's not like that, we just hang out sometimes. Or call. Or something, ya know." This was so uncomfortable, and the more he wanted to get out of this conversation, the more Emma seemed to brighten up.

"You know, we should get going on the office area, and then we have to make some arrangements for you." He tried to steer things in a different direction.

"What arrangements. What do you mean?"

"You can't stay by yourself, and I don't want you staying with Arlene either, because it might put her at risk as well. Frank doesn't have the manpower to have someone assigned to you full-time, and I'm pretty sure whoever came, will be coming back. They'll figure out there is nothing stored on your laptop, and they will need some way to get the information, or, well, whatever. Point is; you can't be alone."

"Are you serious? What the hell? Look, I don't even understand half of what's going on, and I certainly don't understand what any of it has to do with me." Her earlier warm and fuzzy feeling was slowly starting to make her hot under the collar. This was getting ridiculous. What was she supposed to do? Not being in control really pissed her off. "You know, I already can't stand not having any control over my bloody body, now fucking everything feels like it's running off the rails!"

Loudly slamming the remnants of lunch in the sink, she didn't notice Gus coming up behind her until she suddenly felt a hand between her shoulder blades, sliding up to grab her firmly by the neck. He leaned in to her line of sight, so close Emma could count his eyelashes.

Gus's deep voice soothed over her, "Easy, darlin'. I hear ya, and we'll get this sorted as soon as we can, but let's be smart about it, okay?" Leading her to a stool, he nudged her to sit and grabbed the stool next to her. He turned to face her; bracketed his knees around hers, holding her legs.

"This Ernst Corbin I'm looking for has a bit of a criminal history. He was about to rat out a bigger player and either got cold feet, or he was found out and decided to run. Either way, he's running scared, and that is always dangerous, so I'm not gonna take any chances with you, Emma."

"But how long will this take? I mean, how do you know for sure he isn't running for the border already, and you're just wasting time here?"

"'Cause if my guess is right, that truck you described for the sheriff, the one that's been following you into Cortez, is the same truck I saw peeling out of your drive last night. Someone who spends that much time casing you is not gonna give up now, unless he found what he was looking for. I would assume that given the state of your house, plus the fact that I interrupted his business, he isn't done yet. So for now, you're gonna have to put up with me."

Emma had a hard time concentrating on what Gus was saying, but was acutely aware of what he was doing. He was slowly rubbing his thumb over her knee as he talked, mesmerizing her. It felt good. Crap.

"Okay. I'll put up with you, alright," she muttered, as she was enjoying being distracted.

Fucking adorable, Gus thought as he was pulling out of the driveway on the way to the diner for some dinner. She's fucking adorable, and she doesn't have a clue. For all her tough cookie exterior, it was obvious he flustered her, and he liked it; liked having that effect on her. Being a bit of an ass, he held her a little longer than necessary when helping her into the truck, getting her all flushed. Of course, then he had to adjust himself again while making his way around the Yukon, but that was his own doing. Well, technically no, it was all Emma's doing. Fuck. What that woman did to him was unbelievable. Here he was, forty-five years old, for all intents and purposes, his dick should be getting old and tired, but instead it was fired up and ready to go like it was his first time. Wise? Probably not. Hell, he was too tired and too old to play games, or to pass up on good things when they came along. He just needed to make sure to keep his head in the game and keep her protected while he got this asshole off the streets. Good thing he'd had a chance to fill Joe in today, and had the support back from his office, because he had a feeling he might be busy tonight.

Feeling Emma's eyes on him, he glanced over at her. "What's up, darlin', you hungry?"

"Getting there. Pretty wiped out to be honest. Been a long day, but I'm glad it's done. There's not too much damage, and I feel better with that security system in. Although, I still can't figure out how you managed to get them out here so quickly. I'm not buying for one second that they 'owed you one,' so you better hand over the bill when it comes, because I'm aiming to pay for it."

Looking at Emma, he shook his head. "No, darlin', that is on me. Call it part of the service. I toss these guys business all the time, and they work from Cortez as well as Grand Junction, so it wasn't that hard to get someone out to the house on short notice. Don't sweat it, 'cause I don't wanna hear about it." Then he broke out into a grin, saying, "But if you really wanna pay me, you can bake me a pie. I'll take that as payment any day of the week." That drew a snort from Emma, who gave him a half-assed slug to his arm.

"Fine, but you pick what kind." She smiled.

Pulling into Arlene's Diner, he could tell there was a decent dinner crowd. He also spotted Emma's SUV, still sitting in the handicapped spot.

"Why don't I drop you off at the door and see if there is room around the back. Place is busy."

"Just take me around the back with you, and we'll go in through the kitchen. Seb won't mind, so there's no need to make an extra stop here."

Luckily, there was plenty of parking space in the back.

"Do you mind if I grab your arm and leave the walker? It's a pain to move around with that thing when it's this busy."

"Yeah, sure, hang on. Let me get you down safe first." Opening up the door for Emma, he reached up to help her down, but instead of putting her down, he simply held her wrapped in his arms with her feet dangling just shy of the ground. For once he was looking straight in her eyes.

"Short little thing, aren't ya?"

"Gus, what are you doing?" Emma breathed out.

"Holding you. Feels good having my arms full of woman. Are you gonna smack me if I kiss you?"

Before Emma had a chance to respond, his mouth settled firmly over her half-opened lips. Pulling back, he looked at her slightly stunned blue eyes and moved back in at an adjusted slant. With a strong swipe of his tongue, he claimed access to her mouth.

Oh yeah, that woke her up. Her two small hands grabbed the hair at the base of his skull, while her tongue gave as good as it got.

Her body slowly slid down until her feet touched the ground, leaving his hands free to roam over the luscious curves of her ass; more than just a handful and feeling so fucking good. He couldn't help but rock his rejuvenated hard-on against her body, letting her feel exactly what she did to him. Fuck. That woman could kiss thirty-year-old paint of the walls. Her sweet taste and spicy little tongue seemed to satisfy a hunger he didn't realize he had. Her small, but strong hands were kneading the contours of his back and ass; making his skin tingle and his balls draw up tight.

She was rubbing her breasts up against his chest, eager for friction. She made little groaning noises that drove him wild. His hips were involuntarily dry humping into her, and he felt so fucking sexed up and hungry to come. He hadn't felt this way since he was about sixteen and had his first taste of a girl's pussy.

The slam of the trash can lid by the backdoor had them jumping apart. Seb was standing with the door in his hand and a big-ass grin on his face.

"Coming in, folks? Or am I gonna sell tickets?"

"Fuck off, Seb," Emma said, turning all shades of embarrassed. She could barely look Gus in the eye, but the level she was looking at now wasn't much better…holy cow! Lifting her eyes to his face, he was standing there looking all smug down at her.

"Not gonna apologize, darlin'. Although, I came close to throwing you back in the truck and taking you here."

"Seriously? You have no filter! Do you say everything?"

Gus just smiled and shrugged his shoulders. "Pretty much. Don't see the point in beating around the bush, do you? We had an orgasm together, Emma, it's not like we're complete strangers.

And that kiss was fucking hot. I look forward to more."

She just shook her head and laughed it off, because seriously, what else do you do with a declaration like that? Emma grabbed his arm and started moving for the back door where Seb had disappeared inside.

"So what were you and the hunk doing out in the back? Seb said something about walking out and interrupting you? Interrupting what? Dish, bitch." Arlene had followed Emma into the bathroom, of course wanting to hear all the latest.

"Not much of anything. Just parking the car and he helped me out, and instead of taking the walker; he walked me in 'cause it's too busy. Why?"

"Well, let's see. You came in the kitchen all pink and flustered with big swollen lips, looking like you just ate the biggest slice of chocolate cake. Then there was Mr. Hunk, walking beside you, looking like he was feeling mighty good about himself."

"Fine. A kiss, Arlene. Just a little peck."

"HA. A peck, my ass! Tonsil hockey is more like it. That I'll buy, given the way you two looked. Just be careful, okay? Don't want my bestie hurt, even if I do want her to get laid good!"

"Christ, would you drop it already? I'm not twelve years old, Mom. I just want to eat some dinner, and whatever. I don't wanna talk about it anymore. This is freaking me out…all of it."

Washing her hands at the sink and looking up at the mirror, Emma scanned her face, suddenly seeing her reality reflected back at her. Not bad looking, but definitely aging. There were wrinkles around her eyes and a bit around her mouth, with ugly lines in her neck. Oh no, is that a double chin? Fuck!

Turning to Arlene, who was standing there quietly observing for once, she said, "I'm not made for this. I'm too old and too broken...unappealing. I won't be able to think of anything but that!"

"You're an idiot." That's all Arlene said before turning on her heels and walking out of the bathroom.

Sucking in a deep breath, she pushed her way out the door and saw Gus already getting up to meet her halfway. Damn. He wasn't going to make it easy on her.

With the food already on the table, they settled in for a relatively easy conversation. Gus asked her about Boston and Kara, and she told him how proud she was of her girl graduating and finding her way into a great job. She talked about how she struggled a while with the decision to come out here and leave her in Boston, but that Kara had urged her to follow her heart, and so she did.

He told her about his office in Grand Junction and the people that worked for him. It wasn't until she found out that he was forty-five that she instantly lost that relaxed feeling that had started to settle over her.

"You're younger than I am?" She looked at him with abject horror on her face, making him chuckle.

"Two years, so what?"

"Well, that's just great." Shaking her head, her shoulders sagged a little. "Something else to add to the list," she mumbled.

"What was that?" Gus demanded.

"Nothing. Forget it, it's silly."

"I don't think so, Emma. Answer me. Add to what list?" The angry tone in his voice had her looking up at him tentatively.

"Well, don't get pissed at me! It's just…" She let out a big sigh, not quite able to formulate what she was feeling, "I just always…I feel so damn inadequate already! And you! You're like Mr. Perfect or something. You come along and make like some fucking knight in shining armor; all hard, good looking and fit, and…and now you're only forty-five!" Her volume went up toward the end of her little tirade, and Emma was noticing how quiet the diner suddenly was. Looking around, she could see eyes quickly turning away from her, where they were obviously focused.

Shoot me, please, someone shoot me.

Eyes sliding over to Gus in front of her, she saw his head focused down, his shoulders shaking, but as his eyes slowly came up, he was obviously steeling his resolve not to laugh out loud. All she could do now was close her eyes and pretend she was on a beach in the Caribbean. Then she felt his hand grabbing hers. The rough pad of his thumb was rubbing the skin between her thumb and index finger, almost making her groan. She'd just pretend he's a cabana boy.

"Emma."

A cabana boy with a very deep, rumbly voice, making her all tingly.

"Darlin', open your eyes."

Hmmm, cabana boys in the Caribbean give good massages. His thumb was doing amazing work… "Ouch! You pinched me!" She pulled back her hand, rubbing the tender skin.

"I had to. You weren't listening."

"I didn't want to listen. I had a cabana boy, and I was perfectly happy!"

"I'm not even gonna pretend I understand that, but I have something you need to hear."

"Last time we did this, last time I listened to something you had to tell me, you completely freaked me out. I think I have had enough freak outs over the last twenty-four hours to last me a lifetime, thank you very much!"

"Emma, I think there are some things you still aren't clear on that we need to talk about, or perhaps I should say, things that I need to make clear to you somehow. Trust me. I will find a way to make myself very, very clear to you."

Each word he uttered, he moved closer into her space, so that by the end of his speech, she could feel the vibrations on the air. He moved his mouth only slightly to touch her lips, and even that hint of a touch turned her on. She was so screwed.

"But I think we need less of an audience for what I have to say…" Gus leaned in even closer, his lips touching her ear, "and do to you." He promptly moved back into his seat, leaving her blushing, wet, and damn-near panting in a booth in the middle of a damn diner.

Getting up, he held out his hand and said, "Let's head out,

darlin'."

CHAPTER SIX

The drive home was silent; each lost in their own thoughts, but Gus never lost the connection with the woman beside him. Having his hand firmly on her thigh, he rubbed his thumb back and forth, trying to soothe the tense muscles he could feel underneath his hand. He got her apprehension. He got it, but he was not going to let her run with it.

Figuring it must have been a while since she put herself out there, and not liking how vulnerable it made her feel, she was doing a good job talking herself out of something they obviously both wanted to explore. He had no time for that kind of nonsense, not that he had any idea what he was doing. All he knew was that he wanted inside of her badly. Ever since finding out it was Emma on the phone, he started recognizing the vibrations in her voice that he now automatically associated with sex, which obviously meant a constant hard-on.

"Why don't you wait in the car while I check the house," he said to her, as he unbuckled the seatbelt and got out of the car. "I'll just be a minute, then I'll be back to get you, okay?"

Just nodding, Emma kept her hands clasped in her lap. She still hadn't said a word since leaving the diner.

Quickly checking each room and flicking on the lights, he made sure doors and windows were still secure before going back out to get Emma.

"I don't get why I couldn't have brought home my own car.

Now it's at the diner for another night," Emma grumbled, as he let her pass into the house before him.

"Don't pout, darlin'," he chuckled, "We'll end up at the diner tomorrow at some point anyway, and I don't really want to let you out of my sight. Besides, for tonight, I want to pull my truck into the tree line, so it's not visible from the road or the drive."

"I just don't like not having my wheels. I feel out of control in this situation as it is. We haven't even had a chance to go through all of the files on the server yet, like you suggested."

"We will, but first priority was to get fed and get ourselves secure for the night. I'll bring in my laptop so you can sign onto the server, and we can make a start. That is, if you're not too tired."

Emma slumped down on the large grey sectional in the living room, kicking her shoes off and putting her feet on the chaise.

"Exhausted really, but I don't think I could sleep; too much is going through my mind, so I think doing something productive will make me feel better."

Walking over to where Emma is was leaning back; he bent over and put his hands beside her head on the back of the couch, and then leaned in close.

"And don't think I've let you off the hook, darlin'. I'm giving you a breather, that's all, get you used to having me in your space 'cause I aim to be there a bit." He closed the distance, folding his mouth over her lips, and slowly licked them from one side to the other before pulling back. Standing up, he gave a final look from his dark eyes that were now burning with intensity. He turned, walked out of the room, and left Emma sitting in stunned silence.

"Do you want something? I think I may have a beer or two left in the fridge."

They'd been at it for a couple of hours and had singled out most of the files related to Encorb, the company Ernst Corbin apparently used to shuffle money. It was the same company that she was supposed to have received a paycheck from a while ago; guess she could kiss that money goodbye. She had minor administrative tasks that had seemed innocuous at the time, as well as maintained a rather complicated ledger that included some sort of coding instead of creditors or debtors, something she remembered finding rather odd at the time, but she had assumed it had been done for security reasons. The thing that worried her most was that she had stepped outside of her normal scope of responsibilities when she had agreed to perform those small projects. Most weren't more than placing certain files in a dropbox and sending a message to a certain email account. When she checked the dropbox, it was completely empty, but since she wanted to make sure everything she did could be repeated if something went wrong, she had copied each file in her own dropbox as well. Only problem was, the files made no sense whatsoever.

With her eyes getting gritty from staring at the screen, she got up for a drink. Gus was making sure that all of what they found was immediately transferred to his IT guy, Neil, in Grand Junction.

"Would you like a drink?"

"Beer would be nice." Came the response. "I think we'll put

this to rest for now. We've gotten a bit done, so let's see what Neil can come up with tomorrow. We'll also take a drive into Cortez, check the post office, and pay my friend, Joe, a visit while we're there." Gus closed the laptop and walked over to the kitchen, where she had just pulled a beer out of the fridge and was pouring some ice tea for herself. Grabbing both drinks, Gus returned to the couch, while she followed tentatively behind, a bit of anxiety starting to form in the pit of her stomach. Wanting to give herself a little space, she tried sitting down in the big lazy chair across from the sectional, but Gus was on to her, grabbing her hand and tugging her over to the couch where he plopped down beside her.

"Done avoiding me now, darlin'. I wasn't going to let those remarks you made at the diner go, but wanted to give you some time to collect yourself."

Busted, she thought to herself. Squirming in her seat, she was angry that she was allowing this man to make her feel so damn discombobulated. She, who had always been the strong one, always aware of exactly who she was and where she was going, was at a total loss after ten years of preoccupation. She raised her daughter, along with dealing with her own health issues, and now she was faced with this self-assured, strong and capable man. Oh how she hated being such a waffling, insecure, typical female.

Turning to Gus, she found his steady gaze on her, patiently waiting.

"This is not like me," she began. "That person on the phone is not like me. I don't do stuff like that. I mean, I never have...I never would have...before."

"Before what?"

"Before my life started getting out of control, no matter how

71

hard I tried to reign it in. I already did the hardest part, which was packing up all I had and moving here to live a dream just for me. For once, I did something without any thought for anyone else. It still feels self-indulgent and unfamiliar, but it feels good, as well. I guess I figured, why not? I was on a roll when we had our little telephone thing, whatever that was. I had been doing so much 'living in the moment' in the past few months and feeling so good about it, that I didn't think, I just jumped"

"And what is wrong with that?"

"Nothing, I guess, except it was surreal, and I was outside of myself, feeling wanted for the first time in a fucking long time." The expletive made Gus chuckle.

"Don't laugh, I'm serious!" She glared at him. "For too many years now, I've been naked, poked, and prodded more than I care to remember, but nothing about that was sexual. All it made me feel was like a specimen in a petri dish. Ten years I've been a mother, a friend, and most of all, a patient. Not once–not once has anyone made me feel like a woman until I answered that call. I just went with it because it was an amazing feeling. I was greedy and wanted that for myself. I never thought that there was going to be a moment where the 'woman,' who had that amazingly unexpected experience on the phone, would have to be matched up with the person who detached from her body so long ago. That person doesn't really care anymore."

She could feel hot tears trickling down her face. Bending her head, she tried to find a way to undo the past twenty-four odd hours, where she was happily baking pies and had a nice memory to dream of, but then she found herself being lifted on to Gus's lap. His big hand tangled in her curls, pressing her head against his chest as he leaned them back against the couch.

"All I see when I look at you is a woman." His voice

72

rumbled comfortably beneath her, his heartbeat steady and strong in her ear. "Strong, capable, and so damn positive it radiates from your pores. I told you before, I had no idea what you looked like, and you had an effect on me, and then I met you. I didn't know who you were, and you affected me. I come to find the two are the same, and I'm blown out of the water." Pushing her back slightly, he looked in her eyes, as if he was trying to find every answer in their depths. "I haven't asked about your condition, not because I'm not interested, or I don't want to know, because I do. I'm just more interested in getting to know the woman first. That okay with you?"

Lifting her hand to Gus's face, Emma traced the laugh lines beside his mouth with her fingers, before leaning in and softly kissing his lips.

"I'll take that as a yes," Gus mumbled, before taking her mouth in a hungry kiss that sucked every coherent thought from her mind until only sensation remained.

"God, woman, what you do to me…"

Adjusting her carefully on his lap, so she could straddle him, she could feel his hard length between her legs.

"Is this position okay for you? You'll have to tell me if something is painful," Gus said, before renewing his attack on her mouth. With one hand tangled in her curls, almost to the point of pain to position her head for a better angle, the other hand had a firm clasp on her ample ass. She couldn't tell if she was coming or going anymore. The taste of him, beer, and something inherently male were intoxicating. The feel of his stubble over her skin, rubbing through the wetness his soft lips left behind was sexy as hell to her. He placed open-mouthed kisses all along her jaw to her neck. Every part of her body was coming alive as he was awakening all of her nerve endings. Stretching her head back to try and give him maximum access, she groaned at the wet slide of his tongue along her neck as he alternated with nips, and then sharp bites on her skin. She was losing herself in the contrast of sensations he was evoking, and all the while, she was pushing herself on his hard cock, grinding her core on him in a steady, strong, pulsing rhythm, driving herself insane with lust. She was reaching, circling her hips, trying to spread her labia on the hard ridge of his fly through her jeans, just to get more friction. She was getting so frantic, her hands clawing at his hair, wanting more.

She barely even noticed when he removed her top and had her bra undone, she was so lost in the long forgotten feelings. Feeling Gus lay her down, he leaned over her and sucked a nipple into his mouth and pulled hard, getting a response she felt all the way down to her pussy. Restless for more contact, she rolled her hips, looking for something, riding him through their layers of clothing. Gus licked and sucked at each of her breasts while unbuttoning her jeans and sliding his hand inside, finding her bare, as promised, and so wet she had soaked through the crotch of her jeans.

"Please, please…" The incoherent pleas fell from her mouth.

"I know, baby, I'll give it to you," Gus mumbled, not wanting anything to stop the release of built up passion that was setting this woman on fire. Quickly sitting up, he pulled off her jeans and panties all at once, not wanting to give her a chance to think at all. He gave himself a moment to take in her luscious body spread out for him, before making a place for himself between her thighs. He stroked the gorgeous, softly rounded contours of her body. Her skin was so pale; it was almost translucent. She had a slight blush that started between her breasts, climbing up her neck, and flared out over her cheeks. Her plump, wet lips were slightly parted in anticipation, and her thickly veiled blue eyes were staring at him, full of lust and with a fair amount of vulnerability. It made his chest feel full to have this woman, so strong, and yet so vulnerable, opening herself up to him– exposing herself like this to him. It made him hard as rock and eager to taste every last fucking inch of her…Sheer beauty.

Sliding his hands up the back of her legs to her ass, he tilted her a little, and put his mouth on her pussy, sucking as much in as he could while sliding his tongue from her entrance with slow, steady pressure, all the way to her clit. He pressed it with his tongue against the back of his front teeth, causing Emma to arch off the couch and groan. His mouth was flooded with the taste of her, his cock becoming so hard that he was afraid he was going to blow in his pants, but he wanted to make this good for her.

He lifted his head and saw her flushed face and heavy-lidded eyes focused on him. A slight whimper escaped her swollen, smiling lips. Reassured, he slowly inserted a finger into her passage, relishing the wet, tight heat surrounding his digit.

Emma gasped and moaned as he pumped and stretched her, all the while teasing the hood of her clit with the tip of his tongue. Gently inserting a second finger, he had her pussy clasping him so tight, it felt like his circulation was cut off. He knew she was close, so he sucked the little turgid nerve bundle tightly between his lips and alternated sucking and flicking it with his tongue.

"Ahh, Gusss…please…" Emma ground her pussy in his face, reaching for her release. When he hooked his fingers inside of her, he told her, "Come for me, babe. Show me all that beauty!"

The walls of her vagina clutched his fingers, while he looked up to see her throw her head back in complete surrender with tears tracking from the corners of her eyes.

"That makes you even more fucking gorgeous." He lay beside her, gently stroking her soft abdomen with one hand, while brushing a few sweaty curls from her forehead with the other.

"Like a peach, ripe and plump. Perfect to the eye, soft to the touch, and so juicy that once you get a taste of it, you'll never forget the sweet flavor sticking to your lips…it's like sunshine." He leaned over and licked into her mouth to let her have a taste. The combination of a well-sated woman and her juices was almost too much for him as she slid her hands under his shirt.

An out of body experience, that was the only way to describe what she just had. Her entire body was tingling and warm, super sensitized. She felt like any touch would send sparks flying. Before her mind had a chance to engage and interrupt her post-orgasmic bliss with self-deprecating thoughts, he gave her the "Peach" speech, which would have had her in tears if he hadn't kissed the stuffing out of her before she had a chance.

Suddenly realizing her boneless and satisfied condition, versus his raging boner and state of dress, she lifted up on her elbow.

"How come I'm stark naked and you are still wearing every stitch of clothing?"

"Well, that's easily resolved." Pulling his shirt over his head, he revealed a very tempting broad, firm chest with a decent sprinkling of dark and grey hair, as well as a set of big muscular shoulders, both adorned with very unexpected tattoos that curved onto his back as well.

Eager to explore, she ran her fingers through the course hair on his chest, slightly pinching his nipple as she passed by it, which caused him to hiss between his teeth: something for her to keep in mind. Hungry for more skin to run her hands over, she started unbuckling his belt, but just as she was about to lower his zipper to explore the promise she felt there, firm knocking came from the front door, interrupting their sensual haze...SHIT!

"Sorry to interrupt, folks." Ralph said, looking back and forth between Gus, who had quickly slipped his shirt back on to answer the door, and Emma, who was just coming out of the bathroom where she had disappeared to with her discarded clothes to try and make herself somewhat presentable. "Frank asked me to check in on my rounds to make sure everything was quiet here. When I didn't see any cars parked out front, but a light on inside, I thought I'd check it out."

"Pulled my truck into the tree line, so it wouldn't be too obvious from the road. I'm bunking here tonight though, so you can tell Frank there is no need to worry about Emma." Gus intended his message to be clear. He wasn't about to leave Emma's side, and he didn't appreciate the glances Ralph was shooting in her direction.

"Well, I guess I'll be on my way then, since everything here seems to be under control." With a stiff nod in Gus's direction and a hat tip to Emma, Ralph made his exit. Gus stood in the doorway until the taillights of the patrol car disappeared down the road.

Closing the door, he turned around to find the living room and kitchen empty. Turning off the lights and making sure everything was locked down for the night, he made his way to the bedroom. He found Emma curled on her side, her back to the door. Shedding his clothes, and leaving only his boxer briefs on, he slid under the covers behind her, fitting himself against her warm body, his nose in her neck.

"We are not done, but I still have your taste on my lips, your smell in my nose, and with you to snuggle up against me; I'm a satisfied man. Can I just hold you tonight?"

CHAPTER SEVEN

"The spot I've seen that truck waiting is just twenty or so yards back from the intersection, up ahead where we turn left to go to Cortez," Emma told Gus. as they drove into Cortez the next morning to check Emma's mailbox. They also planned to meet up with Joe Morris at the county sheriff's office to touch base and check on any progress.

Emma had woken up earlier with the smell of coffee wafting out from the kitchen; momentarily catching her off guard, until she remembered the events of the night before and the presence of a warm and very comfortable body wrapped around her all night. Her sleep had been deep and delicious, and although customarily sore when she woke up, the strong arm wrapped around her and the big hand grasping her boob, more than made up for that.

She had been lying there for a while, fighting the need to get to the bathroom, just delighting in the sound of slight snoring in her ear and the possessive feel of him holding her down in bed, with a big ass grin on her goofy face before she dozed off again. The next time her eyes opened, she was alone in bed and drooling with a need for the coffee she smelled, when Gus walked in with a cup.

"I've just decided I'm gonna keep you." She smiled at him, holding her hands out for her caffeine fix. She was surprising herself with how unselfconscious she was feeling. It was only enforced when she looked at Gus and saw sheer appreciation reflected in his eyes.

"You have, have you?" His deep voice rumbled over her, as he bent down for a kiss.

"Sure thing. If it means getting rocked to sleep at night and served coffee in the morning, then hell yeah; it's worth the pain of putting up with you the rest of the time," Emma joked, wincing slightly as she tried to get herself up.

"You okay?" Gus wanted to know.

"Oh yeah, I just get stiff during the night; I seize up, so in the mornings it takes a while for me to get limbered up…no big deal." Emma found Gus looking at her intently. "What's up?"

"I'm thinking that's not going to be easy–seeing you in pain," Gus admitted. "Especially knowing there probably won't be much I can do to fix it." Cradling her face, he kissed her lips lightly, and with that, turned around and left the bedroom, saying, "I'll leave you to get ready. We need to get into Cortez today."

-

The post office in Cortez wasn't busy, and opening her box, Emma found nothing but advertising; no check from the elusive Ernst Corbin, not that they had really expected it to show up.

About to head over to Mr. Happy, a local eatery where they planned to grab some breakfast before heading over to meet with Joe, Gus stopped Emma at the door.

"Are you okay to go ahead and grab a table? I just want to ask the postmaster a few questions. You can take the truck, I'll catch up with you."

"God no, it's just across the street. The exercise is good for me. Besides, you'll probably make it there in time to hold the door for me." She smiled at him as she moved past him and through the door he was holding open for her.

"Won't be long." His deep voice was a breath away from her ear and full of promise.

-

Being mid-morning, the temperature was still comfortable, but Emma feared that by noon, the day would turn in to a scorcher. Enjoying the relative quiet of South Beech Street, just off the main thoroughfare of Cortez, she didn't have to worry about traffic. As she rolled her walker off the curb to cross the road, there was only a truck pulling out of a parking spot down the street. Her eyes were already scanning the curb on the other side to find a good spot to lift her walker up, so she didn't notice the truck barreling toward her until the last minute, when the sound of the revving engine registered in her brain. All she saw then was a big truck grill coming toward her before her anger set in. *Hell no!* Trying to dive headfirst in between the parked cars, she didn't quite make it before she felt the impact, and everything faded to black.

-

The postmaster was just about to show Gus into the small office in the back when the roar of an engine, followed by an impact, and the screeching of metal snapped Gus's head around to the window. Seeing a dark truck speed off, he instinctively took note of any details he could grab before turning his attention to the small crowd of people gathering on the opposite side of the street. That was when he noticed the mangled walker, half crunched under the dented side of a parked car, and the bottom fell out of his stomach. Emma…

"Emma!" He ripped open the door and stormed into the street to where he now could see glimpses of a prone figure on the ground through the crowd that was forming. Gus called her name as he started pushing people out of the way. "Emma…" he whispered, seeing her lying half in between two cars, her head bleeding. "Somebody call an ambulance!" With shaking hands, he traced her face and neck, gathering courage to look for a pulse.

A woman who had been sitting at her side put her hand on his arm and looked at him with a small smile.

"We already called. She's breathing, and she has a pulse–I checked. In fact, I saw the whole thing. She hit her head on the parked car before hitting the ground, then the truck hit her legs as she was trying to get out of the way."

Gus leaned in and whispered gruffly in Emma's ear, "I'm not done with you, Peach." Then he pulled his cell phone out of his pocket and called Joe.

"I need you to come to the emergency room. Emma was run down on South Beech Street, just outside of the post office and the ambulance is on its way. I'll give you whatever information I have there…I'm not leaving her side."

Hanging up, he turned to the woman at Emma's side. "I work with the Montezuma County Sheriff's Office, can I have your name and number, in case we lose track somewhere along the way? I'm going in the ambulance with her."

"Sure," the woman said. "Are you her husband?"

"No, not her husband, her…her friend–fiancé," Gus quickly added, figuring it might be the only way he would be allowed to stay with her, given that he was not direct family. He handed her his phone to add her information to it.

Just as he heard the sirens of the ambulance round the corner, Emma's eyelids started to flutter.

"Stay still, babe. The ambulance is here, and I don't want you to move until they have you checked out."

"Mmmmmmm…fucking asshole truck…" Emma mumbled, as her head rolled back and forth over the pavement. Gus held her face and tried to lock onto her gaze.

"Emma, look at me. Keep your head still for me, okay? You're bleeding a bit from your head, and I don't know from where. I need the paramedics to check you out. Can you let them do that for me? Stay still?"

"Such pretty eyes. Chocolate brown. Chocolate's my favorite…love chocolate. Chocolate's yummy." Her pretty blue eyes, still slightly glazed over, were looking at him, a goofy smile playing on her lips. Apparently, she was still a little out of it. "Hi," she sighed, before her eyes slid shut again.

The paramedics had her loaded up in short order and Gus continued his ruse as her fiancé to get himself on the ambulance; not willing to lose sight of her, even for a minute. He gave them as much information as he could, but when it came to her chronic conditions, he hit a big snag and was met with some odd looks when he admitted to knowing few details. That was something that would have to be changed and soon.

Arriving in the ER, Gus was relegated to a family waiting area, even though he didn't want to leave her side. The attending physician assured him it would be faster and easier for all involved if they could simply do their job. She promised to inform him of everything they did and found, as soon as they were done. Given that the waiting room was just around the corner, he could sneak a peek into the treatment room from time to time. He took the opportunity to finally call Arlene, something he had waited with to do until he had Emma in good hands. He didn't know what he had expected, but the sharp intake of breath followed by a, "Goddammit!" wasn't exactly it. However, Arlene did say she was on her way, as in NOW. Okay then.

Finally a moment for his thoughts and feelings to catch up with him, Gus dropped his head in his hands. His hands were still shaking from the experience. When he felt a hand on his shoulder and lifted his head, he saw Joe had found him.

"I got some updates on the way here from the officers on the scene," Joe reported. "So no need to give me all the deets right now. How is she doing?"

"Honestly? I have no idea. She came to for a few minutes, talked a bit, and was out like a light again. If anything, she has a concussion. She sounded pretty out of it. There was also bleeding from her head somewhere, and I have absolutely no idea what kind of impact the rest of her body sustained, let alone what further damage it has done to her. She is already disabled, I imagine she may have some fragile spots more susceptible to permanent injury." He shrugged his shoulders. "I'm just guessing here, I really don't know."

"You care about her," Joe stated.

"Didn't see this that coming, Joe. Did NOT see this that coming. Fuck me."

Just then, the attending walked into the waiting area and nodded at Joe in obvious recognition.

"Chief Deputy Morris."

"Naomi." Joe nodded in the pretty brunette's direction. Interesting. Dismissing Joe and firmly turning to Gus, the doctor introduced herself as Dr. Waters.

"Mr. Flemming..."

"Gus, please." He stood, rubbing his hands on his jeans, trying to look over the doctor's shoulder into the ER.

"Alright, Gus. Here is what we know. Emma has severe bruising along her left hip and leg, and a fairly deep laceration on the side of her scalp. She is conscious at this time and talking, but still a little confused, so we suspect she has, at the very least, a concussion. From what we can tell from our external examination, she doesn't seem to have sustained any broken bones, but given her pre-existing condition, it is difficult to ascertain with any degree of certainty. So we are going ahead and taking her for a round of x-rays and a scan of her head. We would like to first rule out any damage to her brain or skull we can't detect from the outside, and then make sure we are not dealing with fractures or any other hidden injuries we have not been able to pick up on. At this point, it looks like she was very lucky, but let's wait for the results of those tests before we haul out the champagne."

A deep sigh left his lips as he sank back down in the chair, dropping his head down. Feeling a hand squeeze his shoulder, he looked up to see Dr. Waters' sympathetic eyes on him.

"She's been asking for you. You can come in for a minute before we take her for her scan."

Surging to his feet, and practically shoving the doc out of his way, he marched into the room across from the waiting area. Her hair was a mop of curls clumped and straggled together, and her face was pale and scraped from the impact with the parked car and the pavement. Looking at Emma still made his chest do funny things.

"Peach," he managed in a rusty voice, pushing some curls off her forehead and stroking his fingers down her cheek, "How are you feeling?" That came out a little firmer.

"Fine, I'm okay. Really," Emma gave him, noticing the eyebrow he raised. Her lips pulled into a little smile. "I have a nickname now?" she teased. Relief flooded him. Seeing her spirit hadn't been knocked out of her, he couldn't help himself–so he kissed her. His eyes squeezed shut. With all the pent up fear and anxiety that had coursed through his system in the past hour or so, he needed to feel and taste her. Reluctantly letting go of her luscious mouth, he saw his own emotions reflected in her tear-filled blue eyes that smiled back at him.

When he finally responded, he said, "Just calling them as I see them, babe."

Having seen Emma would be okay with his own eyes, it was much easier for Gus to fill Arlene in when she came storming through the door, hell-bent on getting to her friend's side. With Arlene calmed down a bit and introduced as family to the nursing staff, Joe called in a deputy to stand guard at the hospital. Now Gus was ready to rally the troops and run this fucker down.

CHAPTER EIGHT

"I'm fine, Arlene. Stop fussing. The doc said there was just severe bruising and a concussion. She contacted my rheumatologist and neurologist, what more do you want? I've had scans, x-rays; they're observing me until tomorrow. I'm going to be okay." Emma loved Arlene to bits, but she was clucking like an old hen around her hospital bed and it was driving her nuts. She felt like she was putting everyone around her at ease. Funny how people worried a little more just because she already had some health issues, but really, it just made her that much stronger. Pain didn't faze her much, and as long as death wasn't imminent, there wasn't a whole lot that freaked her out, so she tended to be the calm and sensible one in the room. The irony.

Even Gus had seemed completely shaken by this whole incident. That was actually pretty sweet, seeing him so worried about her. She felt little shivers going down her spine when she thought about his newfound name for her rumbling off those delicious lips, 'Peach.' Yeah, not complaining, but she didn't need him to see her any more as an invalid than he probably already did. And teasing him a little to lift the heaviness out of the room seemed like the thing to do. She didn't regret it…it made him bend over close and tease her right back, all sexy and smelling good, putting a satisfied smile on her face.

Turning her thoughts back to the present, she turned to Arlene. "Where did you say Gus was off to?"

"He and that Chief Deputy Morris were going back to the sheriff's office to make up a proper report and 'run some errands'– whatever the hell that means." Arlene scowled.

"Awww, come on, honey. Feeling left out? Is it that bad having to babysit me?" Emma teased her.

"Eff off, Ems. You scared the snot out of me. I almost had a heart attack when Gus called me. I had a blow out fight with Seb, who insisted I shouldn't be driving myself in the state I was in–*hmpf*–but I wasn't about to let him close the diner, 'cause I know you would've kicked my ass for that."

"Damn right I would've…no reason to, but I do appreciate you racing out here for me, Bestie." Emma smiled at Arlene, who rolled her eyes, making Emma laugh.

"Enough mushy stuff, okay? Seb cooked me a good breakfast, and it would be a waste if I hurled those biscuits and gravy all over your pristine hospital sheets."

"Hey Arlene…Bite me."

"Ems–You can kiss my ass."

They were still laughing when the friendly Dr. Waters walked in on them.

"Anybody need spanking? I'm up for that." She deadpanned, sending Emma and Arlene into another fit of snickers.

"I like her…can we keep her?" Arlene turned to Emma.

"Thanks for the invite, but I already belong to someone. Although, I'm sure he wouldn't miss me too much," Dr. Waters joked. "I'm actually here to let you know, all tests came back negative, as did the x-rays and scan. This is all great news, but I do want to do a quick neuro exam before I discharge you tomorrow morning. Is your partner going to be back to pick you up?"

"Partner?"

"The big, hulking male, looking better than an ice cream cone, sitting in the waiting room earlier, looking terrified for you...Gus? Mr. Flemming?"

"Ahhhhh. Lickable, isn't he?...Yeah. Erm–Well, I don't really know. I think so, but either way, I've got it covered, no worries," she said with a side-glance at Arlene, who nodded back at her. Even if Gus wasn't back–she had no clue as to what she had or did not have with him, so she had no way of drawing any conclusions either way–she would always have friends to draw on. God, she loved this small community.

"Well, alright then. I'll see you tomorrow morning. Try and get some rest while you can, because the nurse will come and wake you every few hours or so...standard fare with concussions. Sorry!" Dr. Waters said, with an impish grin and a shrug as she walked out.

Gus had spent the past two hours going over any details he could remember from the hit and run, which wasn't a whole lot. The only thing, a general description of an older navy blue or black pick up, looked to be an F-150, but he couldn't even be sure about that. He had been too preoccupied with Emma at the time. Luckily, the officers at the scene had gathered a little more from witnesses; it had been a rusted, navy colored F-150 with the tailgate missing. It had been sitting in a parking spot down the street, idling, when it suddenly pulled out and swerved to the opposite side. It appeared to aim straight for Emma, who somehow managed to push her walker out of the way and threw herself partially in between the two parked cars. The woman who had been attending to Emma when Gus got to her, managed to get a partial plate, and Joe was running what he had combined with the description of the truck now. Unfortunately, the F-150 was a popular truck and just about everyone owned a pickup truck.

-

Leaning back in his chair, Joe turned away from his computer screen to face Gus.

"You thinking this is Corbin's doing?" Joe voiced what had seemed pretty obvious.

"Sure looks like it. It seems a bit of a jump, ya know? From burglary to murder, no?" Not waiting for an answer, he continued, "I get that he'd be hard-pressed to make sure she doesn't have any information that might point to him, but why hurt her? With her dead, he wouldn't have a clue what she might have held on to, or God forbid, passed on to someone else. It just doesn't make much sense to me." Running his hands through his hair, he gave it a hard pull. "Dammit, I'm so frustrated. I can't get a proper lead on Corbin, I have two suspicious trucks at two separate incidents that seem to be connected, but something feels off."

"I hear you," Joe agreed. "I'm not liking this development either. We've lost track of some of Corbin's former contacts, who seem to have disappeared from the face of the earth, and the man himself is nowhere to be found. On top of that, I'm having a hard time convincing my superiors that round the clock surveillance is necessary for Emma. They prefer to believe they are simply dealing with a bail skip, and since our task force stays mostly on the quiet side, I don't have much weight there either."

Gus pulled his phone out of his pocket and started scrolling through his numbers. "That's it. I'm not taking any chances with her. I'm putting together my own team and calling them out."

"Why don't you take her with you somewhere safe?"

"I thought about that, Joe. It's not that easy. Fuck, I don't know how long this is going to take, and Emma needs her stuff, her meds, her doctors…people she trusts. Besides, from what I know of her, she likely won't budge anyway. No–she's likely safer here, or at least in Cedar Tree, with a small community of people she trusts and friends she can count on."

Joe nodded thoughtfully. " I'll do what I can. Call Frank and talk to him again, but I don't think he has a stable of staff to spare."

"Came with only one deputy, when I saw him–guy named Ralph. Haven't seen another yet. Like I said, I'm setting up shop in Cedar Tree, 'cause no matter what, there is more coming. This isn't going away, and one way or another, Corbin has to show his face at some point…and when he does, I want to be prepared."

-

Dialing his office number in Grand Junction, he got a hold of Dana, his office manager.

"It's me. I need a team over here, Dana. Can you call the motel where you had me booked, just outside Cedar Tree, and book a bunch of rooms? Get Neil to gather up his laptop and gadgets. Call Caleb and see if he can do a couple of days on a job with me…oh, and get in touch with Katie, as well. See if she is scheduled on a detail, 'cause I could use her help too. And Dana? How would you feel about running command center from here?" Listening to his manager read back all his instructions and confirming she would head out with Neil as soon as she had her cats taken care of, made him feel a little more in control already. Good. He was being proactive, which felt a shitload better than being a sitting duck. Or rather, have Emma be a sitting duck. This way he could always have someone covering Emma, so he could react immediately when a lead popped up.

Gus turned to Joe. "Wheels are turning."

"Good." Turning to face him, Joe threw back the last dregs of what passed for coffee in this office and got up. "Let's go pick up your truck in town, since I presume you'll want to get back to the hospital?" he said, quirking his eyebrow.

"Have to run back to Emma's to pick up some stuff for her; they're keeping her for the night. She'll need meds and her things."

"Oh, and you get to pick out her undies? How domesticated." Joe grinned.

"Fuck off. You're a pain in my ass, deputy, and while we're on the subject - what's with you and the pretty doc? You seemed, how shall I put it–familiar?" He flung back at his friend.

"Old news, and none of your business." Was the retort.

"Fair enough, but let's remember that goes both ways!"

On his way to Emma's bungalow, Gus stopped in at the diner to grab something to eat and see if Seb needed anything, while he was out and about. Busy in the kitchen, with an extra server helping out, and a decent lunch crowd on the go, Seb was still more than happy to put something together for him to bring back for the girls. In the meantime, he grabbed a burger.

"Our Ems doing okay?" Seb wanted to know.

"She'll be fine. Was lucky, could've been a lot worse. I don't know how much you've been told about the mess she is in, but some nasty character is after her for information they think she has. Be much obliged if you could keep eyes and ears open for anything unusual."

"Anything for Arlene's friend and the best baker in town," Seb stated solemnly. Strange way to put it, but whatever; as long as he kept an eye on things, Gus was happy.

-

Belly full and a cooler filled with cold sandwiches and salads to take back to Cortez, Gus headed over to the house to pick up some things Emma might need for tonight and tomorrow. It didn't take him long to grab whatever medication he could find, some toiletries, and a change of comfortable clothes. Tossing everything in a bag he found in her closet, and he made sure to leave the odd light on, so as not to alert anyone the house would be empty tonight. Less than fifteen minutes later, he was back in his truck.

Next stop would be the Walgreens in Cortez where he needed to get something before going back to see Emma.

"Oh. My. God!" she exclaimed, as Gus came walking in the door, pushing a bright purple walker, loaded up with bags, in front of him. "Where did you find that awesome color?" She couldn't believe that was the first thing out of her mouth, but she was so excited and touched he had brought her a new walker–and a cool purple one to boot–she didn't know what else to say. Gus chuckled at Emma's exuberance and left the walker by the door. He said hi to Arlene, who was lounging in a chair, and walked straight over to the bed. She couldn't look away from the smug look on his face, the smile lines at the corners of his eyes and the pleased little twinkle she saw reflected there. He walked right up, cupped her face in his rough hands and without a howdy, fitted his lips over hers in a proprietary manner. His tongue demanded entrance, leaving her no choice but to open her still smiling mouth.

"Well, Hello!" That was Arlene, observing the lip lock with keen interest from the edge of her seat. "Somebody got some–and it sure as hell wasn't me!"

Emma could feel Gus's shoulders shaking in laughter, as his smiling lips slowly detached from hers. "Subtle, girlfriend."

"Me, subtle? Hells bells, if I didn't know any better, I'd swear you were trying to give each other an endoscopy by tongue." Arlene grinned.

Oh my, Arlene was on a roll.

"Gross." She wrinkled her nose, as she looked back up at Gus, who still had both hands loosely on her face. Gah, that man did funny things to her insides. She felt sixteen–fine, eighteen. Tops!

"How are you doing?" Gus prompted her, stroking her cheek with his thumb before sliding his hands down to her shoulders and stepping away to grab the stool next to her bed.

"You went and got me a walker?"

"You always answer a question with a question?" He smiled.

"You got me a purple walker. That is the best gift ever!" She couldn't help it, part knock on the head, part medication, and a huge part stunned pleasure at the his thoughtfulness. It had her acting stupid and nonresponsive.

"Okay, I'm getting a coffee. I feel a sudden need to…leave," Arlene quipped, as she got up. "How long has it been? Already you guys are nauseating! Anybody want something?"

"Oh, wait." Gus jumped up. "I whipped by the diner and Seb made you guys some food, so don't get anything to eat. They're in the bags on the walker."

That had Arlene silent for a minute.

"Oh, wow. Nice of Seb," she murmured, turning to head out the door. "Be right back."

-

"Yes, I got you a purple walker. I saw it, it was vivid, and colorful, and unique…it looked like it was made for you."

Emma had to swallow a few times at that. The man was just too much. "Thank you." She managed to squeeze by the frog in her throat. Always a little uncomfortable with intense moments, she fiddled with the edges of her blanket, trying hard not to look at Gus, but aware of every hair that moved on his head. "I uhmm…I really appreciate it."

"My pleasure," Gus said firmly, making clear that subject was closed, before pulling the chair Arlene had vacated closer to the bed.

"Now, I wasn't going to ask, because I want you to understand it makes no difference to me. You are simply Emma, but I realized coming in here with you earlier, that I still have no real grasp on your condition, or conditions. It scared the shit out of me, thinking that I might not have the right information to pass on for them to help you–to do the right things for you. I'd like to know.

Emma struggled to keep the tears that were forming from spilling over. Other than Arlene, who mostly fussed because that's what Arlene did, there really wasn't anyone who had ever made such an effort, or taken such care to treat her right. Even Kara, her own daughter, was so used to having 'Mom' be capable and self-sufficient; she hardly ever asked how she was doing. But this…this was something on a whole different level.

Frankly, she didn't quite know what to do with it. So tempting to hand yourself over to someone and say, "Here, you drive for a while," but not all that easy to do when your butt's been stuck behind the wheel most of your adult life.

"Is it that bad?" Gus joked, as he leaned in and used his thumb to wipe away the stray tear that managed to escape, making Emma snort.

"Hardly. Nothing lethal anyway. Just very annoying, and debilitating and painful. And generally progressive." She sighed with a slump of her shoulders.

"Hmmm," Gus rumbled, grabbing both her hands in his. "Go on."

"It's not just one single illness, or condition–whatever. It's a combination of a few problems. I have some forms of arthritis that have wreaked havoc with my spine, causing damage. I've had a few corrective surgeries, but there is only so much that can be done, and in the meantime, my spinal cord and nerve roots are slowly affected. Then there is the rheumatoid arthritis, which causes inflammation in the big joints. Hence, all my meds. It's how I try to keep on top of the inflammation and minimize pain, so other than that, I'm just peachy!"

Emma tried to lighten the mood with a chuckle when she saw the serious look on Gus's face. He hadn't stopped using his right thumb to massage the palm of her hand, while his other hand would incrementally increase its pressure as she went down her list.

"You are that. Appreciate you telling me. It helps me to know, but it changes nothing." Gus bent toward her to lightly kiss her mouth. "But I'm still not done with you," he mumbled, smiling against her lips.

CHAPTER NINE

After spending a fairly restless night in a hospital chair next to Emma's bed, and being woken every two hours by a nurse checking Emma's vitals, Gus was glad to stretch his legs as he left the room to chase down a cup of coffee for himself. Emma had one with her breakfast, but apparently hospitality didn't stretch to include anyone but the patient. Besides, he had a feeling he hadn't missed much, judging by the grimace on Emma's face after her first gulp. She still drank it, and he smiled, recalling her face with every sip she downed. It obviously hadn't stopped her from her apparent need for caffeine, even though she didn't want any more…he couldn't help but offer her another one.

Stopping at the nurses' station, he asked the charge nurse if she had any idea when Dr. Waters would be in to discharge Emma.

"She does her rounds after 10:00 a.m." Was the answer.

"Thanks," he said, looking at his watch and continuing on his quest for sustenance. Only 7:30 a.m. now…still a ways to go, but not enough to get anything substantial done. Maybe he should check with Arlene to see what her plans were? He might as well stay around, and maybe call Dana to see how she was making out gathering his team. With any luck, she was already on her way.

Armed with his coffee and a couple of bagels from the coffee shop in the hospital lobby, Gus returned to the room to find Dr. Waters already there.

"Hey, you're here already. The nurse just told me you would be by after ten."

"That's when I normally do my rounds, but I was up most of the night anyway, so I thought I'd pop in now."

"Sounds like no one got much sleep," Emma piped up. "I can't wait to sleep in my own bed and not be interrupted every couple of hours to see if I'm alive."

Dr. Waters grinned. "Well, let's see if we can get you out of here."

Less than an hour later, he pulled up to Emma's bungalow, finding Neil's van parked out front. Emma grabbed his arm.

"Somebody's at my house!"

"Yeah, I know," he said calmly, making Emma narrow her eyes at him. "Shit. I forgot to tell you, I had my office manager pull together a team to come and assist out here."

"Here? As in, at...my house? I have no room. Hello–only one bedroom. Where the hell am I going to put a 'team'?" Emma rambled, as she nervously grabbed for the door handle.

"Stop. I'll get you out, and no, they are not staying here. My assistant, Dana, has booked a block of rooms at the motel. Look, I talked to Joe, and they don't have the manpower to secure you twenty-four seven. Also, I figured I wouldn't be able to get you away from here with a tow truck, so until we have our guy, you are not to be left alone."

At that last sentence, Emma scoffed, "Pffft. I'm not a child. I don't need someone telling me what I can and can't do." Crossing her arms over her chest, she tried to stare him down.

He dipped his head down, bringing his face closer. "Trust me, babe. No one, and I mean no one, is going to mistake you for a child." That earned him a full out eye-roll. He got why she would get a little defensive about her life being invaded, so he was straight with her and filled her in on his discussions with Joe. Hearing that the hit and run was deliberate, she was obviously disturbed. Although Emma nodded her grasp of the situation, her face had drained of color.

"Now, let's get out of the car, and I'll introduce you to my team. They're probably just here to let us know they've arrived, and then they'll be off to the motel."

"Great," Emma grumbled. "I have to meet your friends when I haven't showered and look like I was hit by a truck. Just what I wanted after a night of no sleep."

Grabbing her bag from the back of the truck, he had to smile at her sour mood. Putting his arm around her and placing a kiss on her head, he told her, "You could sleep in a dumpster for a week and still look great."

"And you lie for shit," she countered, making him laugh.

"So how long have you worked for Gus?" Emma asked his manager, Dana. A spark plug of a woman: not much taller than Emma herself, with a cherubic appearance, but the demeanor of a drill sergeant. Dana had taken it on herself to 'mother' her a little, while Gus and Neil were discussing hard drives at the kitchen table. Apparently, there were two more to the team scheduled to arrive, but they were coming from other jobs. Neil was the computer and technical specialist, and Dana not only ran Gus's office, but seemed to 'run' Neil as well. If she hadn't been told differently, she would've sworn they were mother and son.

"I've worked for Gus for about six years now? When my youngest was done at the university, and I was pretty sure none of the kids were going to come back home again, I wanted something to do. Good thing too, since my husband passed away unexpectedly just two years after that." She smiled sadly.

"Lord, I'm so sorry. He must have been so young still."

"Yeah, he had only just turned sixty when he was hit with a massive heart attack. Didn't see it coming either...healthy as a horse–always. But it happened so fast, and he was gone instantly." She shook her head. "Figure it was harder on the kids. He was about to become a grandfather."

What do you say to that? Getting older didn't particularly bother Emma much, but that blissful illusion of immortality did start disappearing and that scared her.

"Gus tells me you have a daughter in her twenties already? You hardly look old enough. Where is she?" Dana prompted.

"Kara is twenty-four. She still lives and works in Boston." She smiled at the older woman. "Luckily she has a great job and fantastic friends, so she is quite settled there. She was happy for me when I decided to move here."

"Oh yeah, two months ago, right?"

A little surprised by the information Dana had on her, she quipped, "So I guess I shouldn't be telling Gus any of my deep dark secrets then, should I?" That made Dana laugh.

"I think he's a little sweet on you. He's actually been filling me in on a lot of details of this case, which is extremely unusual. Normally I have to pry information out of him by force, but not this time. Anything to do with you, he seems eager to share with me," Dana confessed with a wink, causing that awful blotchy blush to creep back up on Emma's face.

"Ahhh…" Dana studied her. "So that's how it is!"

"That's how what is?" Gus asked, walking in.

Great. Wondering exactly how much of that he heard, Emma tried for diversion.

"I'm tired, so I think I'm going down for a nap."

"You okay? Here, I'll give you a hand." Gus pulled her up from the couch, wrapping his arm firmly around her waist.

"Need a hand there, Boss?" Dana teased, with a half-smile playing on her lips.

"I've got it, Dana. Thanks." Gus snapped, stopping Emma in her tracks.

"You know, it was on my lips to say–I'm not an invalid–but we all know that would be a lie, now wouldn't we? Anyway, can we tone down the damsel in distress rescue? And I'm. Right. Here. There's no need to talk around me. Geeze." With that she turned around, leaving Gus standing there, too stunned to move. She could hear Dana howling with laughter, saying, "Oooo, can we keep her? You just got told! I wish you could see your face right now. Damn, where's my camera?"

 It didn't surprise her when only minutes later after hearing low voices replace the raucous laughter from the living room, the bedroom door opened and Gus walked in, a sheepish look on his face. "Sorry 'bout that," he grumbled, looking at his boots. "I just don't want you to overdo anything."

Emma stood in front of him, letting her hand stroke the stubble on his jaw, down his neck, coming to rest over his heart. Leaning in, she put her cheek on his chest and slid her arms around his waist, breathing in deep and letting all the stress out of her body on the exhale. The heat of his body soothed her and the steady beat of his heart made her feel secure. Slowly she felt his arms come up around her, one grabbing her firmly around her waist, anchoring her, and the other stroking up her spine gently, but firmly. She felt his big hand slip under her hair and grab the back of her head–his fingers speared through her curls. So safe.

"If I could, I would stop time, right here in this moment," Emma whispered into his shirt, earning a slight squeeze from his arms. Leaning back a little, she looked into his eyes.

"Thank you for caring for me, Gus. Honestly, I appreciate it, but it pisses me off when people talk over me like I'm not in the room. It sets me off. I guess too many times lying in a hospital bed or on an examining table while medical staff discusses you as if you are a specimen instead of a living, breathing person has done that to me."

A small smile played up at the corners of Gus's mouth, and the lines at the corner of his eyes slowly deepened.

"You're right, you know." She could feel his voice rumble deeply from his chest. "I do care for you." His dark brown eyes held her gaze for a moment before pulling her in and planting a quick kiss on her lips.

"Now, let's get you in bed for that nap, while I organize these guys and get them on their way. Caleb and Katie should be arriving at the motel at some point too. It would be nice if things were set up, so they can hit the ground running."

Emma's ears picked up the names for the other two members of the team. "Caleb and Katie?" she asked pointedly, looking at Gus with her eyebrows raised, seeing him wince. Ouch. So her guess was on the money.

Sitting down on the side of the bed, she started undressing, having decided to simply ignore Gus, ignore the awkward situation, and have a well-deserved nap before losing her shit.

"Shit, Peach. I never even thought…" Emma cut him off when she stuck her hand in his face.

"You know, I'm really, really tired, so why don't you go do your thing with your team, and I'll just go have my nap."

"Just let me explain something," Gus started.

"Not now. Please. Just…I need a nap now." Emma rolled herself under the covers and turned her back on him, closing her eyes and willing those dang silly tears away.

"Just so you know, we are not done yet." She heard him say.

Ignoring him, she forcibly slowed down her breathing, until she heard him leave and close the door behind him. Just a minute ago, she had felt safe in his arms, oblivious to emotional or physical threats…now, all those insecurities came washing over her again. The thought of sharing space with his convenient fuck buddy was a bit too much for her emotions right now, even if she couldn't quite pin down where they were, at this point. The fact that it was someone he worked with stung as well. She wasn't just someone he saw once in a blue moon. Did she mean more than he had implied?

Too tired to think anymore, she willed her spinning thoughts away. That's when she heard the door open back up, footsteps approaching the bed and felt him leaning in behind her, whispering.

"Couldn't leave it at that. I'll let you sleep, but not without telling you this. I fucked up. Caleb and Katie are independent contractors, who specialize in personal security, and occasionally, we will hire them on as part of investigative teams. Calling them in was a routine move for me, and I didn't consider the implications this time. I blindsided you, and that's the last thing I wanted to do." Kissing the shell of her ear, he said, "We okay?"

Taking in a deep breath, she forced herself to detach from the slightly nauseous feeling in her stomach,

Emma responded lightly, "Sure thing. We've only known each other for what? Three, four days?" Forcing out a chuckle, she finished. "Just fun and games, right?"

She could feel his growl behind her.

"Fuck no, woman." He bit out. "You know it, and I know it. We'll sort it, but now is not the time. You're exhausted and I have a team to set up. So, when I say 'sort it,' I mean I'll have myself up in your face, under your skin, and into your body so deep, you won't be able to doubt my intentions." Those last words sent a full body shiver down to her toes and had her turning her head, seeking out his eyes. She found them burning with heat and determination into hers.

"Now. Once more. Are. We. Okay?"

"We're okay," she said so softly, the air barely passed her lips. But he heard her and latched onto her mouth with a fierce intensity that left no room for doubt. With one last brush of his lips on her forehead, he pulled back.

"You sleep. I'll be in the living room."

The warm feeling of security at least partially returned, as she rolled back over, closed her eyes, and promptly fell asleep

CHAPTER TEN

"Are you sure you're up to this?" Gus asked Emma, as he turned his truck toward town. The rest of the team had arrived, and he had briefed them all on the case and the events to date. He then sent them off to the motel to set up camp there. They were supposed to grab something to eat at Arlene's after and bring something over for him and Emma. He hadn't heard a peep out of her since leaving her bedroom. She must've been worn out. Of course, neither of them got much sleep in the hospital, and he could feel it too. Then, not thirty minutes after everyone took off, she had come out. When she found out they would all be at the diner, she insisted on going too.

"You were just released this morning. Don't you think you should take it easy today?" He tried again, after she ignored his first attempts to keep her home.

Turning to him, Emma raised an eyebrow and said, "I'm fine! I need to go see Arlene because I haven't seen her all day. I know she is worried, and I won't be able to skip out another day–trust me. I may be a little bruised and battered, but it's better for me to move around than to sit still. I'll just seize up if I do. Besides..." She continued with a satisfied smirk on her face, "I have a strong man who is able to pick me up and carry me off if something happens."

"Smartass." Shaking his head at her, he couldn't stop the smile forming at the corner of his mouth. "Fine, we'll eat there, so you can talk to your BFF and let her know you're alive, and then we go home."

Home. Funny how that came out so naturally. Huh. He never really got too attached to things or places, not even to people. Sure, he had some friends and would socialize from time to time, but nothing or no one he would crave being with. He could see himself craving Emma though. Too soon...too complicated right now. He best just go with the flow and focus on this damn case because it had gotten the best of him so far. Fuck, he even dropped the ball and let Emma get hurt on his watch. He needed his team to help him stay on track.

-

Pulling into the parking space at the diner, Emma put her hand on his arm to stop him, when he was about to get out of the truck. He turned to look at her.

"Does er...have you...? What I mean to say is, did you say anything to Katie? About you and me? Well...I don't really know what there is to say, or what this all means, but I don't want it to get awkward in there."

Shifting in his seat, he cupped her face in his hand.

"I don't owe Katie an explanation, nor would she owe me one. We had nothing. No relationship. Just occasional 'run-ins'."

That drew a snort from Emma and she tried to turn her head away, but he held her firm, forcing her to look at him.

"You and I have something. And even if we can't identify it, just yet, it isn't nothing. It isn't casual; it's something worth exploring the hell out of."

"I think so too," Emma said.

"Good. Glad we have that straightened out." He leaned in for a quick sweep of his mouth over her lips. "Now, I didn't have a chance to catch her alone, but I will make sure it is clear we are together. I promise it is not, nor will it be, an issue."

With one last brush of lips against her forehead, he got out, walked around the truck, grabbed her new purple walker, and helped her down.

Arlene was almost running back and forth between tables when she spotted them coming in. "Ems. What the heck are you doing out of bed?" she hollered across the diner. Okay, so much for not putting Emma on the spot.

"Would you hush, Arlene? I'm fine. I need to eat, don't I?" Emma snapped back, causing Gus to chuckle at the already almost familiar bickering of the two of them. Seb stuck his head around the hood and added his two cents.

"Hey, Emma. Didn't think we'd see you up and about tonight?"

"I'm okay, Seb, and thanks for the food yesterday. That was sweet," Emma said with a smile. Interesting thought Gus. He spotted Arlene watching the exchange like a hawk and rolling her eyes at Emma calling Seb sweet. Could just be Arlene being ornery, but he didn't think so.

By the time they got to the table where his team had gathered, Emma had been stopped by half the patrons, having heard about her 'mishap' and wanting to know how she was doing. Of course, her standard response was 'fine.' He wondered if she would still say that if the pain was killing her–probably.

"Hey guys, Dana, Neil you've already met Emma. Katie,

Caleb–meet Emma Young, reason we're all here in Cedar Tree."

Caleb, a former ranger, was an excellent tracker and private investigator. He was a large man, dark and regal, in part due to his Native American ancestry. He rose out of his chair and shook Emma's hand.

"Pleased to meet you, Ma'am."

"Oh cripes, please. No ma'ams! I know I'm no spring chicken, but that is not a title I deserve yet!" Emma laughed, squeezing a smile out of the stoic giant.

Next up was Katie, personal security expert and a P.I. as well, who also towered over Emma as she got up to introduce herself. Of course that wasn't hard to do, since Emma was pretty short. He could see the two women scrutinizing each other, but only pleasantries were exchanged.

"Let's order something. Have you guys ordered yet?" He glanced around the table.

"Yeah, just did," Caleb said, his eyes following Arlene around the tables. "Although I'm thinking your friend's got her hands full."

"Arlene will be okay. She's just grumpy 'cause she's been worried, but she manages crowds twice this size and wouldn't break a sweat. The woman is impossible to fluster, except when it comes to me apparently," Emma responded.

"So…uhm, how are you feeling?" Gus turned, curious to see Katie address Emma.

"I'm fine. Thanks for asking." Was her standard answer, delivered with a reserved little smile. Yep, this was awkward, obviously. Damn. He really should've thought this through.

"You were lucky then, very lucky there won't be any lasting

effects. There won't be, will there?" Katie added quickly.

"Nope. Fortunately, I was blessed with a hard head, apparently, and enough padding to cushion my fall."

"Good. That's good."

Eager to break into the slightly uncomfortable exchange, Gus shoved a menu in front of Emma.

"Here, order up. Then we can get you up to speed and discuss our moves for the next few days. I'm tired of sitting like bait on a hook waiting for a fish to come by. I want to shake things up a little; make things happen before they happen to us."

With Seb working away at their orders in the kitchen, Gus filled Emma in on Neil's findings first. He had made some headway with the coded files from Emma's drop box they had sent him a few nights ago. Apparently, the combinations of numbers and letters looked to be dates and bank accounts, with two or three letters in each code he wasn't quite clear on yet. Emma suggested perhaps initials, since that's how she would always number her invoices–a combination of the date and the payee's initials. Gus was stunned when he looked at her. He knew he was a goner. Fucking smart too, he smiled. Reaching over, he grabbed the back of her head and pulling pulled her close, resting his forehead against hers.

"You are fucking amazing, you know that?"

A blush creeping up from her neck, Emma glanced around, before turning her eyes back on him.

"I was just thinking logically, that's all." She almost whispered, "Everyone is staring, Gus"

"Don't care." And he planted one on her right in front of the team and the entire diner. Fuck! For a middle-aged guy, his hormones were feeling all kinds of jumpy around this woman: horny all the damn time.

Looking up, he checked the faces around the table. Dana looked back with a pleased smile. Neil was trying to look everywhere else. Caleb was wearing a shit-eating grin, and Katie–dammit, Katie had a smile plastered on, but it's it was as fake as tits on a bull. Fuck.

Could've handled that a shitload better.

Over dinner, details for that night and plans for the next day were hashed out. Gus would stay with Emma in her house. Caleb would take first shift outside, Katie second. Neil and Dana were going to work on the codes at the motel. Tomorrow morning, Joe was going meet up at the house for a briefing. Things had better start moving soon.

Emma was quiet on the way home. Tired and wondering what the sleeping arrangements were going to be for the night, but too chicken to start up a conversation about it, she let her mind wander back over dinner instead. That was a bit awkward, and not just a little intimidating. Dana and Neil she could handle, Dana felt like a contemporary, even though she was probably ten or fifteen years older. Neil was young enough to be her child, so no threat there. But Caleb was an imposing figure with dark penetrating eyes and a stern chiseled face, almost without expression, and she couldn't get a read from him. And then, of course, there had been the infamous Katie. She was tall, and very athletic...and probably a good ten years younger than she was.

Not to mention being beautiful. Of course she had to be beautiful. Her frustrated groans had Gus turning around in his seat.

"Everything alright?"

"Just tired. The day is catching up to me now, I guess." Emma smiled at him, and he reached over the console, put his big hand on her leg and gently squeezed.

"We'll be home soon. You can put something comfy on and put up your feet. I'll make some tea or something, if you like? Catch a movie? Just forget about everything for tonight. Sound okay?"

Emma leaned her head back and closed her eyes. "Mmmmm, sounds perfect, actually."

With her eyes still closed, she could feel the heat from his hand leave her leg, before the backs of his fingers slowly stroked down her cheek. She sensed his eyes on her. Perfectly content for now to hide behind her eyelids, she stayed where she was, not wanting to give away how much his care was starting to affect her. Why did her life have to be so complicated? Well, it wasn't for her, she was used to it, but why would someone who didn't have to deal with all of her issues voluntarily stick around? She really didn't have that much to offer. Nothing really, when you thought about it. Sure, she baked a good pie, and she wasn't exactly horrendous to look at, but in terms of offering someone the possibility of a future? She couldn't do that. Not when she might well end up being a burden.

Peeking from the corner of her eye, she could tell Gus's focus was back on the road, and they were almost at her turn off. If only she could fast forward for a minute, just one minute, to maybe six months from now, to have a peek at what they had turned into…if anything, just so she could shut up her overactive brain. She was making herself nuts, and she had vowed a year ago when she started making plans to move to Cedar Tree, that it would be the start of a new attitude. She would let no opportunity go by the wayside; take everything at face value and grab at happiness with both hands. So, here she was, beginning to break every damn rule she had made herself.

"Mighty loud thinking goin' on over there, Peach," Gus rumbled in her ear, as he leaned in to undo her seatbelt. She hadn't even noticed they had pulled up to her house, and he had gotten out already.

"Are you planning on sharing what you've been chewing on? Or is that not for public consumption?"

Looking at his warm dark eyes, set in that ruggedly handsome face staring down at her, she made a decision right there. "I'll be happy to share, but later. Get me inside, Big Guy. I feel like some tea and a cuddle." She smiled at him. Raising his eyebrows a bit, Gus didn't hesitate. He threw her walker back in the truck bed, put an arm around her back, and one under her knees, and lifted her off the ground, making her laugh.

"At your service, darlin'."

CHAPTER ELEVEN

Feet curled up under her on her nice big sectional, comfortable in her favorite grey yoga pants and a long sleeved shirt, Emma was enjoying the sounds of someone puttering around in her house.

"Do you have an actual teapot somewhere?" Gus called from the kitchen. "I thought I'd just make a whole pot, save us from getting up, if you don't mind."

Before she even had a chance to answer, he followed up with; "Never mind. Found it!"

Go figure, a domesticated man. One who actually looked and found. Lucky girl–she was thinking, chuckling to herself.

"And what, pray tell, are you chuckling about alone in here?" Gus asked, walking into the room with teapot, mugs, sugar, milk, and a pie on a tray.

"Where did you get that pie?" She wanted to know.

"From the diner. I had to bribe Arlene to get Seb to defrost one in the oven. I had it in the truck bed and brought it in when you were changing." He looked so sheepish; it made Emma laugh.

"Are you so hard up for pie? You could've told me. I would've baked you a fresh one."

"No baking for at least another couple of days yet. Then you can go nuts on me. And yes, I'm that 'hard' up for pie. Your kind of pie," Gus said, wiggling his eyebrows.

"Oh Lord, you need new material, Mister," she said, rolling her eyes. "That was pretty sad."

Flopping down on the couch beside her, Gus picked up the entire pie plate and two forks. He sat back, handed a fork to Emma, pulled her snug to him, and told her, "Dig in, woman, before it gets completely cold."

"The whole pie?"

"Sure, why not?"

"Uhmm, we just had dinner…"

"Dinner. Yes, but this is dessert, they're different parts of the meal. Besides, we're sharing, right?" Turning a suggestive look to her, with a cheeky grin on his face, he teased, "Come on, it's my favorite; peach pie!"

Giving up the argument and completely disarmed by his playful charm, Emma settled into Gus's side and dug in with her fork.

"So, are you going to let me in on what you were thinking on so hard back there?" Gus mumbled through a mouth full of pie.

Damn. Should've figured she wouldn't get out of that one easy. "I was just a little…overwhelmed." She put down her fork and picked up her mug of tea for something to keep her hands occupied. Gus mimicked her moves, but slipped one arm around her and drew her in close.

"How? At dinner?"

"Yeah, a bit intimidated by Caleb, and–well–Katie, to be honest. It was a bit awkward to say the least. I felt out of place. Maybe I should say I felt confused…about my place, that is."

"Hmmmm." A slight squeeze on her shoulder encouraged

her to go on.

"I used to be active and outgoing, athletic even, but since my physical issues started limiting my mobility, I withdrew. I allowed people to slowly disappear from my life. I have no family left, other than Kara, and she was angry with me because I was withdrawing from the outside world. Then I met Arlene online, and found out she was still living a full life while dealing with her own issues; it shook me awake. I got mad and realized I wasn't ready to go through life as a 'sick person.' I really felt too young to label myself like that. About a year ago, I decided I would grab every opportunity thrown at me, taking chances, opening myself up. The new me has been here with you the last few days, living in the moment. Unfortunately, the old me showed up at dinner. Still insecure, I guess. All these beautiful, capable people with so much to offer, and I couldn't help but start to compare. I don't have a hell of a lot to offer, but pie." She nodded toward the half eaten plate on the table, before turning to face Gus, who remained silent. He was looking at her with a near scowl on his face.

"Are you done?" he asked.

"Well, other than to say that I managed to shake myself out of my funk most of the way before we got home. I was about to withdraw from…whatever it was we had going on here, because I was scared. Then I reminded myself I had made a promise not to be that person anymore. So here I am."

"And thank God for that."

Lifting her so she was sprawled half over his lap and leaning against the armrest of the couch, he planted his hand beside her hip and leaned in close. "I've said this before, and I don't mind saying it again. I don't know where this is going. I didn't plan for any of it, but I like what I see. I also like what I feel when I'm around you, Emma. I want more of that. Fucking thrilled that you decided by yourself not to start running, 'cause I would've given chase, but I'd much rather be doing this." Before she could respond, he had her mouth covered with his.

Firm delicious pressure, the taste of peaches and hot tea lingering on his tongue as it slid into her mouth, seeking out hers. God, he tasted so good: the combination of his flavor and scent, a mix of sweetness with a citrus musk leftover from his morning shower and a smell all his own. Her hands skimmed over the flexing muscles in his back as he struggled to keep most of his weight off her. Her hands searching for purchase, somewhere, anywhere, while she was drowning in the sensations of his kiss. Finally finding a handhold in his hair as his lips left her mouth and trailed along her cheek and jaw to her neck. She couldn't help but move her head out of the way to give him full access, wanting to feel his wet mouth on as much of her skin as possible.

"Gus…" she breathed out, "So good…"

Without warning he pulled away, standing up, gingerly adjusting what had to be an uncomfortable erection by the looks of it, and reached for her. "Not here, Peach. Not the couch."

Grabbing his hand, she allowed him to pull her up, and help her into the bedroom. He sat her down on the edge of the bed and kneeled before her with his hands on her thighs. "I almost forgot you were hurt. We should stop," he said regretfully.

"No. I don't want to stop." Emma draped her arms around his neck and pulled him toward her. "I want this. I want you. I'm fine, I promise."

Groaning, Gus leaned his head on her chest. "I promised myself I would give you at least twenty-four hours, darlin'. It hasn't been that. You have a concussion and you're bruised all over. I'm gonna hurt you."

"Please, Gus. I want to feel you. I want to touch your skin."

Not saying anything, Gus stood, stripped his t-shirt off in one swift move and was down to his boxer briefs in no time flat. Finally she could study his gorgeously fit body and the beautifully tattooed designs gracing it. Her eyes traced over the dusting of hair covering the hard planes of his chest and abdomen, leading to the band of his boxer briefs. Leaning forward, her face now at the level of his stomach, she put her open mouth on his stomach, pressing her tongue against his skin. His flavor burst over her taste buds. Feeling a slight shiver run through him, she wrapped her arms around him, pulled him between her legs, and pressed herself against his prominent erection. Sliding her hands down the small of his back, she cupped the swell of his firm ass before pulling down his briefs. With her chin, she nudged his waistband down as far as it would go in the front, trailing her tongue down from his navel. Gus's breathing turn erratic, as the fabric of his briefs was caught tight around the head of his cock. Pulling back and looking up, she could see him looking down at her with dark heavy-lidded eyes and parted lips still wet from their kisses. His chest fell and rose fast and shallow. Holding his eyes, she edged forward and very purposely swiped her wet tongue along the rim of the head of his cock through the fabric, causing him to draw back his lips with a quick intake of breath. Again she licked him around the rim, this time following with a slight scrape of her teeth along the same path. A soft growl rumbled from his chest–his fists clenched at his side. Craving the feeling of his length filling her mouth, she relieved his cock from its fabric confinement, barely able to wrap her hand around the base. Then in one big slide, moved her mouth and lips down to engulf him tightly, until he was seated as deep as he could go.

"FUCK! Emma…" Gus, who had been so controlled just a moment earlier, suddenly grabbed her by the hair. Holding her head firmly, he started fucking her mouth. Emma clutched his ass, trying to find purchase while revelling in the power of having made this beautiful man come undone. The trembling of his muscles under her hands was evidence of his fight to keep his plunges into her mouth from going too deep. Not usually one to give over control, Emma couldn't believe how satisfying it was to offer yourself up so completely to someone else's pleasure. Right in that moment, with her head immobile, she was more turned on–felt more alive than she could recall ever being. Her eyes conveying the passion and newfound strength, she looked at the powerful man above her who was taking what he needed, wanted and desired–from her.

"Stop. I don't want to come yet, Peach. Not yet," Gus barely managed to get out, as he gently pulled himself away from her mouth. Looking down, he was momentarily shaken. Emma made a stunning picture sitting there, even still dressed. Her hair was a wild riot of curls where his hands had tangled, cheeks flushed, her lips wet and swollen from being stretched around his cock. So giving and the fucking sexiest thing he'd ever seen. And her eyes…her eyes were like deep pools of a timeless ocean, shiny and full of knowledge, hidden depths, endless promise, and soft warm comfort. He was losing himself in her.

"Too many clothes, baby…let me take care of you."

Without waiting for a response, he grabbed her shirt by the hem and pulled it up and over her head. Having foregone a bra when she changed earlier, she was left bare-chested. Pulling her up, he leaned down to take one nipple in his mouth, lightly tugged on it, released and kissed it, before repeating it on her other breast.

"Hold on to my shoulders." Bending down to his knees, he pulled her yoga pants and underwear down at once. Emma did as he asked and stepped clear of her clothes. Throwing the pants out of their way, he sat up on his knees and wrapped his arms around her. He rested his head on her breasts, feeling the length of her lush, soft body against him. "You feel so damn good…" he said softly, deeply breathing her in. Soft skin, yet firm and padded under his hands, but underneath still fragile. Leaning out, he gently pushed her back a little.

"Let me see. Lay down for me, babe. Let me check what those bastards did to you properly." Skimming his hands over her body, he noted the large dark bruising, which extended from the middle of her ribs, down her left side and her hip, almost to her knee.

"Jesus!" Burst from his lips as he tried to reign in his temper. "Babe, I'm so sorry. I didn't realize. I should've been much more careful with you. This is a really bad idea." Noticing the slightly shocked look on her face, her teeth firmly biting down on her bottom lip, he moved onto the bed on her right side: her good side. Wrapping himself around her, he insinuated his leg between hers. With his hand on her soft belly, he stroked her skin with the tips of his fingers.

"Feel my cock against you? Feel how hard you make me? Understand this; I will be inside you, but I don't want to run the risk of hurting you. When I fuck you, I want to enjoy this gorgeous, luscious body the way it was meant to be enjoyed. Do you hear me?"

Emma simply nodded, leaning over the edge of the bed to try and grab her shirt.

"What are you doing?"

"Grabbing something to sleep in?"

"Nope. No covering up. I like you just like this, so I can feel every inch of you." Pulling her back down, he curved her against him. Then he reached to turn off the bedside lamp, wrapping his arms around her and burying his nose in her curls. Closing his eyes, he hoped his dick wouldn't spontaneously combust during the night with that fragrant bundle of warm skin rubbing up against him.

CHAPTER TWELVE

She must have dozed off at some point during the night, because when Emma opened her eyes, she could see early morning light filtering in through the blinds. Slowly becoming aware of her surroundings, she noticed she was naked and had a very warm, firm body pressed against her backside. She lifted her head off the pillow, turned slightly, and found Gus's rugged face, relaxed in sleep beside her on the pillow. His full lips were slightly parted and a small grunting noise escaped with every exhale. His full dark head, with streaks of gray, had hair sticking out in every direction, as if he had rubbed his head all night, and his thick eyelashes fanned over his cheekbones. It was quite the contrast between the sharp, alert, imposing Gus, and this soft, rumpled, endearing Gus. It put a smile on her face.

It didn't take long for Emma's brain to register the customary morning pain and seize ups that came with being in one position for too long. She knew she would be better off getting up and moving, before things got any worse. Trying to be as quiet as was possible for her, she tried to slide out from under the total body hold Gus had on her, stifling her usual morning groans. When she made it to the bathroom without waking him, she couldn't resist turning around to take a peek at the gorgeous naked man in her bed. Not something she'd ever thought she'd see again. She took a quick mental picture…one long, hairy, muscular leg draped over the sheet, the full side of his body exposed. The tight hard globe of his ass curving into a broad nicely muscled back where another piece of ink adorned his olive toned skin. Delicious–she grinned to herself, like the cat who got the canary–and all mine, at least for now. In the bathroom she turned to look at herself in the mirror, and her smile faltered. Ay...not the prettiest sight, she was. Her hair resembled a bird's nest, and her normally rather pale and floppy body was now black and blue as well. Ugh. She wasn't sure what he saw when he looked at her, but whatever.

With a quick finger comb through her hair, a pair of yoga pants, a shirt and her teeth brushed, she made her way into the kitchen. The plan was to maybe get some muffins going, when she was stopped in her tracks at the sight of Katie standing at her counter, pouring coffee.

"Morning." Katie had obviously heard her approach, because she hadn't even turned around yet, giving Emma time to gather herself. Yikes, this was a little awkward to say the least.

"Hey. Morning to you too. Guess you got stuck with the early morning shift? Glad you were able to find makings for coffee. I should've thought to put something to eat out as well. I was actually about to see what I have lying around to throw some muffins together. That is, if you're hungry? Of course you may have already eaten..." Emma rambled on as she moved around the kitchen, trying to avoid any eye contact with Katie. She was painfully aware that Gus was sleeping in her bed.

A hand on her arm stopped her mid sentence. "Emma," Katie softly implored. "Let's sit for a minute?"

"Okay. Sure." She followed Katie's example and pulled out a stool at the counter. "Look, this is a bit awkward..." she started, before the younger woman interrupted her again.

"Sorry, I know. Let me. I feel I need to clear the air." Emma looked up to find Katie's eyes fixed on hers. "Look, I realize you know about Gus and my...previous 'arrangement,' and I swear that's all it ever was. It didn't mean anything."

But Emma noticed her downcast eyes as she added the last.

"Perhaps it wasn't for Gus, but what about you? I get the feeling maybe more for you than you've let on. Am I right?"

Katie opened her mouth to presumably deny, but thought better of it, and shrugged her shoulders instead. "I never realized it until I saw him with you, to be honest. Was too wrapped up in work. I guess our little set up was too…comfortable." Resting both elbows on the counter, Katie clasped her mug in both hands staring into her coffee. "Funny, it was the way he looked at you–touched you, that showed me this was an entirely different ballgame. I wasn't even in the same ballpark."

"I'm sorry. I honestly don't know what to say, because anything out of my mouth would seem wrong. But one thing I do know; Gus has no idea." Emma got off her stool. When she moved around Katie to the coffee pot for a refill, she gave her shoulder a brief squeeze. "Can I get you a refill?"

Katie planted both her hands on the counter and pushed herself up off the stool. "No thanks, I've had enough. I might come back for those muffins, if you're still planning on baking some?"

"Absolutely," Emma said with a smile.

"Are you okay with me being here, Emma? Do you trust me to take care of you?" Katie stopped with her hand on the front door; concern evident on her face.

"I don't doubt that for a minute," she responded firmly.

Nodding once in acknowledgement, Katie turned the knob, slipped outside, and closed the door behind her. Through the kitchen window, Emma stared into the early morning, feeling a little guilty about this turn of events. Who knew?

The earlier sound of voices had briefly woken Gus, but the lack of sleep, for the last few nights, soon pulled him back under. The next time he woke, it was to the feel of lush warm lips against his own, and the smell of apples and cinnamon in his nostrils.

"Hmmmmm…" he groaned appreciatively, as he licked his way between those lips and folded his arms around the gorgeous body attached to them. "You taste and smell delicious, Peach."

"Ditto, Big Guy."

That made him chuckle. "Morning breath and all, huh?"

"If it tastes like you and smells like you, then yeah…" Emma snuggled up against him, her hands playing through the hair on his chest. When the pads of her fingers skimmed over the tips of his now sensitive nipples, he was barely able to contain the growl it drew from him. "Dangerous game, babe. If you move your leg half an inch, you can feel why that is."

Emma immediately lifted her head to peek, then turned her eyes back. "Oops." With a mischievous half-smile, and biting her lip, she tried to sit up and move away from him, but he wouldn't have it.

"Oops? You come in here, kiss me senseless, smelling like baked goods, and tasting like sin, play with my chest, and all you can say is 'Oops'? Na ahhh. Not buying it, Peach. You have my dick hard as rock and you are not getting away with; 'Oops'." Rolling over, he gently forced Emma to lay back down again, wedging himself between her legs, careful not to put weight on her injured side. "How're you feelin'?"

"Better."

"Better how? Better than yesterday?" he pushed.

"Better with you right where I want you," Emma confessed, earning her a shit-eating grin and liquid heat-filled eyes.

"Really. Then prepare to be devoured, 'cause I can't fucking wait any longer to be inside you."

His instinct was to take her wet mouth and plunge his tongue in to taste her, like he was dying to do to her pussy, but he needed to see her–touch her, first. Moving his knees outside her hips, he slid his hands under her shirt and eased it up, pulling it from behind her back, and over her head, exposing her soft, natural rosy-tipped breasts.

"So pretty…" Was about all he managed before his hands cupped and molded her mounds. Then his mouth was eagerly sucking and licking at a hardened nipple, drawing nonverbal encouragement from Emma, who had a hard time lying still. He feasted on her, taking as much of her breast in his mouth as he could, pressing the nub against the roof of his mouth with his tongue and sucked with long deep pulls. He was unable to stop his hands from roaming over her soft and yielding skin, wanting so much to mold himself to her–inside her.

A small sound of distress escaped her when he sat back to continue the task of undressing her. Eager to feel all of her, the yoga pants and underwear were next in line. One swift tug had those taken care of, and in the early light of day, he finally had a full view of all that was Emma Young; spread out before him. Embarrassed by his blatant perusal, she tried to cover herself with part of the sheet. But he wouldn't let her, pulling it from her hand,

and he sat back on his knees between her spread legs, looking down at her.

"No. Don't. You are absolute perfection. Just the way you are supposed to be. Don't cover up, don't hide, and don't change. I see all of you and you are breathtaking," he said with blatant appreciation and lust evident on his face.

Stretching out over Emma, he rested his forearms beside her head and slid his hands in her hair.

"I know you are safe. Do you trust me when I tell you I'm safe?" He wanted to know. When she nodded, he held her eyes, while he slid the tip of his erection through her slick labia.

"So wet for me, baby…I could come from this alone."

Emma pleaded with him, "Don't tease…I need to feel you. Please."

With his arms and hands firmly anchoring her, he surged his straining cock into her tight, wet heat in one solid move until he was seated so deep, his balls pressed against her ass. Emma's mouth opened on a silent moan. So hot. He had to freeze his movement to gain some control, his body trembling with the effort.

"You okay?" he managed, looking at Emma's lust-filled gaze. All he got in response was a moan, but when her hands made their way down to clutch his ass and pulled him deeper, he knew he had a green light. "Hang on, Peach. I need you comfortable for this." He lifted her ass a little, giving her hips some support with pillows he grabbed from the bed. Pushing his own knees wide underneath her spread legs, he had that little bit of height and extra leverage he wanted. He bent over and took her mouth, slowly moving in and out of her, trying to find her sweet spots. He took his time to register every response from the expressions on her face and her movements. Being inside Emma was unlike any experience he ever had, and he wanted to make it last. His body trembled with the effort to fight his release back, each time he threatened to go over.

He could sense she felt teased when Emma tried to speed him along, but Gus was determined to set the pace. "Patience, baby…I need you to brace against the headboard, because I'm about to fuck you hard."

Doing as she was told, Emma raised both her arms and held on to the bed frame. He lifted himself to his knees and pulled Emma's hips toward him a little.

"Eyes on me. I want you to see me come apart for you."

The man was cracking her heart wide open.

Having teetered on the edge of an orgasm for far too long already, all it took was Gus pulling his substantial cock almost all the way out, before slamming home hard. When he hit her clit on impact, it was enough to make Emma come instantly, the first time. His eyes with burning intensity on hers, she couldn't keep her hands from clutching at his butt cheeks, spreading them wider, to try and pull every inch of him inside her.

"Fuck, babe, I like that. You playin' with my ass; it feels fucking good."

Emboldened by his encouragement. she felt her way as close to where the two of them were connected as possible, slicking up her fingers. She slid one hand back up his ass crease to find the place she read about, the one that would increase his pleasure. Keeping her eyes locked on him, she firmly slid a finger up his ass, curving it slightly to try and find that certain spot.

A list of expletives left his mouth, but Gus's pumping increased and turned erratic. Shifting his weight slightly to one side, Gus used the other hand to pinch and pull at her clit, highly sensitive and swollen right above where they were joined. It sent her body into the eager spasms of a loud and prolonged orgasm.

"Ohh, holy fuck! Gussss!"

"Coming, Peach. Eyes on me–for you." Head thrown back, his neck strained, mouth gasping for air, and with her finger still curving in his ass, his hips pumped furiously. Then he stilled– jerking and groaning his own release.

She gently eased her finger out, stroking his ass and back, easing down his breathing. He was lying half on her and half on the mattress. Emma could feel tears trickling down the side of her face. Talk about losing yourself in the moment.

Gus lifted himself up on an elbow and looked at her. "Hey, darlin'. Tell me I didn't hurt you?"

Palming his face, she pulled him close for a sweet kiss. "No, honey. Not hurt." She smiled up, tracing his beautiful rugged face with her eyes. This kind man, who simply walked in to her life, embraced her, all her issues and shortcomings, and looked out for her. She'd never been on the receiving end and it was an amazing feeling. Letting her watch him become vulnerable in her hands was an incredible gift of trust.

"You simply undo me," she whispered to him.

CHAPTER THIRTEEN

"So how is Emma doing?" Joe wanted to know, when Gus walked into his office in Cortez, pissed that he had been called in.

"Black and blue, but her head's feeling fine and she should be all right. She's tough."

"Noticed that about her," Joe agreed.

"That better be all you notice," Gus bit out, his eyes conveying he was not playing games.

Joe threw his hands up and chuckled. "Whoa there, buddy! It's not like that for me, but I can see she got to you."

"Just tell me what this meeting is about that had you call my ass in here, instead of henpecking me. I wasn't too happy about have to leave my charge."

Joe burst out laughing. "Your charge? Man, you're killing me here." Propping his feet on his desk and linking his hands on his belly, Joe watched him pour the black sludge they swear was coffee.

He could feel Joe's observant eyes, trying hard not to let the self-deprecating grin tugging at his mouth escape. "Enough busting my balls. What's the deal?"

Still chuckling, Joe sat forward in his chair. "I got a lead on the hit and run truck yesterday."

Gus was about to demand why in hell he hadn't been notified, but Joe already had his hand up and explained, "You were up to your eyeballs in looking after your 'woman'…" Joe threw him a glare.

"Besides the lead was thin to start with, so hear me out…"

Joe swiped a hand through his hair, and Gus noticed for the first time that he looked like he might not have seen his bed last night. Rumpled and bleary-eyed, Joe looked like he was ready to pack it in.

"Go on," he urged.

"DMV came back with a hit on the partials we got from witness accounts at the scene. A navy 1994 Ford F-150 belonging to a Kelly Janssen from Mancos, who turns out to be the seventy-six year old widow of a former Colorado State Trooper. Now here is where it gets interesting. When one of our deputies went to talk to Mrs. Janssen, he found no one at home, but the truck was parked in the back of the property. From neighbors we discovered the lady has been in the hospital here in Cortez for the past two months."

Frustration was starting to slowly gnaw away at Gus's patience.

"So basically fuck-all."

"No. Not quite. Mrs. Janssen has cancer and hasn't been given very long to live. She obviously wasn't driving the truck, said it used to be her husband's and only her son drives it on very rare occasions, to move stuff."

At the mention of a son, Gus's head snapped up. "Do we have a name?" He leaned in, eager to move on something– anything, but especially the bastard who fucking hurt Emma.

"Randolph. I already checked. He hasn't visited her since last week. We weren't able to get more out of her at the time; the woman was exhausted already and the doc kicked us out. We'll have to go back to see what more we can find out, 'cause the name Randolph Janssen doesn't bring anything up. We are on it. We're bringing in the truck, and I've got someone going back out to Mancos today to talk to the neighbors again."

"So a name and possible access to what might have been the vehicle used to run Emma down. Anything else you've got? Something I could sink my teeth into?"

"The newer black truck Emma described following her, and you saw pulling out of her drive, may have been rented from a National car rental office here in town. They reported a truck with a similar description rented a week or two ago for one week. When it wasn't returned immediately, they didn't think much of it at first. A corporate card had been used to rent it. It's not unusual for cars to be kept a day or two longer, but when it hadn't shown up yesterday, and they called the number they had been left with, it was not in service. They contacted the PD to report it. So now we have a BOLO out on the truck."

"Still nothing connecting anything to Corbin. I feel like we're treading water, and it's just getting muddier and muddier."

"It always happens before shit starts floating to the surface." Joe got up from his chair. "I'm quickly going to check with the guys in the shop to see about the truck. They should have it in there by now. Just hang tight a sec."

Gus dropped his head in his hands, rubbing his temples to try and clear some of the pressure that was trying to build.

His thoughts were inadvertently drifting back to the morning, when he left the bed rather abruptly after receiving Joe's call. He was an ass. One moment he had a fucking beautiful woman wrapped around him, opening up to him, telling him in so many words the effect he was having on her, and the next he walked out the door with barely a goodbye. Thing of it was, it had been on the tip of his tongue to give her everything. Every last little bit of what he had been pretending didn't affect him anymore. The friendly but firm demeanor he displayed to the outside world had become part of him. It just wasn't all of him, and for some reason, he wanted Emma to know every scarred and ugly bit. That's why he had asked her to look at him. He really wanted her to see him, to see all of him. He hadn't held a thing back, letting it all show in his eyes, on his face. Yet she still cared, still stroked, still held. It had been on his lips to break the seal on his fucked up past; to bring it out, have her see and acknowledge it, and then to be able to leave it behind him for good. He would know he finally had the balls to face someone without any reservation, who could reflect back all that he was feeling, and trust it wouldn't change a thing. All of that had been right there: on his lips, in his eyes and in his heart. Then the fucking phone had pulled him away from the moment. Coward that he was, he had jumped on it, leaving Emma looking sated but a little hurt and confused in bed. He dressed, gave her a quick kiss, and told her he'd be back as soon as possible, leaving the team to cover her while he was gone. Asshole.

For a minute, she thought she had reached him with her words, but then the phone call had interrupted their 'moment.' She could see a hint of relief flick over his face when he took the call and told her he had to meet up with Joe in Cortez. He left her lying in bed, wondering if perhaps she had shown a bit too much of herself too soon.

Emma felt a little tender in areas that hadn't seen the kind of action they had just been subjected to in many moons, but otherwise surprisingly good, considering. Carefully rolling out of bed, Emma made her way into the shower. She would make it a quick one, because as soon as she heard low voices coming from her kitchen, she was pretty sure her babysitting crew had arrived.

-

Still slightly damp from her shower, she was grateful for the AC the little bungalow boasted; otherwise she'd never dry completely. Emma pushed her walker into the kitchen, needing its stability this morning. She found it in the corner of the bedroom where Gus must've left it.

"Morning–again." Katie said, once again hanging out by the coffee pot, wearing a little smile. "You have two less muffins, I'm afraid. I pounced when I smelled them."

Emma grinned. "Good. That's what they're there for."

"I wasn't alone, though. Gus was stuffing his face with the other one on his way out the door. Guess he needed some quick energy," she said with a snicker.

Flicking a glance at Katie, Emma was relieved to find no malice in the other woman's eyes. She still wasn't going to touch that. "He said something about Caleb coming too?"

"Yup. Called him in. He's having a quick shower and will be over after. I told Gus to go ahead and go. We can manage for those fifteen minutes."

A knock at the door had them both turning their heads.

"That'll be him. I'll get it," Katie said, making her way to the door, while Emma headed for the coffee pot, eager to grab a cup. She would get a new pot started before the next team member

135

came in. She could hear Katie talking to whoever was at the door, which didn't sound like it was Caleb after all. Curious to see who it was, Emma looked down the hall to the front to see Ralph standing on the doorstep.

"Oh hey, Ralph! What brings you out? Any news?" She turned to grab another cup down from the cupboard, and added, "Come on in, I'm just making fresh."

She barely registered the shuffling behind her at first, but the slam of the front door, and the loud crash, quickly snapped her to attention. When she whipped around, she found Ralph standing only two feet behind her. Looking beyond him, on the hallway floor she could see Katie lying on her back, unmoving. Frozen in shock and disbelief, her body seemed rooted to the spot, while her eyes slowly drifted back to a man she though she knew. When she saw the cold, calculated mask on his face, the hot tendrils of terror broke through her apathy and she opened her mouth to scream. But before she was able to shriek , the last thing she saw was the arm arcing down toward her–and then nothing.

CHAPTER FOURTEEN

"It might be our truck," Joe said, as he walked back into his office. "The guys just got it in, but they didn't have a lot of time with it yet. A preliminary look showed the left front end had some damage and a trace of possible red paint on the underside of the driver's side door was found. We're trying to confirm if that sample is consistent with Emma's walker. They're running some tests now, but they'll be limited. We don't have a full lab here."

"I don't care, I'm not worried about building a court case, I'm just interested in nabbing this guy before he tries something again."

Joe nodded his head in agreement.

"Oh, and another thing. The deputy at the hospital called; Mrs. Janssen was awake and had something interesting. When he prompted her on the whereabouts of her son, she said he shouldn't be too hard to find, since he was one of us. When he told her there is no deputy Janssen with the sheriff's office, she threw him for a loop. She said he wouldn't be called Janssen, but Murphy: his father's last name. State Trooper Janssen had been his stepfather and her second husband. Her son's name is Deputy Murphy, Deputy Randolph Murphy."

Gus had already been halfway out the door before Joe had a chance to finish his sentence.

"Where the fuck you off to?" he yelled after Gus.

"Randolph is Ralph, Frank's deputy in Cedar Tree," Gus barked back, taking the stairs two at a time, on his way down to the parking lot and his truck. He was already pulling out his phone to try and reach his team.

"Gus! Get in my truck! I drive, you call," Joe instructed.

Without objection, Gus changed direction immediately toward Joe's vehicle. He knew he'd get a lot further in the speeding truck of a well-known Cortez chief deputy than he would in his own. Besides, it would leave his hands free to make calls.

Joe intercepted a young deputy in the parking lot and yelled at Gus to toss his keys at him. The young man was instructed to hold onto them until further instructions. Gus was trying to get through to Katie's number, once again, as he was getting into the passenger side of Joe's truck. Impatiently pushing end, he was about to call Caleb, when the phone rang and Caleb's name showed up.

"We have a problem," Gus started, not giving Caleb a chance.

"I know, boss. I'm at the house, Emma is gone, and Katie is down and hurt. Call an ambulance, she's lost a lot of blood," Caleb sounded grim.

"Fuck!" Slamming his fist on the dashboard, he turned to Joe to fill him in. He had been on his phone getting teams mobilized, while working his way through traffic, trying to get out of Cortez as fast as humanly possible.

"Boss!" Caleb called again for his attention. "Katie was in the hall, but there was more blood in the kitchen…Emma was nowhere in the house. I have to go, I've gotta take care of Katie."

The line went dead and all feeling seemed to flood into Gus's stomach…swirling around and threatening to pull him under.

"Ambulance for Katie. Emma's gone," He bit out, barely holding it together.

"Got it," Joe said and immediately relayed the information to the station on the other line.

A rage was slowly fighting through the shock and numbness, at the thought of his Emma hurt, in danger–or worse. "Gonna kill that fucker with my bare hands," he ground out, his hands clenching his own thighs so hard, he'd likely leave bruises.

"We'll get her," Joe placated him, before turning his attention back to Frank, who was on the phone now.

"Put Frank on speaker"

Joe took one look at his clenched jaw and fierce eyes and did as he asked.

"Frank, you're on speaker," Joe warned him.

"Frank." Gus was trying to reign it in. "He driving a department car or his own?"

"Uhh, I'd have to go check. Sometimes he'd take a patrol car home, if he had an early shift next day."

"Why don't you fucking go check, Frank? Jesus. Fuck me!"

"Hey, listen now, I'd hate for anything to happen to Emma as much as you do, you ass. So get off your high horse, and my back, while you're at it!"

"You know fuck-all about me or my woman, you dick. Your fuckin' deputy harms one hair on her head, and I'm not fuckin' responsible for what I'm gonna do!"

"Pissed because once again she got hurt on your watch, Big Guy? Huh? Mighty fine job you're doing protecting that 'woman' of yours."

With the sheriff now taunting him, and an already volatile situation rapidly getting completely out of hand, Joe jumped in sending everyone to their corners. "Shut the fuck up. Both of you!" Joe bellowed, "We've got one woman with unknown injuries and another missing and possibly injured. We have a suspect, who also happens to be a law enforcement officer. We have limited resources, little time, and a fucking humungous amount of area to disappear into around us. So both of you, save your energy, 'cause we are going to bloody well need it."

Red in the face from his tirade, Joe took a few deep breaths before continuing, "Getting back on track; we need details on the patrol car and his personal ride. Frank, can you get that? Inform the Durango State Patrol office. Have them ask their boys to keep an eye out and maybe notify New Mexico and Utah as well. Just in case. We don't want them to be able to get too far. If they get over state lines, we lose all control of the situation. It's going to be enough of a challenge working together, without adding more agencies to the mix. Unless it becomes absolutely necessary, let's avoid it."

Listening to Joe take charge of logistics helped settle Gus's mind. It left him to solely focus on Emma.

When they pulled up beside Caleb's truck, the wheels hadn't stopped turning yet before Gus had the door open. He was running full speed in the open front door, only to stop dead in his tracks at the scene in front of him. Sitting on the floor in a large puddle of blood was Caleb, with kitchen towels clamped around

Katie's head, looking like he was trying to hold her together. He looked up at him with a defeated look in his eyes that sent chills down Gus's back.

"Ambulance?" Caleb croaked out.

"Right behind us. Flight For Life from Durango is also on the way," Gus assured him, sinking down beside him on his knees, afraid to take a closer look, but needing to do something. His hand felt for a pulse against her neck, and he could faintly make out a flutter under the pads of his fingers.

"Been afraid to remove my hands. Just trying to keep blood in her body. She's…she…" Choked up, Caleb simply closed his eyes, laid his head back against the wall, and gave up trying to talk.

Sirens announced the arrival of the ambulance and the first of the back up teams Joe had called on.

Barely clinging to life, Katie was loaded onto the helicopter and taken to Durango. Gus had called Dana and she and Neil were on their way to stay by her side. As shocked and scared as he was for Katie, Gus was taken aback by the depth of Caleb's reaction. He offered for Caleb to stay with her, but he wouldn't hear of it. Said she'd be pissed if she found out he ditched his job to hold her hand.

Now with the first responders out of the way, he had his first opportunity to have look around. When he walked into the kitchen, and saw the blood on the counter and the floor, it hit him; that was likely Emma's blood. But when he spotted the purple walker, with her cane in the clip, standing abandoned off to the side, his knees about buckled. That was her independence.

The nausea he had been struggling to keep down at the thought of Emma hurt surged back up, and he all but ran to the bathroom where he lost the contents of his stomach until there was nothing but bile left.

"You okay in there?" Joe asked from the other side of the door.

"Fine–Be right out."

He rinsed his mouth, splashed some water on his face, looked himself in the eye in the mirror, and pulled himself together. No time to lose it. She needs you.

He would find her and tell her what he didn't have the balls to tell her only a couple of miserable hours ago. If it was the last thing he did.

CHAPTER FIFTEEN

Voices.

She could hear voices, but they seemed far away. And movement. She was moving…or at least being moved. Carefully lifting her eyelids, only to squeeze them shut again at the instant pounding pressure it released inside her head.

What?

Bits and pieces drifted back through the red haze of pain, running from her skull, all the way to the base of her spine. A sick feeling settled in the pit of her stomach. Not even beginning to understand the why and how, Emma could figure out the possible implications of her situation; and none of it was good.

Oh my God…Katie. The memory of the still body in a pool of her own blood almost froze Emma in fear.

Those voices. She could still hear them. Carefully trying again to open her eyes to scan her surroundings, Emma fought down the bile that came up at the sudden surge of nausea when light hit her retinas. She was on a dirt floor–packed sand or something by the feel of it–in an old stone shed that looked like it had been loosely stacked. It reminded her of one of those Pueblo Indian dwellings Arlene had shown her at Mesa Verde on a trip. Through the opening in a wall, she could see two men facing off just outside the shed. Ralph was one, and she didn't know the other, but his back was turned toward her.

Her brain was trying hard to cling on to every detail, but the pain and exhaustion were overwhelming. About to close her eyes, she heard Ralph shout, "No!"–before a loud bang rang her ears. Then she saw him crumpling down to the ground. Numbed with fear, Emma wasn't quite able to process what she just witnessed. When the second man turned around to face her, she recognized his face from a picture she was shown just a few short days ago. She wished she had kept her eyes closed; tried closing them now. Ernst Corbin.

She could sense him walking up to her, nudging her in the ribs with his foot.

"Good, you're awake, so don't even try to fake it. There are ways to make sure you stay alert, but you won't like them."

Cold chills broke out over her skin and trembling started in her fingers. It slowly spread in spasms over her body and made her breathing come out gaspy and thin. She tried hard to control her body's response, not to give this man any satisfaction. Focusing her eyes away from him, she prayed for Gus. For him to be able to find her, because she knew he'd move heaven and earth to.

"You shot him," she breathed out.

"I killed him," Corbin corrected. "He won't be getting up. Fucked up what should've been an easy job and almost got himself caught. Bringing you here was his last chance, he delivered–but he won't be needed anymore."

"I don't…un…understand any of this." Emma had a hard time getting her words out, she was shaking so hard by now. Positive he wouldn't hesitate to shoot her. But why hadn't he yet? Why not just point and pull the trigger and be done with it? There must be more. Keeping him engaged was her only chance at dragging this out long enough to give Gus a chance to find her. If he even had one.

"You don't need to. Do you know who I am?"

Deciding to go with honesty for now, she responded, "Yes, I've been shown a picture."

"Good, saves me an explanation. Any copies ever made or printouts made of the ledger I had you do up?"

This was where she didn't want to give everything away, so she opted for obscurity.

"I never make copies, or save to USB keys. And if I make printouts, it's only to work on mistakes and those copies are run through the shredder when I'm done. No hard copies are kept." Technically, nothing she told him was a lie, even though she did leave out the online drop box, but she couldn't help dropping her eyes away as she said it.

The small move didn't escape Corbin's attention. Before she could take another breath, he was up in her face, one hand in her hair. He had her head pulled back so far, she was afraid her neck would snap.

"You're lying!" he spat out, shaking her body like a rag doll from the precarious hold on her head. She could feel the hair ripping from her head in chunks, as blackness started to encroach on her vision. Barely able to cling to consciousness, she defiantly forced out: "Fuck you!" Which earned her a vicious punch to her jaw with his free hand and sent her over into welcome darkness once again.

Ten minutes after the Flight For Life helicopter lifted off

with Katie, Emma's house was crawling with law enforcement personnel. Frank had arrived as well and had just informed them that he had found the patrol car at Ralph's house. His personal Jeep Cherokee was missing from the driveway however. With an APB out for the car and driver, the limited forensics team on scene, and the Montezuma County Sheriff's Office aligned with the Cortez PD; a network was being thrown out to attempt to cut off exit routes. Officers were also venturing out, trying to actively pursue any witnesses they could find in and around Cedar Tree.

He figured that was how Arlene came to be storming up the porch steps, right for him. The diner was likely one of the first stops they made. Gus didn't step back from the hard slap she delivered to his face.

"You fucking asshole! You promised you would look after her." Overtaken by anger and fear, Arlene continued to pound him with her fists, when Joe stepped in, trying to pull her back.

"Leave her," he all but whispered at Joe. "She's right. I was supposed to…"

Wrapping Arlene up in a tight hold, feeling the struggle seep out of her as slowly her body sagged in his arms, he bent his head to her shoulder and softly repeated, "I was supposed to, I'm so sorry. I promise, I'll find her."

Taking a deep breath in, Arlene pulled back and with a tear-streaked face looked at him.

"You'd better, and not without me. Now what have we got?" she asked, getting a smirk from Joe.

"Lady…" Joe started, "This is a police investigation that is ongoing, and right now…"

"Oh save the official bullshit lines, will ya?" Arlene bit off. "That is my soul sister you are talking about. Closer than any blood relative of mine. Now, I know everyone and everything that goes on in this county. See if I can't be of help. I need to help."

With a look at Joe, who nodded his assent, Gus told Arlene what he knew. When he mentioned Ralph's Cherokee, her head shot up. "Is that thing green?"

"Why? What do you know?" Joe jumped in before Gus could.

"It's just that my waitress just came in half an hour ago, complaining about being nearly forced off the road. Some idiot cut across the county road onto that back road that leads to the cemetery, the one north of the reservation. She said he was driving a forest green Cherokee."

Joe was immediately on the radio, relaying the information. Both Gus and Joe took off for the Yukon the deputy just dropped off, leaving Arlene swearing at them from the porch. As Gus tried to maneuver the truck around the fleet of law enforcement vehicles cluttering the drive, he could see her and Caleb running at her truck, parked at the end. "Fucking stubborn woman!"

"Who?" Joe wanted to know.

"Arlene is behind us with Caleb. Fuck. She better not get in the way." He slammed his fist on the steering wheel.

"Tell me where to go," he instructed Joe.

"Go back through town, past the diner. On the other side is a turn off on the left only. It won't have any markings. I'll tell you when."

Joe was beside him, alternating between cell phone and radio, barking out instructions. Gus's focus was on the road, trying to steer clear of any traffic as he floored it. Trying to keep his mind as balanced as the truck was another matter. His thoughts were bouncing between what he was going to do to Ralph Murphy, when he got his hands on him, and what might be happening to Emma. All the while, the road took forever to be eaten up by his wheels. Finally he resorted to praying Emma was going to be all right, but the whole time he felt like he was going to crawl out of his skin. For the short period he'd known her, he could sense there was something unique and unguarded between them. For most of his life he had worked hard to simply live on the surface. He was good at not letting things touch him too deeply, but with Emma he didn't seem to have a choice. The woman was made up of such courage. She had an open and welcoming attitude toward life, without trying to block away or deny the tough parts. She simply accepted them and brought them into her positive attitude. He wanted to have more of that; be a part of that. Of her. At least have a chance at that. He was not going have this fucking asshole take it–take her–away from him.

"Hey!! Watch it!" Joe grabbed the wheel and pulled them away from the ditch.

"Don't fucking get us killed. Stay focused."

"Sorry," he mumbled, forcefully clearing his mind from anything but driving.

"Turn coming up on the left." Joe pointed ahead.

Slowing down at the last minute, he almost had the truck on two wheels as he made the turn sharply.

"Jesus Christ! Next time I'm driving." Joe swore beside him. "Slow down a little. Lots of little turn offs here into the bush, mostly dirt roads. I want to check for tracks."

Just then Gus's phone rang. Pulling it from his pocket, he

looked at the screen and handed it to Joe to answer.

"It's Caleb, put it on speaker. He's still behind us. Maybe he's seen something."

"Caleb. Talk to me."

"It's Arlene, Gus. Caleb and I were talking. The cemetery is on the edge of the reservation and fairly closely patrolled for vandalism. I doubt anyone would go there, but there is something I just thought of. There are some old Anasazi ruins just a mile or so this side of the cemetery. A dirt road–well, more like a set of tracks really–going into the sagebrush on the left hand side. They go in for about half a mile to a bit of a clearing. The ruins should be only fifty yards or so straight north from there. Caleb said to call you. We're almost on your tail."

"How much further up ahead is it, Arlene?" Joe asked, checking his mirror to see Arlene's truck closing in on them.

"Just a minute or two."

Gus looked at Joe, trying to gauge his thoughts.

"Stay on the phone," Joe instructed. "Give us a heads up for the turn off. I want to check for tracks. If there are any fresh ones, we both turn in, but you stay well behind. Should we be heard or spotted, and they get around us somehow, you will be second tier. Reinforcements are not far behind us, so if anyone is in here, we'll get them."

Relaying the same instructions to the teams in the rear, all eyes were now focused on the left side of the road.

Fresh tracks had led them onto the trail. Trying to drive on it, making a minimum of noise wasn't easy. Aside from the engine noise, the uneven surface jolted and rattled the big Yukon. Gus almost had to slow down to a crawl by the time they reached a clearing of sorts and spot two vehicles.

Joe immediately got on the radio, with the phone line still open to Arlene's truck far behind them, giving updates.

"Forest green Jeep Cherokee confirmed and a tan Toyota 4Runner unknown, looks to be a rental. National ZRE-839, Colorado plate. Run it. We're going in.

Leaving the Yukon at the opening of the clearing, so it faced the trail out, Gus and Joe carefully scanned the surroundings for any movement. Not able to spot anything, Gus was the first to get out, leaving the door unlatched. Then he saw Joe do the same. Weapons drawn, both made their way toward the north side of the clearing, eyes and ears peeled for anything unusual.

Gus could hear his own heart pounding in his ears with the heightened level of adrenaline that was pumping through him. He could somehow sense Emma was close, but he shut down any emotions. He had a job to do. Keeping Joe in his vision from the corner of his eye, he saw him motioning to the right. Changing direction, he followed closely behind. Joe led them through an old burned out patch of spruce. On the far side, he could see what looked to be some piles of stone.

Stopping in his tracks, Joe crouched down, motioning him to do the same and whispered, "Right there. To the left of that tall burned tree trunk, half behind those bricks."

Looking where Joe indicated, he spotted the shape of what appeared to be a man's head and torso, half hidden by the rocks.

Freya Barker   SLIM TO NONE

His back was toward them. Pointing to his right, Gus started moving, while Joe automatically circled around in the opposite direction.

Two separated targets were more difficult to control than one. Besides, they had two cars in the clearing, which meant there was at least one other person they didn't have eyes on. One other person, who might be in a position to harm Emma, if they were discovered.

The snap of dry wood sounded on the other side of the ruins, and the figure suddenly disappeared completely from sight. Gus could only hear was some rustling and then the loud reverberation of a gunshot. Spurred into action, he abandoned all attempts at staying hidden and ran in a direct line for the roofless structure, terrified of what he might find.

Coming up on the side of the small building, he kept his back to the wall, inching his way around. He was constantly checking in front, behind, as well as above him, to make sure he wasn't walking into an ambush. Other than sounds of movement from within the walls, he could hear nothing else. Coming to the end of the wall, he carefully snuck a look at the other side, but there didn't seem to be anyone. Turning the corner, he saw an opening to the building and made his way toward it. At the last minute he spotted a body laying off to his right. Ralph. Dead. Fuck. That was not good, not good at all. Was that the shot he had heard? Looking a little closer, he noticed that the pool of blood under the body had started congealing around the edges. Flies had started collecting on the body already. He must have been dead longer than the few minutes since the shot rang out for sure, especially in this heat. It would've taken longer than fifteen minutes for that blood to start clotting. Damn. Would Emma be lying dead somewhere too? Was that gunshot the one that ended her life?

151

The thought almost made his knees buckle. And where the fuck was Joe?

Tamping down his emotions once again, he turned his focus on the doorway; pretty sure he wouldn't like what was waiting inside, but moving toward it anyway.

"Mr. Flemming, how convenient to have you join us here. I'm afraid your partner has been slightly indisposed."

Corbin, the cock-sucking weasel had one hand wedged under Emma's jaw, the webbing between his thumb and forefinger all but cutting off her air. His other hand held a gun to her thigh. Emma looked to be passed out, and her lips were tinged slightly purple from lack of oxygen. One side of her was covered in blood, and Gus couldn't hold back the growl that started low in his chest, or the inadvertent step forward his body made. Fucker must have taken down Joe.

"Hold it right there, lover boy. One more move, however slight, she loses a leg. Another after that she's done. And so are you." Using the gun in his right hand to stroke up and down Emma's leg, he smirked at Gus.

"Juicy piece of pussy, is she? A bit too old and chunky for my liking, but I guess there is no accounting for taste, is there?"

"Leave her the fuck alone! You'd be lucky to have a woman like that even look at you twice. Mother-fucking bottom-feeder…" Gus was struggling to rein in his rage, knowing he had to keep a tight control or this situation would get completely out of hand. "What is it you want, Corbin? What was Ralph Murphy doing with the likes of you?"

"Ah…poor Ralph, I'm afraid the promise of the almighty dollar proved to be too much for him. You know, it is surprising how easy it is to find a weak link in every chain. Ralph's was his ailing mother and his increasing gambling debt. Living so close to the reservation does have its drawbacks. He served his purpose."

Keeping a close eye on Emma, Gus thought he could see her eyelids twitch a few times. He hoped to God she would keep them closed, even if she was awake. Having to look her in the eye would make him completely lose his cool.

"Ah yes, what I needed from the lovely Emma here, is some information. You see, I know she copied my files to somewhere…but she has been too…let's say, indisposed, to inform me of the where and how. I need those files." Corbin finished with an angry shake to Emma's neck, causing Gus to clench every muscle in his body, in an attempt to stay still.

"But now, Mr. Flemming, unfortunately the game has changed a bit. Unless you can provide me with the information I need, I will have to…" He didn't get any further. As he had begun to suspect, Emma was awake. She chose that moment to throw her entire weight sideways, away from the hand that held her by the throat. At the same time, trying to knock the hand with the gun out of the way. Gus reacted and moved forward instantly. He tried to get to Corbin before he was able to lift up his gun to aim at either Emma or him. He wasn't fast enough.

Two shots rang out, one followed on top of the other.

CHAPTER SIXTEEN

Once again, Emma found herself waking up with a massive headache at Southwest Memorial Hospital in Cortez. This time, however, she was surprised by who was at her bedside.

"Kara!"

"Hey, Mom." Her beautiful daughter was there, in the flesh, but with an angry frown on her face.

"Honey, what's wrong? What...How come you're here?" Her voice was raspy, her throat still sore from the pressure that bastard put on it.

In one terrifying wave, all recollection came flooding back. Emma struggled to sit upright in her bed, panic clutching at her chest.

"Mom! What are you doing? Lay back down, you have a head injury, please!" Kara begged, trying to hold her down in her bed.

With the sound of gunshots still vivid in her mind, deep sobs tore through her body and tears streamed down her face unchecked. Kara tried to wipe them away, and kept asking her what was wrong. She couldn't seem to form any words, so overcome with fear of the loss she would have to face. Rolling on her side, she curled in a fetal position, her back to her daughter, who resorted to stroking her back. "Mom, I'm going to get the doctor, okay? I'll be right back, I promise."

Not responding, Emma couldn't help but let the last few seconds she remembered play out again and again, hoping against hope to come up with a different conclusion. But each time the outcome was the same. She had managed to get away from Corbin, but as a result, he shot Gus. Two shots, that's what she heard before she passed out again. She was sure of it.

In the next moment, someone was rubbing her back. She hadn't heard anyone come in. A warm breath skimmed blew on the shell of her ear, and she heard a familiar deep voice rumble, "It's over, Peach. He's dead, won't be hurting you any more. No need to cry, darlin'."

Her body tensed up completely. It took her a minute to register, before she turned in her bed to find Gus leaning in on her. Totally overwhelmed with relief, she threw her arms around his neck and pulled him on top of her, sobbing loudly.

"Hey, hey, hey. What's all this?" he asked chuckling.

Barely able to draw proper breath, she hiccupped, "I…I…thought you we…were gone."

"Right here, babe. Right here," Gus mumbled into her hair, while hanging half in half off her bed; trying not to put any weight on her. He was drawing big soothing circles with his hand on her back. "Shhh. I'm not going anywhere, Peach. There isn't anywhere else I'd rather be."

"It may be a little too early for this kind of activity, folks." Dr. Waters said, walking into the room, followed closely by Kara. She looked on with her eyebrows up in her hairline. "And Emma, we really have to stop meeting like this." The doctor quipped, smiling at her. "Your daughter tells me you were in near hysterics, are you in pain? Although you do seem better now…"

Slightly embarrassed, her face buried in Gus's shoulder, Emma was not quite sure how to respond with the doc's inquiring eyes and her daughter's piercing ones focused on her. Luckily

Gus decided to take the lead. "It seems Emma had limited recollection of the events. She was under the impression that I didn't survive our, erm…encounter." He looked down at her with warm eyes. "As you can see, I was able to set her mind at ease."

"Thank goodness for that. You folks are keeping our little hospital busy enough. While I'm here, let me check your vitals. Unfortunately, this time you are not going to go home so soon. You have now had two head injuries in the span of a few days, and have about twenty or so cool stitches keeping your scalp together. We'd like to hang on to you for a bit. But don't worry, you'll have company." A small smirk formed on Naomi Waters face.

"What do you mean, I'll have company?" Emma wanted to know.

"Oh, I guess Gus here will have to fill you in on all the details, but Chief Deputy Morris will be our guest for a few days as well."

As Gus ended up telling her and Kara, after Dr. Waters had left; Katie was in Durango in serious but stable condition. She had undergone surgery to remove a piece of her damaged skull that had caused substantial bleeding to her brain. Apparently she had drains placed to keep the pressure off. Caleb was holding vigil there now, along side Dana and Neil.

As far as the events by the Anasazi ruins; the initial shot had been Corbin shooting at Joe, when the two of them were approaching from opposite ends. Joe had the bad fortune of disturbing one of the Ute wild horses that tend to roam in the area. He drew the unwanted attention of Corbin and ended up shot in the stomach as a result. Then as Gus had faced down with Corbin inside, what she now knew, were the remains of an Anasazi pit-house, Caleb had caught up with them. Managing to come up just outside of the door opening. He had listened to what was going on inside, and had waited for an appropriate moment to intervene. When the first shot from Corbin's gun, narrowly missed Gus, Caleb hadn't hesitated. The second shot had been from his gun and hadn't missed its target.

Joe had needed surgery but would be okay and was apparently just down the hall. It was a shock to Emma when she found out this all happened the day before…She had been out of it for almost twenty-four hours. Apparently Arlene had gone home to sleep after spending the night.

-

Emma turned to Kara. "So how did you end up here, love?"

"I got a call from Mr. Flemming, and I…"

"Name's Gus, darlin'. Told you that." A small smile played at the corner of his mouth.

"Fine. Gus. And mine is Kara, not darlin'," Kara snapped, rolling her eyes at him.

"Kara! What in hell's gotten in to you?" Emma wanted to know "You're being rude."

"Whatever, Mom. Anyway, after talking to Arlene as well, 'cause of course I didn't know Gus from Adam," Kara said with great emphasis, making sure her mother understood she was put out. Oh yes, Emma got the message.

"So I heard a bit of what went on here and hopped on a flight, thinking you might need some help." Shrugging her shoulders, Kara looked a little like when she was fifteen and had felt left out.

Emma reached for her hand. "I'm so happy you're here, honey. I just didn't want to worry you, or God forbid, have you come out here when there was still danger. I was in good hands."

Kara snorted hard at that. "Yeah, I can tell. What did that doctor say? Second time in a few days you end up in the hospital?"

"Kara, stop. You're being unreasonable. You have no idea of the stuff that has gone on this past week. But now you're here, the danger is past, and I'd be more than happy to fill you in." Emma tried to appease her daughter. Knowing once her girl got her hackles up about something; it would take a lot of work to smooth them down again.

Smiling at Gus, who sat beside her, she nodded. "I gather you two have met?"

"I had Neil pick her up in Durango this morning." Gus smiled back, still holding on to her hand.

"That's good of you, thanks." Squeezing his fingers briefly. Turning to Kara, she noticed the keen way with which they were being observed.

Kara looked at her with a question in her eyes. "Are you guys an item or something?"

Not quite sure how to respond appropriately, Emma took a few moments to collect her thoughts, but before she had a chance to answer, Gus jumped in.

"I like your mother. A lot. We met under unusual

circumstances, so we really haven't had a chance to 'date' or get to know each other in a normal way. That doesn't mean we didn't get to know each other, or that we are not involved, 'cause we are. It simply didn't take a traditional route."

"Bit fast, all of this. Don't you think?" Was Kara's retort.

"Yes, it is. One of the benefits when you've been around the block a time or two is that you're clear on what you like. You don't tend to waste time playing stupid games." Slapping his hands on his knees, Gus moved to get up. "I'm going to have a visit with Joe and leave you girls for a bit. Can I bring anything back from the coffee shop?"

Kara shook her head no and Emma wasn't sure what she was allowed to have. Before he left, she pulled him down for a chaste kiss, and whispered her thanks against his lips. She decided to ignore her daughter's presence.

With Gus gone from the room, Kara turned her attention to Emma. "Mom, how do you know he isn't taking advantage of you?"

"Seriously, Kara? I think you have our roles reversed, and for your information, my lack of mobility has not affected my ability to take care of myself. I stopped controlling your life a while ago. I love you. But don't start messing with mine now." She looked sternly at her daughter, who had her lips pressed together in a straight stubborn line. "Now, that's as much of an answer as you're going to get, seeing as this is all new to you. I understand your concern, but I've got it from here. Now get your skinny ass over here and give me a hug for Christ's sake. We haven't even had a proper hello."

Tilting her head, she tried to coax a smile out of Kara, who finally gave in, sat down on the bed, and wrapped herself around her mom.

"Sorry, Mom, I was so scared the whole flight over here. So worried about a head injury and what it might mean for you, or if it would have long-term effects. I didn't intend to be a bitch, really."

Stroking her daughter's hair, Emma reassured her. "I know, love. I know that, and I'm sorry too. Sorry I didn't tell you, and that you had to find out this way, and especially that you were scared." Pulling back and cupping Kara's face in her hands, she held her eyes. "Please give Gus a chance, he is unbelievably good to me. I promise you."

With a typical Kara eye-roll, she muttered her assent. "Fine. I'll try."

"That's all I can ask for, honey," Emma said, grabbing her back in a hug.

CHAPTER SEVENTEEN

Three days later, Gus was helping Emma get ready to go home. Kara had been staying with Emma most of the time. During the days, he was working hard with the sheriff's office to try and tie up any loose ends of the investigation here. He also had frequent contact with other members of the task force trying to bring down Bruno Silva. It was slow going with Joe still laid up in the hospital. Too many questions were still unanswered, even with Corbin out of the way permanently. Without everything tied off neatly, Gus didn't think they would be able to ease up completely.

He hadn't spent as much time with Emma as he would've liked, but with her daughter in town, it would've been stupid not to make use of the opportunity.

He and Kara had been like ships that pass in the night, quite literally at times. They would take shifts staying with Emma at the hospital during the nights; so they would both have a chance to catch up on some sleep. Things between them weren't quite on friendly terms yet, but cordial enough. He was sure she would figure out eventually that he wasn't going to hurt her mother. If he had to be completely honest, he hadn't spent a lot of time thinking about the future yet either, but what he did know was that he wanted a chance at one.

Arlene would pop in early mornings and after the lunch rush. Emma had bullied her into keeping the diner running, when she got wind that Arlene planned to close early to sit with her. They compromised on the two shorter visits during the day. Still a lot, since Arlene had to drive out from Cedar Tree each time. He got a call from her this morning, letting him know she wasn't coming in but would instead get Emma's house ready for her.

Dressed and waiting for their final walking papers, Gus ran the plans by Emma. "Kara wanted to go to the house and wait for you there, and Joe was wondering if you'd come say bye before you go. He has to stay for another day, maybe two, but wants to see with his own eyes that you're okay."

"I'd like to see him too," Emma agreed. "Honestly, I won't be sad if I never see this hospital again. So sick of white coats and scrubs."

Just then, Dr. Waters popped her head in.

"Can't blame ya," she snickered. "I hope I don't see you here anymore either, at least not under these kinds of circumstances. I just came to give you these." She handed Emma her discharge papers. "You'll find an appointment sheet for a week from today. I will just want to have a quick look at those stitches and follow up with you. Other than that you should be good to go. Anything changes, I'm sure you know where to find us now. Next time let's try to meet somewhere a bit more fun." She smiled as she walked out the door.

-

With a quick visit to Joe, Gus had Emma settled in his truck and were on their way in short order. Grabbing her hand off her lap, he pressed his lips in her palm. "So glad I'm taking you home. I was starting to get pretty sick of that hospital, and I'm sure you even more so." He smiled at her.

"Amen." Emma leaned her head back against the headrest, closing her eyes. "I still can't get over all that has happened in the last week. My boring and simple little life turned into this big drama. And it's not just me; I hate that Katie and Joe got hurt so bad." Letting out a big sigh, she turned back to him, drawing his eyes. "Do you think this is it then? It's all over now?"

This was the part Gus had not been looking forward to and had hoped to push off a little longer, but he wasn't about to lie to her. "We've been busy tracing Corbin's movements back as much as we can, trying to tie up all loose ends. Darlin', the one thing we haven't been able to tie off is that black truck. The truck I saw speeding off the night of the break in at your place and what we think was the same one that had been following you into Cortez those weeks." It killed him to have Emma looking at him with a look of worried shock on her face.

"But…how is that possible? Who else would have an interest in me? I don't get it. Are you sure he didn't have someone else working for him? Someone like Ralph?"

"Pretty sure. A black rental truck that was reported missing was just found yesterday at the bottom of a gulley. VIN confirmed it was the missing truck, and although most of it was wiped clean, the lab found a single print and a few partials in a few obscure places. The owner of those prints is known to the police, Emma." He looked over at her, gauging her reaction. "He's a known criminal who has close ties with Bruno Silva."

Frowning at him, Emma seemed confused. "The crime boss guy? What would he want with me?"

"Think about it, darlin'. Corbin skimmed money off him and used you to keep track of it, even if you had no clue you were doing it."

"Fine, but that still doesn't explain how that guy, Silva, would know. Not like he and Corbin were speaking, were they?"

"True, but I'm getting the impression that Silva was onto Corbin turning state's evidence, right from the start. He must've had someone keeping an eye on Mr. Corbin's every move. Probably didn't want to stick his neck out with law enforcement around all the time and really, with tabs on Corbin, he wouldn't have to. Could just let him lead the way to his money."

"Right." Emma turned her head away, leaning her forehead against the side window. "And now he wants me to show him."

Sounding so tired and flat, as if her usual zest had left her, cut Gus. So he pulled the Yukon to the side of the road and turned off the engine.

"What are you doing?" Emma wanted to know.

Unclipping his seatbelt, he moved his seat back, unclipped her seatbelt, and gingerly lifted her onto his lap; where he anchored her with one arm wrapped tightly around her waist and the other at the back of her neck. "Babe, hear this. I know I fucked up. I shouldn't have left you–should've taken you with me into Cortez, I know that…"

"You couldn't have known that…that's ridiculous!" Emma exclaimed.

"Hush, and let me finish. It was my responsibility to keep you safe. I didn't do that. But I swear to you, I won't let anything happen to you. They will have to kill me first." He firmly held her head in place when she tried to avoid his eyes. "You're important. You hear me? When I heard you were gone, saw your blood." He squeezed his eyes shut at the memory and fought to keep his emotions in check. Swallowing hard he continued,

"Having no fucking clue where to start, made me crazy. Then finally being able to do something and finding you at the mercy of that cocksucker, bleeding, your air being cut off; I have never in my life felt such fear."

She could feel the shudders run through his body as he relived those moments, and the emotion was stark on his face. Leaning into him, she simply rested her head on his shoulder and held him the best that she could.

"Thank you, for saving me. I knew you'd come, that's all that was in my mind. I was terrified, but I knew you would find me."

Gus pushed her back a little and fastened his lips to hers like a starved man, kissing her voraciously. His tongue made strong, dominating sweeps through her mouth, and curled around her tongue as it penetrated deep. With his hands crushing her to him, he made sure she could feel every hard inch of him claiming her. She could taste his hunger, fear, and desperation, but also something else, something richer, deeper: a heady flavor that had her spinning and her body aching for his rough hands. Unlatching himself from her, Gus took in a deep breath. "Fuck me. I would take you right here but, darlin', I gotta bring you home or I'll have two already pissy females after my ass. And there is only one female I like on my ass," he said as his voice dropped another octave, or so it seemed.

"But, my sweet Peach, it has to be said. You taste like hot sin."

With a soft swipe of his lips over hers, she was lifted back in her seat and buckled in. Gus started the truck and took them home, a satisfied smile on his face. All Emma could do was think about how easy it had been for him to completely distract her from her predicament. Letting fatigue take her, she simply closed her eyes.

-

Feeling herself being lifted out of the Yukon, Emma blinked her eyes open to find herself at home, Arlene and Kara waiting on the porch.

"Take the long road, hot stuff?" This from Arlene, who couldn't let an opportunity go by to try and needle Gus. He was virtually unflappable and lifted one corner of his mouth.

"Decided to stop and blind Emma with my mad fishing skills, if you must know, Arlene. Diner food is getting old."

"Oh puleeze," Arlene scoffed, "The only fish that impresses Emma is one that is cleaned, cooked, and on her plate, ready to eat! She hates the fishing. Struck out on that one, lover boy." Cackling, Arlene shoved his shoulder.

"Leave the man alone, Arlene," Emma admonished her, with a big smile on her face. "You are such a pest."

"Yeah, but isn't that why you love me?" The normally slightly gruff and abrupt Arlene threw her arms around Emma as soon as Gus deposited her on the porch to get the rest of the stuff from the truck. "This better be the last time you scare me like that, woman," Arlene sniffled in her ear. "I had no one to fucking bicker with for days!" Making Emma laugh through the tears that wanted to flow.

Turning to her daughter, Emma could see worry and irritation in conflict on her face.

"Come on, sweetie, lead me inside. I could use a cup of tea."

CHAPTER EIGHTEEN

A week had passed since Emma had been discharged from the hospital. Joe had been sent home to recuperate in the meantime, and Katie was still in the hospital. She was hanging in there, tough as nails, Dana having taken up residence in Durango to be closer on hand. With Neil back in the motel in Cedar Tree, monitoring things, Caleb was able to make regular treks to see Katie. He was still adamant about not leaving his post in town. Gus had considered calling in some additional manpower, but after last week's events, the sheriff's office had finally decided to assign a few more man-hours. It meant they had better local coverage than before. But being already short by one deputy, they had some reinforcements on loan from a neighboring county until the vacancy could be resolved.

Nothing much had happened in the past few days. Other than running down the occasional potential lead, there hadn't been much movement at all. Silva appeared to have gone silent, but Gus knew very well that looks could be very deceiving. Not trusting for one minute that the danger might be past.

Today Kara was scheduled to fly back to Boston. She had missed a full week and a half of work, but with her mom back up and about again, she really couldn't miss more work. Emma assured her that she would be fine, and would call every day, keeping her up-to-date. In the meantime, Gus had made himself scarce, trying to give mother and daughter some time to visit. So he had spent most of his time working outside, fixing the rickety steps on Emma's porch, making a start on a ramp, or driving them to and from the diner to hang with Arlene. Every day, Caleb would come and take over so he could drive into Cortez and work from the sheriff's office. Then at night, Kara would head over to Arlene's to sleep, since Arlene had offered her spare room. Emma didn't have one, and Gus would bunk down on Emma's couch. This out of respect for her daughter, but also because he didn't trust himself in bed with her while she was still recovering.

It was getting old though, the couch wasn't that comfortable, and he missed having her soft body to wrap around. Not to mention every time he touched or kissed Emma, he received a glare from Kara if she was around. Even having only the best of intentions, she managed to make him feel like crap. He had to give it to the kid though; she was fiercely protective of her mom. Little did she know that her mom could hold her own and didn't need her protection.

"Morning," Emma said, shuffling into the kitchen, her hair a wild mess, as usual, and sleepy creases covering her face, looking absolutely kissable. Moving right up to her, he palmed her face and did just that.

"Mmmmm, what was that for?" She wanted to know, a soft smile on her face. Leaning her cane against the counter, she slid her hands up his chest.

"I love the rumpled, early morning look on you. Makes me want to crawl back into bed with you and 'rumple' you up some more." Taking her hands, he pulled them up and around his neck, sliding his own hands down her arms and sides, grabbing her hips and pulling her close. Angling his head down, the took her lips for another taste, stroking his tongue along the seam of her mouth, forcing her open and sinking himself in the warm, sweet taste of her. When he felt her fingers tugging on his hair, and her breasts rubbing up against his chest, he groaned. Lifting her up, he sat her on the counter, moved between her legs and forced his full hard length against her hot core. Hearing the small moans come from the back of her throat, when she sucked his tongue, drove him wild. His hand slipped under her shirt and over her soft breast, pinching her small peaked nipple. Dropping his head, he pushed her shirt out of the way and latched on, lips wide, sucking hard on a mouthful of her luscious tit. So fucking delicious, he could come in his jeans right there.

"Oh God!"

Feeling her hands tighten in his hair, he renewed his efforts, until he noticed she was pulling on his hair. Hard.

"Oh my fucking God, you've got to be kidding me!" Kara said from the doorway. "I did not just see that."

Closing his eyes momentarily, Gus, as calmly as he could, pulled down Emma's shirt and straightened up. When he cupped her face and looked her in the eye, he saw panic reflected there. Leaning in, he kissed her sweetly before he lifted her down from the counter and handed her the cane. Turning to the cupboard to pull down mugs, he said, "Coffee everyone?"

"Please," Emma said, still a little shell-shocked.

"Are you serious?" Kara sneered, throwing attitude.

"Serious about what, Kara?" he said, turning to face her. "About your mother? Yes. Very serious. I'm sorry you had to walk in on that. I'm sure finding your mother making out with me was less than comfortable for ya. But if you're waiting for me to apologize for it, you'll be waiting a long time. I'm not sorry for kissing her. I plan to be doing that and then some, a whole lot more. So you might as well get used to it."

"Mom!" She turned to her mother next.

"Stop. I mean it, Kara. I love you, but you have to stop this. I honestly don't know what's gotten into you. Gus is right, you weren't meant to walk in on that, obviously, but you are acting like a child–not the adult I know you are. What's going on?"

With that, Kara burst into tears.

Figuring now might be a good time to make himself scarce, Gus kissed the top of Emma's head–who now had a sobbing Kara folded in her arms. He squeezed Kara's shoulder, grabbed his mug, and went out to sit on the front porch to make some calls.

-

He checked in with Neil, who finally had some good news; after 'cracking' the code on Corbin's ledger entries, he was finally starting to pull some information together. He had found out about half the entries were traceable to overseas accounts, where large amounts of cash had been deposited in the last few months. Not only that, but each entry had also left an imprint of the source. All of those were pointing squarely in the direction of Bruno Silva. Those flapping loose ends were coming closer to being tied up. It was a double-edged sword, the need to keep their findings so tightly under wraps but absolutely necessary for the investigation. If anything leaked out, Silva would disappear, and all the work the task force had put in would be lost. But until they had every T crossed and I dotted, it meant there was ongoing danger for Emma, and that didn't sit particularly well with him.

The sound of gravel had him lift his head to see Arlene's beat up truck pull in. She got out with a mischievous grin on her face.

"What'd you do? You get kicked out?" She chuckled at her own joke.

"Ha. No, more like I escaped," he shot back. "Kara caught us in a...let's just say, compromising position this morning, and it didn't go over too well. She had a little melt down, and I thought I'd let the girls work it out," he said with a shrug of his shoulders.

"Coward. Little girl got ya running?" Arlene tried to needle him.

"Hardly. If you can't scare me off, Arlene, then how do you figure a waif like that could?"

"Good point, my man, good point. All right, even though I suck at tears, I'm going in. I have to get that girl to the airport. Wish me luck."

Grinning at Arlene's antics, Gus gave her the thumbs up.

He briefly considered following her into the house, but opted instead to use his time. So while waiting for the tension to clear a little, he continued the work he started on the ramp leading off Emma's porch. He had overheard Arlene say something about Emma needing one. He had seen her struggle with the steps on some of her bad days, especially on those when she was dependent on her walker. Agreeing it would vastly improve her comfort and independence if she could simply walk down a ramp, instead of struggle with the walker down her steps, he had gone to work.

In the past week, he had spent a lot of his 'idle' time working out here, needing to keep his hands busy, when they were really aching to be all over Emma. He hadn't wanted to add to the slightly tense atmosphere and had limited any public displays of affection to the odd stolen kiss and hug, whenever Kara was not around. Except for this morning, they had been able to avoid any confrontations. But now it seemed there might be more going on with Kara than simple dislike of him or concern with her mother.

The outburst in the kitchen reeked of some deeper issue he wasn't privy to. Damned if he could figure it out. The girls would probably be better at digging that up.

Lost in thought, Gus hadn't heard anyone approach until he felt a tap on his shoulder. Turning around, he was surprised to find Kara standing behind him with a fresh mug of coffee.

"Hey. Thanks, I needed another one." Accepting the mug from her, he smiled, taking in her swollen, downcast eyes and hunched shoulders.

"You're welcome. And...I'm uh...sorry about earlier. Actually..." Shaking her head lightly, Kara sighed deeply and raised her eyes to meet his. "I'm sorry I've been a shit this whole time. I'm really not like that. It's just..." Turning to look out at the mountains in the distance, Kara seemed to gather her courage, while Gus patiently waited her out. "Like I just told Mom, I am still adjusting to her being all the way over here. Even though I wanted her to do this–to move–I feel like I need to be on high alert all the time. I made taking care of her my responsibility, but I guess it isn't."

Seeing a few tears escape from her eyes, Gus used his knuckle to wipe them away then tilted her face so he could look her in the eye. "I get it, Kara. Trust me. I do. Since meeting your mother, I've wanted nothing more than to wrap her up and put her on a shelf to keep her safe. But I figured out fairly quickly that she'd have me out that door so fast, I wouldn't know what hit me."

Kara couldn't hold back a giggle. "Probably."

"So it's gotta be worse for you, given that you've seen her go from healthy and able-bodied, to physically challenged as she is now. But you have to realize that she likely hasn't changed a lick.

In fact, she probably has gotten a whole lot stronger and smarter since. Don't you figure? Smart enough to know when something is too much for her, or when she needs help."

"I guess," Kara sniffled, and throwing caution to the wind, Gus wrapped his arms around her, feeling her stiffen up momentarily, before slowly snuggling into his chest.

"Trust her, Kara. If you can show her you won't go overboard with the protective instincts, and remember it is she who is the parent and not the other way around, I would bet she'll confide in you and call on you for help."

Kara's arms squeezed around his middle and for a while, they simply stood there on the porch. Warm in the morning sun, his cheek resting on her hair and her head snuggled against him. Looking out at the view, he felt a sense of contentment settle over him, a warmth that settled deep in the darkest corners.

When Kara finally stepped back and smiled up at him through tear-streaked cheeks, he felt her settle herself in his heart, right along with her mother.

"I'd better get ready or I'll miss my flight. Thanks, Gus." Lifting up on her toes, she kissed his cheek.

"Any time, Pumpkin'. Any time."

CHAPTER NINETEEN

With her baby on the way home to Boston, Emma felt a little conflicted. She was sad to see Kara go, it had been wonderful to spend some time with her. But with the potential for danger still around, she preferred Kara to be safely in Boston and not underfoot, where something could happen to her. Of course, she also had missed Gus. After the hot and heavy start they had, things had slowed down to a crawl, and it was making her a little antsy.

She had almost interrupted Gus and Kara on the porch this morning. Getting a glimpse at their moment settled her right down. She had no idea how that man could know her so well, yet he did. The way he then handled her baby with such care, it had made her cry. After the week of tension they had just been through, it was a thing of beauty to see Kara snuggled up against Gus's large frame. Not to mention the look of pure contentment that had settled on the big man's face.

Now she wanted to jump his bones.

-

"Penny for your thoughts."

She had been washing up the last breakfast dishes at the sink, gazing out the window, deep in thought. She hadn't heard him come up behind her, when she felt his lips move against the shell of her ear. His strong arms stole around her waist and pulled her tight against his front. A slight shiver ran through her body.

"You cold?" A note of concern sounded in his voice.

"No. I just missed you." She smiled at the view, settling back against his chest.

"Hmmmm...missed you too, Emma." He buried his nose in her hair. "So much," he added.

A little taken aback at his serious tone, she turned around in his arms and tilted her head to the side, looking him in the eye.

"So much, huh? To tell you the truth, I was just thinking the same thing. I mean, it's not like you haven't been around, but… Well you know, with Kara here, we haven't really spent a lot of time together. Alone, I mean."

"Exactly. There is so much more about you, Ms. Young, that I would love to learn." Gus slid one had down to her ass, pressing her body into his rather prominent erection. A mischievous smile lifted one side of his mouth.

"Is that so, Mr. Flemming?" she countered, running her hands down his back to where she reached the hem of his shirt and found skin, just to slide them back up again along his spine without any barriers between them.

"Hmmm-mmm... There is a whole life's history to catch up on: favorite colors and foods, dos and don'ts, family and friends, books and music. Lists and lists of need to know," he teased, punctuating each item with open-mouthed kisses and nibbles along her neck and her shoulders, sensitizing her nipples and flooding her lower stomach with a warm surge.

"Shall I make us a pot of tea, then? So we can sit down and compare notes?" she teased back, as she tried to turn away and pull out of his arms. Growling, he yanked her back against him with some force, weaving his hand in her curls and tilting her head. His fierce eyes burned into hers, and he shook his head no as he bent down and took her mouth.

And take he did; without apology. Hungry, impatiently and thoroughly: his mouth eating at her lips and her chin, his tongue probing and prodding deep. She clenched up on her thighs, trying to ease the ache between her legs that wanted to be satisfied. As if he could sense her need, he slid one of his knees between hers, and with his large hand cupping her from behind, pulled her over his thigh. Tucking her close to his body, her clit and pussy riding his strong thigh muscle. The feeling was enough to steal her breath. "More…please, give me more." She panted out, her heart racing; she was grinding herself as best she could against his leg.

"Arms around my neck, Peach. Hold on to me. I've got you, love." He grabbed her hips firmly in both hands and lifted his leg on the rung of a kitchen stool. Silencing her moans with his mouth, he moved her back and forth along his thigh. Her panties were slick with her arousal and the friction on her clit was almost too much to bear. Clutching to Gus's shoulders and hair, she tried finding purchase as she reached for completion. Teetering on the very brink of orgasm, she grunted when he suddenly lifted her off. He set her on her feet, and in one move, stripped off her yoga pants and underwear, and planted her on the kitchen counter, buck naked from the waist down.

"Gus..." she pleaded.

"Let me give it to you, Peach," he said, spreading her legs, going down on one knee, and latching onto the little bundle of nerves at the apex of her thighs, sucking hard as he plunged two fingers in her pussy. A long keening sound came from her as she tried to hold herself up with one hand, while pulling his head tighter into her. His fingers pumping, she could feel them curving up at the same time his teeth bit down on her clit, catapulting her into euphoria.

Fucking nothing like it. Her face; as she gave herself over to him, as she came. The taste of her. Fucking beautiful. He never took his eyes of her as he tongue and finger fucked Emma to orgasm. His balls about to burst, he stood, slid an arm around her shoulders and under her knees, and carried a limp but sated Emma into the bedroom.

"Where are you taking me?" She wanted to know.

"Not done with you yet."

That made her giggle softly. "Dunno how much help I'm gonna be. I'm like Jello."

"You can have a little time to recover, while I play with you some more." He wasn't going to let the opportunity pass him by, now that they finally had the house to themselves. Not in any hurry, he divested her of the remainder of her clothes and got himself naked as well, with Emma observing him from her position in bed. Watching her eyes taking him in, her eyelids getting heavier with lust, made his own libido rage out of control. His woman. Resilient, smart, warm-hearted, and so fucking beautiful it made his chest ache. He climbed on the bed and slowly lowered himself on top of her, mindful to keep some of his weight on his arms. The sensation and contrast of his hard and coarse body being pillowed by her softness and pliancy felt like a safe haven. Sanctuary.

"Gus…" she whispered in his ear, hands skimming over his back and through his hair. "You feel incredible. I missed you."

Lifting up, he held the top of her head while looking down

into her eyes. "Missed you too, baby. Your smell, your sounds, the feel of you, your hands on my skin; I missed it all." Lowering his mouth to hers, their kiss started soft and gentle, but it didn't take long for the pent up hunger and frustration of the past week to catch up and spark it into something more carnal. His hand restlessly skated along her side, shifting himself partially off her to gain access to her luscious body. With each skim of his hand, he got a little distracted when passing her breast, plucking at her nipple, just to hear the catch in her breathing. His own breathing became erratic when those little hands of her started doing their own exploring. He'd better put a stop to that before things were over before they started.

"Easy, tiger." He tried to soothe Emma, who was growing more restless underneath him. "Got lots of time and nowhere to be. Besides, I almost forgot...I have a surprise for you."

"Surprise?"

He had to chuckle, in some things women were so easy. "Yeah, it's in the back of your closet, let me grab it quick."

"Now?" She lifted herself up on an elbow and shot him a look of incredulity.

"Trust me. You're gonna want it now." Grinning, he got up off the bed to grab the box that had arrived a few days ago at the post office. He had hid it on top of the shelf in the back of her walk-in closet. He hoped she would like it, although he had to admit, after seeing it on the website and thinking about all the possible scenarios, he probably bought it as much for himself as for her.

Emma was waiting in the middle of the bed, eager to see what the surprise was; all but forgetting she was completely naked. With the remnants of her orgasm still flush on her face and the excitement over her surprise in her smile, he felt something settle in him. He put that flush there. He made her smile. He made her happy.

Sitting down beside her on the bed, he handed her the unmarked box to open.

"What are these?" Emma wanted to know when she pulled out the different sized foam wedges.

"Just what they look like. Wedge pillows, with multiple purposes." Wiggling his eyebrows suggestively, he urged her to lie down and moved the smaller wedge under her shoulders so her head was elevated enough to be able to look down her body. The bigger one he slid under her hips so that her butt was lifted off the bed.

"Oh boy! I see what you mean." Emma chuckled. "This is actually really comfy. Where did you get these?"

A little embarrassed, Gus shrugged. "Was trying to figure out ways to be adventurous but still safe and comfortable for you. Found them online, some website I found for people with disabilities. Stuff to help them maintain an active life."

"Come here," Emma pulled on his arm, trying to get him closer. "Come here, you. I'm trussed up like a holiday turkey here, I can barely move, you'll have to come to me." Her voice was husky with emotion.

Rolling over on his side, his head rested on one arm, he stroked Emma's hair back from her face. "You like?"

"I love them, you big oaf." She smiled at him, sliding a hand around his neck and pulling him close. "But what means most to me? Is the thought behind it: the care, the encouragement, the support, the acceptance and, Gus? The depth of the feelings."

The last took him by surprise. He must have mentioned he cared for her, but surely he would remember if he had told her, well…he loved her. He did.

"Love you, Peach. I do. Never expected it, but you make it so fucking easy. I never stood a chance." With a little trepidation in his heart, he lifted his eyes to look at her and saw nothing but the big smile on her lips and in her eyes. "You're just gonna smile at me? Leaving me hanging?" By now two big tears were making tracks down her cheeks, but given the crazy big grin on her face, he figured those were happy tears, and he wiped them away with his thumbs as he claimed her mouth for a kiss.

"Ditto." Was the choked up response he got, forcing a laugh from him.

"What the fuck? Ditto? Oh hell no, you're not getting away with that, missy!" He grinned, settling himself over her, grabbing her hands and raising them above her head.

"Feel those handholds at the top of the pillow? I want you to hold on to those and don't let go." Settling in between her legs on his knees, he pushed the wedge further back under her, so that her ass almost hung off the edge. Then he spread her legs, exposing her completely to his view. She was wet with her arousal already.

"Liking this, are you?"

"Hmmm …" Was the only response he got, as she impatiently rocked her hips, looking for some friction. Bending down, he swiped his tongue through her folds from her ass all the way to her clit, taking the distended bud between his lips and sucking hard. He could hear her mewling and looked up to see her watching from her slightly elevated position.

"More, please," she pleaded, lifting her hips off the wedge.

"Keep those hands where they are, but turn on your

stomach."

Helping her to flip over, the wedge now supporting her hips, her ass was high up in the air, without putting any pressure on her legs or knees.

"Beautiful." He traced her back with both of his big hands, from her shoulders all the way down to the globes of her ass, kneading her flesh.

"I can't fucking keep my hands of you, darlin'. Are you ready for me?"

"Fuck me already. Gus, please…"

Her skin felt oversensitized. With every pass of his hands, she was struggling harder and harder to keep her own from moving. Restlessly shifting her hips, she wanted to spread herself as wide as possible for him, wanting to feel him fill her. Fuck her hard. This little control game they were playing had her turned on so much, she was going to come from skin contact alone.

She could feel his hands slide down the back of her thighs, and as they traveled back toward her ass, her cheeks were spread wide open. The sensation of his tongue between her legs, gave her a full body shiver. This time he licked her front to back, briefly tonguing her pussy before sliding further up. His thumbs slid from her labia into her passage, and she involuntarily clenched down on them. God, she wanted to feel his cock.

"Patience, my delicious Peach," Gus rumbled from behind her.

He pulled a thumb from her and trailed moisture up to her ass, started gently probing and pushing through the tight ring of muscle. Never had she been breached there before, and Emma briefly fought the instinct to pull away, but wanting to experience it all, she instead pushed back against his finger.

"Oh my God, Emma. What you do to me. I have to get inside you."

With his thumb still firmly lodged in her ass, he slid his painfully erect cock through her folds, probing for her entrance. With one big thrust he planted himself balls deep inside her, with a groan, causing her to gasp for breath.

"You okay, my love?" Gus whispered to her.

"God, yes, yes. So good," she whimpered. "Please move…"

She could feel a hand anchoring her hip and then he moved. Pumping slowly at first, but with increasing speed. He matched the movement of his cock, sliding in and out of her, with the thrusts of his thumb. She was overwhelmed with a sense of fullness, a feeling of being completely consumed.

"One of these days, darlin', I want to fuck you here." Gus said, as he twisted his digit in her ass, which woke up a whole new set of nerve endings and jump-started an explosive orgasm, causing her to buck and scream his name.

Using both hands now, Gus grabbed onto her hips with a strong hold sure to leave imprints. Moving more erratically, he pumped into her until he found his own release. Finally collapsing, completely spent, and gasping for air, on top of her. She welcomed the weight of him, the give of the wedged pillows taking most of it. He had his head buried in her hair, and twisting her head slightly, so her lips could reach him, she kissed him. "I love you too, Big Guy."

CHAPTER TWENTY

"We really should talk," Gus said, as he walked into the kitchen.

Hard to believe it had been only three hours since Kara left. It felt like so much time had passed already. Her plane should be leaving in twenty minutes or so, and Arlene should be back sometime soon. Although, Emma was pretty sure Arlene would wait around with Kara until the last possible minute.

Then there had been Gus sucking up snippets of time and expanding it a hundred-fold, creating memorable moment after moment. He felt so huge in her otherwise rather limited life. Sweet, bossy, presumptuous Gus; who could bring her to her knees with his thoughtfulness and fierce protectiveness. Not to mention the dirty thoughts he didn't hesitate in sharing and his calm presence.

But calm was not what she felt radiating from him at the moment. When she turned to him, she could see tension in his jaw and in the balled fists he was hiding in his pockets. Something was wrong.

"Talk about what?"

"Us. You and me." Gus stayed on the other side of the counter at a safe distance, looking uncomfortable.

Swallowing down a ball of nerves that had suddenly taken up residence in her throat, Emma forced her next words out. "Is there a problem?"

His eyes met hers briefly before looking beyond her, out the kitchen window. "I…um, maybe. I was thinking while I was having a shower. We haven't really had a chance to talk much. About our pasts. Our lives."

"Okay…" She was trying hard not to panic at his changed demeanor from earlier that morning. "What is it you're saying exactly, Gus?"

"Just that there is some stuff in my past that you should probably know about. Before, you know…you make any decisions about me." He looked so uncomfortable; it tugged at her heartstrings. Making a decision to throw caution to the wind, she turned around, grabbed two coffee mugs down, filled them, and set them on the counter.

"Here, you grab these and let's go sit down for a bit."

Walking right past him, she went ahead into the living room and sat on one end of the couch, waiting for him to follow. It took him a minute to move, but he grabbed the mugs and brought them in, sitting down next to her.

"Talk to me."

He still avoided looking at her directly, but hesitated only for a minute before taking in a deep breath and letting it out. "I married young, too young probably. In part to get out of the house, wanting to start my own family. Getting away from mine. Dad was a cop. Mom was a stay at home mom, who really had nothing much going on outside of taking care of us. Dad ruled the roost, so to speak. With a firm hand."

"He hit you?" She wanted to know.

"Nah. Occasionally if we'd really stepped out of line, but nothing abnormal for those days. He was just…overbearing, controlling. Had high expectations."

"You mentioned 'us' and 'we', do you have siblings?"

"A brother. Five years older. He followed in my dad's footsteps and became a cop: the apple of my father's eye, two peas in a pod. I was the odd one out, more attached to my mom. More like her, too. Too soft for my dad's liking." Gus picked up his coffee and took a swallow. "Still, I followed in his footsteps too. Got hitched young, went to the police academy, and ended up joining the Detroit PD along side him and my brother. He always pushed me to join in with some of his 'fraternities.' A bunch of cops hanging out together, trying to find ways to manipulate department policies from the bottom up. I was never one for politics, so I passed. Time and time again. That pissed him right off. Of course my brother was into it, he was right in the thick of things."

Getting up, he started pacing the room restlessly, and Emma could sense they were getting to the meat of his story. Determined for him to tell her everything, she wasn't going to move or even look at him differently. She simply continued to sit there, sipping her coffee, waiting for him to finish at his own pace.

"One day, two cops were found dead, our colleagues. Murdered. They had also been part of one of my dad's fraternities. No discernible leads were found, but Internal Affairs suddenly showed up asking questions about those. Apparently they had been part of an ongoing corruption investigation. We were all questioned, but when they got to me, they started asking me about my dad and my brother. Wanted to know about their association with the two murdered cops. I told them what I knew about that particular fraternity and mentioned I'd been to one meeting and wouldn't like ever go again. Just not really interested. Still, they came after me hard, basically accusing me of being a corrupt cop. They had nothing on me, since there was nothing to have, but they did scare the shit out of me. During the interrogations, they asked me to identify a number of fellow officers who had been present the one time I had joined my dad and my brother at their weekly get together. I didn't think I was doing anything wrong, I simply told them what I knew."

His voice had dropped so low; Emma had to lean forward to catch every word. Shame and guilt were evident in his eyes, which were completely unshielded. "Turns out their innocent little 'fraternity' was a front for organized extortion from local merchants and small businesses. They took pay offs for covering up crimes and eliminating evidence. The two murdered officers had been informants for IA, been found out, and murdered. My dad and brother were deeply involved. It made me sick. Mom didn't believe it, continued to believe in their innocence. Both were convicted and did time. Dad ended up dying in prison. Mom completely lost it and now lives in a seniors' home. It's a small blessing she doesn't recognize anyone anymore, because now I can go visit her from time to time without her kicking me out. After my brother, Will, was released, he disappeared."

With his back to her, Gus stared out the window as he recounted the tragic history of his family. She simply sat on the couch, with her hands covering her mouth; tears streaming down her face. Her heart ached for him, but still she waited him out.

"Right after the IA investigation, I started receiving threats. Some were anonymous, but most were right in my face. I was transferred when it became impossible to work for the department anymore. But each new placement, and later in every new town or city; the stigma of having sold out my 'brothers' caught up with me. My marriage was never strong, so Karen left after the second transfer, having had enough of my fucked up family and me. I bided my time the best I could. Barely made it to early retirement age and hightailed it out of there. That's when I started out on my own."

Making love to Emma this morning had been mind-blowing, and not just the release after a week's pent up sexual frustration, but so much more than that. Years of restraint seemed to be released when in Emma's arms, something he had no experience with. A need to strip himself of all pretence and veneer, and simply share this real, honest connection with her, had urged him to voice his feelings out loud. But that was not what had set his mind spinning. It was Emma's responding declaration of love that followed their intense moments of shared bliss, which sparked up his insecurity.

Anyone who had ever professed to love him had ended up turning their backs on him and walked away when the going got tough. So even though he was convinced of his own words and the feelings they conveyed, he couldn't help his knee-jerk reaction to Emma's. It wasn't so much that he questioned her integrity, but he would simply have felt a whole lot better if she knew the dirty truth about his past before she had expressed those sentiments.

Now he was questioning the wisdom of laying his whole sordid past out there for her. Fuck. He was a hot mess and felt gutted after dragging all that shit back up again. Looking over, he found Emma curled up on the couch, head in her arms, bawling. Now fucking what? How was he supposed to take that?

Unsure, pissed, and hurting, Gus got up and walked out the front door. He needed some air. Halfway down the steps of the porch, Emma's voice coming from behind stopped him.

"Where the fuck do you think you're going?" She was leaning against the doorway, hands on her hips, looking furious.

"You're going to tell me you love me, fuck me, and lay the most horribly tragic story on me, just to walk out the damn door without another word? I don't fucking think so, Big Guy." Her eyes were daring him to move another inch. "Give a person a goddamn minute to process this shit, okay?"

Startled, he realized she was right. He hadn't given her any chance to respond, so he sat down on the porch steps. He had made all the wrong assumptions, based on past experiences. That hadn't been fair to Emma. "You're right. I'm sorry," he admitted, when she sat down on the step and leaned into his side.

"You realize that's a pretty messed up burden your family left you with, right?"

"They'd probably argue things the other way around, seeing as my dad and brother are the ones who paid the price."

That earned him a snort from Emma. "For real? They're the ones who got what they deserved in the first place. They broke the rules; they pay the price. How is that your fault? Any of it? I don't get that kind of thinking. The only people who think like that are criminals; people who don't think twice about pulling others into their shit, or making them pay for it. Face it; you have paid through the nose for all these years. Except you didn't deserve it. All you did was the right thing."

"Yeah, but they're my family…"

"If you're gonna throw this on family loyalty…" Emma interrupted sternly, "Then let me remind you that they broke that bond, the moment they expected you to defy the law. Assumed you would lie to your superiors and asked you to risk your own hide in order to save theirs. I call bullshit on family loyalty!"

During her little tirade, Emma had sat up straighter and moved back from him, her small fists flying, punctuating her fierce words. The entire picture filled his chest with a huge warm bubble and caused a lump to form in his throat. But when she indicated she was done with a cocky little nod of her head, it was all he could do not to burst out laughing. His Peach was a tiger.

Hauling her back over to him, he curled her into his chest, stuck his nose in her curls, squeezed his eyes shut, and breathed her in deeply. He was an idiot.

Tilting her head back a little, she looked up in his eyes, put a hand to his cheek and smiled.

"Hey. Gus Flemming, I love you."

Yup. Idiot.

CHAPTER TWENTY-ONE

"Hey, Seb, what's up?"

It was coming up on 4:30 p.m. Emma was in the kitchen making some inroads on a marinade for the barbecued steak skewers on the menu for tonight's dinner, and Gus was on his cell phone, checking in with his team, when the phone rang.

"Have you heard from Arlene?" Seb's concerned voice came over the phone.

"Not since she left to drop off Kara at the airport this morning. She had a few errands to run in Durango, but that's all I know. Why? Is she not back yet?" Looking at the clock and realizing it was nearing the dinner hour at the diner, an uneasy feeling started forming in the pit of her stomach.

"Haven't seen her. She was supposed to be back around one, and she is not answering her phone. Have you talked to Kara?"

"Not yet, but she isn't scheduled to land until sometime around six p.m. She was going to call me." The thought of not being able to get a hold of her daughter for another hour or two didn't sit well with her all of a sudden. "Hang on, let me get Gus, he may have an idea."

Gus had picked up on part of the conversation already, because he was standing right behind her when she turned around, startling her. When he put his hands on her shoulders and leaned down to look in her eyes, she realized how much she had come to rely on him, his touch settling her right down.

"Talk to me." Was all he said.

"That's Seb on the phone. Arlene hasn't shown up yet, and she was supposed to be back at the diner three and a half hours ago. She's not picking up her phone."

Taking the phone from her hands, Gus wrapped one arm around her and pulled her tight to his side, while getting as much information from Seb as he could. After telling him he would look in to things, he promised to call him with whatever he found out.

When Gus turned back to her, he asked her to pull up Kara's flight information.

"Why? I can tell you she is supposed to land at a little after six p.m. We won't be able to reach her until then anyway." A flicker of uncertainty passed over his face and suddenly the full force of that nagging unease came over her in the shape of paralyzing fear. Raising her hands as if to shield herself, she backed away, shaking her head. "Oh God. Please. No."

Ignoring her retreat, Gus stepped in and enveloped her in his strong arms. "Easy, my love. No borrowing trouble. We're just checking she got on her flight. That's all. Just making sure. Hush now."

But it was no use. The thought of anything happening to Arlene or, God forbid, her Kara had her stomach lurching up in her throat. She just had time to pivot around and hit the sink, before throwing up violently. A cold towel pressed to the back of her neck and another wiping her face made her feel moderately better, as she struggled to get herself under control. No falling apart now. She couldn't afford it.

After Gus installed Emma on the couch with a glass of water, her phone and the laptop, pulling up necessary information, he was on his phone contacting Joe. He quickly informed him of Seb's call and passed on Kara's flight number, with a promise to keep each other up-to-date with any developments. His next call was Caleb, whom he'd hoped to catch in Durango, visiting Katie. In luck, he caught his friend just as leaving the hospital. Caleb promised to check the airport parking lot, ask around at the United Airlines counter, and would drop in on the couple of stops Arlene was supposed to make. He too would keep Gus in the loop.

It didn't take Joe long to call back, but the news wasn't good. Kara had never boarded her plane, and Gus felt his own precarious hold on his emotions start to slip. With one glance at Emma's questioning expression, he steeled himself before hanging up with Joe and turning to her.

"Apparently Kara didn't make her flight, love. That was Joe. He just got word back from United that she never checked in or boarded."

Expecting her to fall apart, he took her hands in his, ready to promise to find her. But she surprised him. She yanked her hands back, pushed herself off the couch and made her way to the door without a word.

"Hey. Wait a minute..." He barely got the words out of his mouth before she swung around, facing him, her cheeks flushed and her eyes wild.

"I can't. I don't have time. I've gotta go get my girl." Then she was out the door, and almost down the steps, before he caught up with her.

"Darlin', let's hold on here." When he tried to step in front of her to slow her down, she shoved him out of the way, single-mindedly focused on her car. Again he intercepted her, but this time from behind, putting his arms around her body, effectively trapping her arms so she couldn't lash out at him.

"Let. Me. Go." She struggled to get out of his hold, only making him pull her in tighter.

"Emma. Listen to me. " Bending close to her ear, he continued quietly, "I'm going to find her and Arlene. I promise you, my love. But I can't have you going off half-cocked on me; you'd slow us down. It wouldn't help. Do you hear me?"

The struggling stopped and when he loosened the hold on her, and turned her around, he was struck by the determined look in her eyes.

"My phone. Where is the phone; I need to try and call her."

Pulling out his cell, he asked her for the number, but even punching them in, he knew in his gut she would not be answering. Judging by the sudden slump of Emma's shoulders, she had come to that realization as well. "Straight to voicemail, Peach. It's out of juice or been turned off." Watching her pull herself together again, he encouraged, "We'll get her back."

"I hear you. Bring me back my baby, Gus. Please bring me back my baby." The last she forced out on a barely contained sob, and Gus had to admire the fiery strength this woman hid.

"I will. Don't doubt it." With a kiss to her hair, he led her back inside, where she headed straight for the kitchen, pulling out bags of flour and mixing bowls.

-

Leaving Emma to work through her fear and frustration in her own way, he thanked God for his foresight not to get too complacent and send his team home yet. Then he got hold of Dana, who was still managing their impromptu command center at the motel. Dana promised to be over within the next half hour, after leaving Neil with specific instructions to dig up what he could on any movement from Silva or any of his known associates.

Gus had no doubt he was the one behind Arlene and Kara's disappearance. Felt it in his gut. But what he couldn't figure was why. Why them? And for what? Corbin was no longer an issue for him. Sure, he probably wanted to get as much of his money back as possible, but he had to know Emma would have passed on any information she might have had to the authorities by now. He was missing something. There had to be something he was overlooking.

-

Baking normally calmed her, but Emma didn't think anything would be able to still the hurricane of emotions tormenting her right now. A mix of unspeakable fear and anger on behalf of her daughter and Arlene, and an unhealthy dose of frustration and rage at her inability to do anything. Gus's off-hand implication that she would slow down efforts and be a hindrance in finding her own child had been a cold splash of disappointment and hurt. Oh, she was sure he hadn't meant it in a mean way, but my Lord…the implications behind those words. The shock of having felt faultlessly complete in this man's arms one minute, only to be found lacking by him the next, was a painful truth.

Steeling herself against her slowly crumbling heart, she chose to concentrate on the pie dough that was shaping under her hands, forcing her mind to fill with positive thoughts, in hopes the universe would be kind to her loved ones.

By the time Dana arrived, Emma had six pie shells lined up and covered with damp tea-towels and another six balls of pie dough wrapped up in plastic, waiting to used to cover whatever filling she ended up making.

"Keeping busy?" Dana stated the obvious, as she came in the kitchen and observed the disaster Emma's 'therapy' had left in its wake.

"Not done yet." Was all she could bring herself to say, afraid she'd lose the frail hold she had on her emotions if the older woman so much as looked at her kindly.

Appearing to catch on to her way of coping, Dana went to wash her hands and simply asked her what she could do. Grateful for the pretence at normalcy, Emma directed her to the crate of peaches Arlene had dropped off this past week, while she checked the pantry for almonds.

At some point during the time Emma had been working the dough and pointedly ignoring Gus, she had lost track of his whereabouts. The heavy footfalls in the hallway and looming presence behind her in the small storage space, where she was scrounging for ingredients, alerted her to the fact that he hadn't been too far away this whole time. But when she tried to get past him with her bag of almonds, he wasn't moving out of the way. "Excuse me," she said, rather sourly. "I tried staying out of your way. If you'd be so kind and return the favor?" Forcing her way past him, she glimpsed the look of confusion on his face, before she felt herself being grabbed around the waist and caged in against the wall, his front against her back and his hot lips at her ear.

"I'm gonna give you that, even though I don't have a fucking clue what I've done. But this is not the time to get into whatever it is. Know this though, my sweet angry Emma. I'm not done with you."

Sucking in deep breaths, Emma tried to regain her equilibrium after he pulled his body away from hers. Both physically and emotionally she needed steadier ground. Hearing him talk to Dana in the kitchen had her moving in that direction, only to catch the last few words.

"… in Joe's office."

"What's happening in Joe's office?" She wanted to know.

"Caleb is meeting Frank and Joe there. He hasn't had any luck in Durango, and is going to be my contact in that office. I'm not leaving here. I have a feeling this is only the beginning, and my guess is Arlene and Kara are not the objective, but merely a means to an end."

Slowly the realization dawned on her. "Me? Using them to get to me? Fucking why? Why me? What is so goddamn special about me?" Anger had eclipsed all other emotions now. Good. She was about ready to rip someone's throat out with her teeth if they came close enough.

"My gut tells me it is still Silva, but something doesn't quite make sense. I wouldn't be surprised if we didn't hear something soon."

Emma wasn't sure if that insight from Gus was supposed to make her feel better, because it didn't. But at this point, she would welcome some action, any action, because waiting without knowing anything was starting to drive her insane.

CHAPTER TWENTY-TWO

Three times the fucking phone rang, and not once was it anything that brought them closer to finding out what happened to Arlene and Kara. The first time had been Seb, whom he should have called back. He felt bad about that; the man was a mess and ready to close the diner down. His sneaky suspicion that there was more going on between Seb and his employer was only enforced by the man's tangible fear when hearing it might involve kidnapping. Gus expected him to show up any minute. He was getting rid of the last customers and sending the wait staff home before locking up.

The second call had been Frank, who should've known better than calling the house phone. Of course, Gus didn't hesitate to inform him of that. He still hadn't quite gotten over the way the sheriff had dragged his feet when one of his own turned out to have been involved. Things like that rubbed him exactly the wrong way.

Frank called to give Gus a head's up that aside from state patrol, the entire task force had been notified. They were apparently contemplating putting the FBI on standby, given their close proximity to the various state borders. But until they could confirm any wrongdoing, or contact was made, their hands would be tied.

Dr. Naomi Waters had been the third one on the phone, checking in to see how her patient was faring. By this time, Emma was almost coming apart at the seams and about ripped the phone off the kitchen wall. When she heard her doctor's voice, she simply shoved the phone at Gus, and dropped her head on her arms on the counter. In as few words as possible, Gus told Naomi that Kara and Arlene were missing and she should call Joe at the sheriff's office for more information, but that they needed to keep this phone line open. Then he apologized and hung up.

When he went to rub Emma on her back in comfort and support, she immediately straightened up and moved over to the sink to start on some dishes. Hmmm, still in the doghouse. Dana looked back and forth between the two of them and raised her eyebrow questioningly at him, but all he could do was shrug his shoulders. Damned if he knew.

=

It was getting close to eleven o'clock at night. Seb had long since arrived with some leftovers from the diner. Neil had also shown up and brought most of his equipment, not wanting to be too far from the action. Caleb had run over some recording equipment borrowed from the FBI satellite office in Durango. Luckily they had Neil, who would be able to install it right away.

They all had managed to eat some of the food Seb had brought over. Finishing off copious amounts of coffee, they also made a serious dent in the peach and almond pies Emma had been baking. Those had been hard to resist when the whole house had smelled of the freshly baked pastry all night. Two and a half pies gone, just like that. Damn, that woman could bake. Seeing people enjoy the fruits of her labor had done her some good, judging by the small, pleased smile on her face as she kept serving slices. In some cases seconds and thirds.

Coffee and the comfort food had soon worn off and with Emma's small house full of anxious people and way too few answers, tension was beginning to build to near cutting quality.

When the house phone rang, Emma about leapt off her perch

on the kitchen stool, right by the wall unit. Quickly standing up and placing a hand on hers, preventing her from snatching it off the hook right away, he softly reminded her, "Give Neil a chance to start recording, darlin'." To which she curtly nodded in understanding.

Keeping one hand on her neck for support, he indicated for her to pick it up, pressing his ear close so he could listen in.

"Hello?"

"...Mom?" Gus could hear Kara's voice, confused and scared.

"Oh, sweetie. Are you okay? Is Arlene? Is she with you?" Clutching at his free hand, Emma was fighting hard to stay strong. "Honey? Talk to me please..."

But all they could hear was a soft crying. "Kara?" Emma tried again.

"I'm okay. I'm scared, Mom. Arlene, she's here, she fought...she...she got hurt. She's hurt." With Kara sobbing now, it was difficult to understand what she was saying.

"We'll do whatever it takes to get you both help, sweetie. Where are you? Are you alone?"

Gus gave Emma an encouraging squeeze.

"No, not alone. I'm not allowed to say anymore, only that you will receive instructions tomorrow in your post office box. And they're saying only you and Gus–no one else–or they'll hurt us."

"Honey, please. I'll do anything to get you, I love you."

Wrapping his hand around the receiver, Gus twisted it against his mouth.

"Kara, doll, listen to me. You sit tight and do exactly what they ask. Don't fight them, okay? Don't argue and don't fight. We won't stop until we have you. I promise."

"Make it a point to look out for Mom, Gus. If something happens, take care of her. She loves Mesa Verde; you take her around, take her fishing. She'll love…" Just like that the connection was broken, but not before they could hear a man's voice softly bite out, 'Enough' in the background.

Emma's carefully maintained control crumbled. He wrapped her up in both arms, trying to hold her together as she was falling apart. His eyes found Neil's over her shoulder, hoping he might have had enough to trace the call, but the curt shake of Neil's head told him enough. But Kara had been very clever.

"Did you get everything on tape, Neil?"

He took Emma by the hand and walked her with him to sit on the couch.

"Yep, have it all."

"Play it back, will ya? The last few sentences Kara directed at me. I need to hear them again. She was telling me something."

Emma looked at him with disbelief on her face. "A message? She was scared, Gus. She was looking out for me." Her eyebrows drawn together, he could tell she was confused.

But as soon as Neil played back Kara's words, and Emma actually listened to them, her eyes opened wide. She turned to him with a smile on her face. "My girl fucking rocks!"

Glad to see some life back on her face, he planted a quick hard kiss on her lips.

"She sure does, darlin'. She sure does."

"Sorry to interrupt this love fest, but what the fuck are you talking about? All I was able to make out was that Arlene couldn't keep check of her temper and got herself hurt. Also we have a whole night to wait and worry some more." Seb obviously had reached the end of his patience in letting Emma and him take the lead. He couldn't blame the man and quickly enlightened him.

"Anyone, who knows Emma, knows she can't stand fishing. I'll admit, when she started talking I was listening to the message, not so much the words, until she mentioned taking Emma fishing. Then I knew I had to pay attention."

"Well, I'll be damned." Was Seb's response. "Let's hear it again."

Caleb had already transcribed her words and highlighted the possible clues. Mesa Verde was an obvious one. They figured out that 'around' was an odd way to phrase something.

"So we have fishing, around, and Mesa Verde. Anyone have any ideas?"

Neil had pulled up a map of the area and Gus was looking over his shoulder.

"What about the Mancos River?" Neil suggested. "It runs almost all around the other side of Mesa Verde before it intersects with the 160 in Mancos, and again south of the Ute reservation. But that is a lot of area to cover."

"It's mostly unpopulated area, so it's not like there are a lot of access roads. I'm thinking this would be a good time to fill in Joe and Frank at the sheriff's office. They can put the right calls out to the state patrol, and perhaps park officials to keep an eye out. At least we can be pretty sure they aren't too far from here, but given that it is near midnight, and pitch dark out, I don't think there will be much point in looking tonight. So I suggest we all try and get some sleep and wait for daylight."

Neil and Dana went back to the motel for a few hours of sleep. Gus handed Seb a pillow and some blankets, so he could take the couch, since he wasn't about to leave. Then Gus talked with Caleb on the porch for a minute. "You going to be okay out here?" He wanted to know.

"Yeah. I don't want to leave you alone here. I don't like that they are basically inviting you to come along tomorrow. That doesn't sit right. Seems odd. Everything about this seems odd. Not at all the way I would expect Silva to conduct business. So I'm gonna be around."

"Okay, if you're sure. Need a break, come get me. All right?"

"Go look after your woman. Keep your eye on the prize." Caleb winked at him and stepped off the porch into the darkness.

CHAPTER TWENTY-THREE

Drained and in a significant amount of pain, Emma was struggling to get her kitchen clean before she could settle enough to go lie down. She had no illusions about sleeping, but would need to give her body a chance to rest, or she wouldn't be any good to anyone by morning. She was realistic enough to know that.

Seb walked in and took the dishrag out of her hand, nudging her to the side. "You go get ready for bed. You look about ready to drop. I'll finish cleaning up." Ignoring her protests, he simply picked up where she left off until finally she gave in, wished him a good night, and headed for the sanctuary of her bedroom.

Sitting down on the side of her bed, she considered having a shower. Wash the remnants of what surely had been the worst day of her life away, but she couldn't bring herself to spend the energy. A bath would be nice now. Although she normally loathed baths, it wouldn't require much more of her than to simply lay back and soak. Oh, and attempt not to drown in the process. Which, given the current weight of her eyelids, was a distinct possibility. Hell, she didn't even have the energy to undress. She simply allowed herself to fall backward on the bed and rested her eyes. Just for a minute, just until Gus came to bed.

-

She could hear Kara crying, but she couldn't get to her. Her arms and legs wouldn't move, and no one was listening. They kept walking around her like she was an obstacle in their way, deaf to her pleas–her cries to be seen, to be heard. And all the time, her daughter's sobbing was moving away, further and further out of reach, to where she couldn't even hear her anymore…and the silence was quietly killing her.

-

Rough calloused fingers wiped at her wet cheeks. Confused, she opened her eyes to find Gus's deep brown fixed on her. "You were having a dream, darlin'. Crying and screaming. You okay?"

She could feel his deep voice resonating in his chest. Then he chuckled, shaking her a little in the process. "You scared the stuffing out of Seb. He came poundin' on the door, convinced I was trying to harm you."

Still a bit rattled and trying to compute the dream, the memories of the day that came flooding back, along with the emotions that came along with it, she looked at Gus.

"Did you undress me?" she asked, not remembering how she ended up wearing one of his shirts and wrapped tightly against him.

"When I came into the room, you were dead to the world, fully dressed and only half on the bed. You didn't even blink when I moved you all the way up, so I decided you would probably be more comfortable out of your clothes than to sleep in them all night."

"Oh. Thanks, I guess." She might still be a little dazed, but she could clearly remember now how angry and disappointed she was with him. Upset enough not to be too friendly, but not enough to deny herself the comfort of his warm body wrapped around hers. Frig. She could be such a pushover.

"Are you ever gonna tell me what I did wrong?"

Yeah, she figured he wasn't going to let it go. He had told her so plainly enough. Turning around to face him, she decided to give it to him straight. "You know what pisses me off more than anything?" A raised eyebrow is all the response she got. "The fact that you don't even realize you screwed up. That's what eats at me most."

"I obviously realize I messed up something, or I wouldn't be asking you what I did wrong, would I?"

Oh lovely, attitude. Just what she needed.

"Come on now. Let it out. Not good to let it eat at you." He urged her on.

"You know what? You're a sanctimonious prick! You led me on. You made me believe you saw more than a cripple. That you simply registered it like the color of my hair and nothing more, but that was a lie, wasn't it?"

Not quite connecting the dots, Gus shook his head as if to clear the cobwebs. "Come again?"

"You. When the chips where down, you couldn't point out my limitations fast enough before you pushed me to the side."

Okay. Now he was getting a little pissed himself. Pointing out her limitations? What? "Emma, I swear to God have no idea what you are talking about. I have never pointed out your 'so-called' limitations. And let me remind you those are your words and not mine. Where is this coming from?"

Getting worked up to a full head of steam now, Emma sits up in bed and points at him.

"Ha! You did so. You told me outside not to get in your way, or I would slow you down. You can't deny you said that."

Realization dawning, he closed his eyes and shook his head in exasperation. "Emma…" he groaned. "You can't tell me you don't realize I would've said the same thing to anyone in your situation?" Noticing her triumphant look, he quickly clarified. "As a parent; your situation as the parent of a missing child. Or as someone whose loved one might be in trouble. In fact, when I heard and saw Seb's reaction to Arlene's disappearance, I told him the same damn thing!"

Seeing her eyes widen, and her shoulders slowly drop in sudden understanding, did a lot to abate his anger. Scooting closer to her, he cupped her face, hating to see the doubt lingering behind the tears. "Oh, sweet Peach. Don't you see it's you who labels? Simply by how you choose to interpret the things I say." Understanding the concept of the knee-jerk response quite well from personal experience, Gus felt pretty awful for her. "Come here, you." Leaning back, he gently pulled her back down beside him, her head tucked under his chin.

"I'm such a tool," Emma sniffed.

He busted out laughing. "Pretty much, darlin', but I love you. Tool and all." Earning him a swat on his chest and a snicker from the hollow of his neck.

"Come on, let's try to at least close our eyes for a bit longer."

Turning her head, she pressed a kiss to where his heart should be.

"You're a good man, Charlie Brown. Too bad Lucy can be such a bitch"

"Good thing Lucy's such a hot piece of ass then." He smiled.

CHAPTER TWENTY-FOUR

It was barely seven o'clock in the morning and already Emma's house was packed with bodies again.

Gus had slept only a couple of hours, off and on, playing out the events of the previous day in his head. Frustrated that he couldn't go out and hunt the girls down was eating at him. But the thought of leaving Emma alone terrified him, because he wasn't sure if would have played into the kidnappers' hands. Leaving Emma for any length of time was simply no longer an option. Not after seeing her in a hospital bed twice already. They'd literally have to kill him to get to her.

He looked down to the woman in his arms, who finally succumbed to her exhaustion. This woman owned him, as much as she was his. Unfamiliar with this sense of belonging, it had taken him a while to identify it for what it was. Home. Her smell, her smile, her friends and daughter, her house, her life…hell, even her anger and grief felt a part of him. And something he wanted–no–needed in his life.

If only he could figure out Silva's ongoing obsession with her. He needed to find a way to put his own demons to rest, before he allowed any of them to fuck up the best thing that happened to him.

As soon as light started filtering through the blinds, he had slid his arm from around her, trying not to wake her, and disappeared in the bathroom for a quick shower. With light would come the opportunity for some action, and he wasn't about to let any of it go to waste.

-

"Neil…" he called over the young whiz kid. "Have you found any movement around Silva? Anything we might be able to use: airline tickets, rental cars, sudden moves, increased telephone calls; anything?

"No, Boss, sorry, nothing so far on that front. None of my alerts have gone off. But I am actively tracing back connections from Silva and any of his crew to see if I can find something that might look familiar or raise a flag. Unfortunately, most of that has to be done manually, so it takes time, but Dana's been helping me."

He indicates Dana, who is sitting across from him at the dining room table, with another laptop in front of her.

"Okay. Keep at it. But as soon as you have even the slightest suspicion you might have something; fill me in."

"Will do, Boss."

-

Emma was at her usual perch in the kitchen, pouring coffee for the assembled crowd and baking pancakes. She looked so damn fragile this morning; it made his heart ache. Walking up behind her, he slid his arms around her and kissed her neck. "Hey, baby, did you take your meds? You're wincing like you are in pain, and I haven't seen you take them yet."

She shook her head. "I have to eat something first, but I don't know if I can keep anything down."

"Okay. How about some milk to start off? Maybe a cracker or something? Just to get a bit of a base in your stomach. I know it doesn't seem important, but as soon as the post office opens, you and I have to get out of here, and both of us have to be at our best for the girls."

He kept his fingers crossed that his suggestion wouldn't sound too patronizing and instead would jumpstart her into taking care of herself. If only so she could be strong for Kara and Arlene. Lucky for him, it worked. He could feel her spine straighten as she gathered her resolve.

"Seb, honey?" She called over the diner's cook. "Would you jump in for a sec? I'll be right back."

She disappeared into the bathroom and he knew she needed a minute.

Caleb and Joe had come in early this morning, as well, and were in the living room when he joined them.

"Frank had patrols keeping an eye out as soon as the sun was up this morning; all around the Mesa Verde perimeter roads. Keep in mind it's a fucking huge area to cover, Gus." Joe filled him in.

"I know. If we can concentrate efforts along the Mancos River, I'm positive they're being held along there somewhere. Or at least, they've been there."

Pulling up a satellite map of the area on his laptop, he zoomed in closer on the river's run.

"Here, Joe, come have a look at this. You're probably more familiar with the area than anyone. Can you see any areas, any spots that would be a good hiding place? Anything stand out to you at all?"

"Can I see that for a minute?" Caleb turned the computer to face him. Leaning in, he seemed to be focusing on a particular area. With a satisfied grin, he pointed at the screen.

"There. Point Lookout," he said, with a smirk on his face.

"Yeah? What's with it?"

"You know how Kara said to 'Make it a point to look out for Mom,' last night? I thought that was odd wording, but now it makes sense. That girl is smart, it was another part to her clue."

He looked at the screen and could see where Caleb indicated a geographical mark inside Mesa Verde. It was one of the higher points in the park, which had a view toward the east.

"Okay. Good. At least we can focus on the east side and can fairly safely forget about the portion of river that runs the south of the park." He gave Joe a pointed look, he immediately got on his phone to relay this new theory back to the sheriff's office.

"Nervous?" he asked, glancing over at Emma, who was sitting next to him in the Yukon, hands clenched tightly in her lap.

They had managed to eat a little, got cleaned up, and worked out a plan of action in the past thirty minutes. With the post office opening at eight-thirty, he wanted to make sure they were outside and waiting by the time the doors opened. The instructions had been for just Emma and him, so they assumed they would have eyes on them. It didn't necessarily mean they were going in alone, but there wouldn't be any back up visible. Thanks to Neil, the inside of his truck was now equipped with a hidden microphone in the center console; the easiest place to hide the necessary wiring. Although no patrol cars would be visible, Caleb was somewhere behind them in Seb's borrowed truck. A nondescript beater, of which there were many on the road. Seb himself had to be virtually tied down, to prevent him from hopping in the backseat of the Yukon, and could only be appeased with the promise he could ride shotgun with Caleb; provided he keep his mouth shut, his hands to himself, and his ass in the truck at all times. But if Gus was anywhere near correct in his suspicions about the man's feelings toward Arlene, he couldn't blame him for insisting on the ride-along. He would've moved heaven and earth himself, had the shoe been on the other foot. Joe had been forbidden by the sheriff, Dr. Waters, and Gus himself to leave the couch in his condition, but no one was able to deter him from running the control center. The county sheriff's office had whatever eyes and ears they had available tracking their progress. Gus trusted Joe implicitly with that and didn't even bother to get all the precise logistics. That was Joe's strength, and given the circumstances, he had no choice but to leave it all in his hands.

"Nervous, anxious, scared. You name it, I'm feeling it," Emma said. "I'm wound so tight I'm afraid I'm gonna hurl all over your leather interior." She eyed him sheepishly.

"That's the thing about leather, darlin'. It's easy to wipe down. It's the least of our worries." He grabbed her hand, putting her cold clammy fingers on his thigh, and covering them with his own wide palm. "We are going to focus on getting them back today. Open your mind and be ready for whatever comes. Please trust me."

"I do trust you." Her slightly defensive tone had him squeezing her hand.

"I know. I mean, trust me enough not to question me today. Enough to know I'm good at what I do, and when I say something, listen to me right away. It might mean the difference between success and failure."

When it was quiet beside him, he looked over to find her swallowing hard.

"I will…I mean, I do–trust you–that is. I'll take your lead. I'll do whatever it takes."

Picking up her hand, he pressed his lips to her palm.

-

When the postmaster showed up at twenty-five minutes after eight, Gus was by Emma's side of the truck, already helping her down.

"Morning. You folks are early," he commented over his shoulder, but when he saw Emma he startled.

"Ms. Young! How are you? I haven't seen you since…well, since the accident."

"Morning, I'm good thanks," she answered him, trying to keep a normal front. "I was told there is an important message waiting for me this morning, do you know anything about that?"

Looking at her quizzically, he repeated, "Important message? Not that I know of. But maybe something was dropped in the bin overnight. I can go check. It's usually the first thing I do in the mornings; check whatever U.S. mail has delivered in there overnight. Sometimes locals drop their mail right in the slot as well, trying to avoid postage. I don't really mind. Not many folks know about it. I figure if they're so hard up they come out at night to drop their letters in a slot that only opens between midnight and six a.m., to save a few pennies, they probably need a little help."

Shrugging his shoulders apologetically, he went off in the back, only to return moments later with a large canvas bag stretched open on a metal frame. Dumping the contents on a sorting table behind the counter, he started putting the accumulated mail into piles. Waiting as patiently as she could, Emma felt the barely controlled frustration course through Gus, whose fingers were starting to squeeze her waist tighter and tighter. Shifting slightly to loosen his vice-like grip, she apparently caught his attention.

"Fuck me. Sorry, Peach. I didn't mean to..." Stopping him mid-sentence, by grabbing his face, she kissed him once, hard, on the mouth.

"It's okay. It's getting to me, too."

"Here is something addressed to you."

Waving an envelope around, the postmaster was barely able to take two steps before Gus was on him, snatching the paper from his hand.

"Hey. Wait a minute!"

Emma quickly intervened. "I'm so sorry, we've been waiting for this news and are a little impatient. Thanks so much for your help. We'll get out of your hair now." With a raised eyebrow at Gus, she turned to the door, expecting him to follow behind her.

Once outside, she turned to him.

"Can you hold off until we're in the truck?"

"Yeah, sorry. Hang on." Opening the doors, he lifted her in, tossed her walker in the back and jogged around to the driver's side. Once seated, he ripped open the envelope, and she scooted closer to read along with him.

-

DRIVE TO ENTRANCE MESA VERDE NATL. PARK

TEXT THE WORD "ARRIVED" TO 970 734 0234 FOR INSTRUCTIONS

-

Flipping the note over to check for anything else, Gus repeated the contents out loud for the benefit of those listening in.

"Do you think that means we interpreted Kara's words wrong? You think maybe she is inside the park?" Fear that perhaps they had been making all the wrong assumptions was crawling over Emma's skin, causing her to shiver.

With a quick flick of his eyes, Gus assured her. "No. Not necessarily. I'm thinking perhaps whoever has them, thought they might throw us off by directing us there; a place that would seem easy to disappear in. They know it would take a huge amount of manpower, equipment and time to search, so that makes it the perfect tactical distraction possible. They must figure we'd come somewhat prepared and might want to throw whoever is tracking us off their game, right?" When Emma nodded her agreement, he continued. "I am expecting to have to leave my truck behind at the very least, since that would be easiest to keep track of. But what they don't realize is that we already have a good idea of their whereabouts. Near the Mancos River on the east side of the park, somewhere visible from Point Outlook and somewhere that has good fishing. Or at least somewhere that reminded Kara of fishing."

Directing his voice to whoever was listening at the other side of the microphone, he added, "Check the area for anything along the river. Bait shops, fishing hangouts, any restaurants in the neighborhood that serve fish or seafood, even outfitters. It may be a long shot, but we have to consider she may have relayed anything she saw as landmarks as well."

214

Radiating confidence and completely in his element now, Gus was a sight to behold. As unsure and anxious as she had been before, looking at the big hulk of a man beside her with the intense and determined look on his face, she was amazed to feel her resolve and faith returning. There was no doubt in her mind they would find her girls. Not with Gus so focused and sharp.

Turning to face her, he even flashed her a grin. "Eyes sharp, Peach. We're looking for signs, businesses, and buildings, anything that has any of the words, or combination of the words in Kara's message. Counting on you, love," he said with a wink.

God, she loved this man. She wanted him in her life.

-

By the time they arrived at the turn off for Mesa Verde National Park, her eyes were gritty with the intense focus on every sign they passed by on buildings, road signs, or billboards. Other than Mesa Verde and some signage for the town of Mancos, a little further down the 160, she hadn't seen much that piqued her interest.

Gus pulled the Yukon into an empty parking spot to the left of the entrance gate and killed the engine. "Nothing on your side?" He wanted to know.

"Nope. Not a damn thing. So what do we do now?"

"We follow instructions and see what happens, but we have to try and leave some direction behind. If we can. We'll think of something, just be ready to improvise and remember that Caleb is still somewhere behind us. He can hear us and would've kept a safe distance." Pulling his phone out of his pocket, he started typing.

"Wait." She covered the phone with her hand. "Just one sec, please." Leaning her head back against the seat, she kept her eyes on Gus, as he waited her out. "*I love you*," he mouthed at her, making her smile.

"*Back atcha, Big Guy*," she replied soundlessly, all too conscious of all the ears that were listening in. Reaching for him, she slid her hand around his neck, and gently pulled him toward her, meeting his lips and pouring everything she couldn't say at that moment into their kiss. His hand came up to cradle her face as he pulled away and she could see a myriad of emotions swirling in the depths of his eyes. With one last kiss on the tip of her nose, he released her and went back to the text on his phone. Then they waited.

CHAPTER TWENTY-FIVE

The five minutes it took for a response to come back felt like an eternity. Gus looked at the screen and read it off out loud. "It says: Leave the car. Walk to exit and wait for Cortez cab. Do it now."

Turning to Emma, he smiled at her encouragingly. "Okay, here we go, darlin'. We're being picked up on the road. Assume we are still moving east of Mesa Verde, so focus in that direction. Keep an eye out for Cortez taxi cabs." The last was directed at their silent audience, the ones they were about to leave behind and had to trust would find other ways to keep track. Pulling out Emma's walker, he was just in time to catch her trying to jump out of the Yukon. "Easy there, tiger. Don't want you getting hurt. I was coming to get you."

"I know. I just want to go get her. Now."

The tightness around Emma's mouth was evidence of the determination and strength this woman had in spades. She completely blew him away. Almost running with her walker, he threw his arm around her shoulder, trying to force her to slow down a bit. "Darlin', you run off all that energy now, you might not have enough left later. Save it."

Irritated, she tried to shrug his arm off, but she must have seen the validity of his point, because she slowed down her gait.

They didn't have to wait long at the side of the road. As promised, a cab pulled up with the passenger side window rolled down. When Gus leaned down to peek in, an elderly man was at the wheel.

"You Emma Young?" He tried looking past Gus at Emma, but Gus persisted in standing in his way, glaring at him. "Look, young feller, I was told to pick up an Emma Young and her companion, who had some car trouble here. Now if it ain't you twos, I'm gonna hafta find 'em."

"It's us," Emma said from behind him, slipping around to the window. "Can you pop the trunk for my walker?"

"Sure thing, missy, need my help?"

"No thanks, we've got it." Pulling his sleeve as she moved to the back of the cab. "He seems pretty clueless, Gus. I doubt he's involved," she whispered.

"Of course he is, he just may not be aware of it. He may have some answers though."

He folded her walker into the trunk, closed it, and took her arm to help her in the backseat. Before he could close the door, she grabbed his arm and pulled him down.

"Don't do anything that might endanger the girls. We don't know who's watching or listening." Well damn. There was that. For all he knew they had this cab wired for sound, or would harm the old man, if he said anything. He couldn't go in demanding answers, but that didn't mean he couldn't chat a little.

"So," he started, "Did Triple A contact you?"

"Hell no. That'll be the day, won't it? Nah, he said he was her brother-in-law or something. Babysitting her little girl? Didn't sound too friendly, if you ask me, but what do I know? Said to drop ya'll at the Outlook's yard. Belongs to a buddy of his, he says. I'm guessing they'll pick up yer truck, too."

One look over his shoulder told him Emma had been listening as closely as he had to the ramblings of the old man.

Brother-in-law, Emma mouthed at him questioningly. Apparently that one caught her attention as well, and damned if that didn't send shivers down his spine. What kind of sick perverted game was being played out here? He wasn't allowing his mind to wander in the direction it wanted. Because at this point there was no way of exploring all the possible scenarios.

"So, erm…where is this yard you're taking us to? I'm none too familiar with the area, so I've never heard of it."

"Round the other side of Mesa Verde, right where the 37 and the 38 meet; just this side of Mancos on the river. Not too far. Pretty area. You drive down that road a ways, and you've got the high cliffs on the one side and the river on the other. Me and the missus used to drive all the way down to where the dirt road turns into a trail, and you can get close to the water. We'd bring a picnic or somethin'; spend a nice afternoon every now and then. Not soul around for miles. Fun times."

The hearty cackle that accompanied the old man's trip down memory lane elicited a snort from the backseat. Gus had a hard time not to crack a smile himself.

A shove in his back from the rear seat snapped him to attention. "Look. That sign says Outlook Point Yard right at the next exit," Emma pointed out.

"Yup," their driver confirmed. "Next exit is the 38. I purposely skipped the 37, 'cause it's full of potholes this year. The county and the town of Mancos are still bickering over who's gonna pay the bill to fix it up again. So it ain't getting fixed. 'Sides, turn in for the yard is off the 38 anyways. Coming right up."

-

The first hundred or so yards were paved, but after that the

38 was nothing but a packed dirt road. Emma's heart was pounding in her chest. She thought for sure she was going to be sick. Gus was trying hard to keep a light and easy banter going with the old man. All the while, she looked around her for something, anything that could prove to be helpful. Although at this point, she figured it would probably be moot. They were about to find out what it would take to get her girls back. Though she knew Gus was sure their back up was solid; she had to admit her confidence had wavered over the last half-hour. As it stood now, she was mentally preparing herself to hand herself over willingly. She would, without hesitation, as long as Kara and Arlene were let go. That was the only thing that mattered. And Gus. Oh God, he would fight tooth and nail over her. She would have to try and…

"Put that thought right out of your head, darlin'." Speak of the devil. He was leaning over the back of his seat, glaring at her. "Whatever it was that put that frown on your face, you can drop it right now. We're in this together. Just trust me, please?" His eyes were imploring her to comply without argument, which she grudgingly did. If only not to drag the old man in any further than he already might be.

They had only passed a handful of buildings before the cab turned into a driveway on the right, which was partially obscured from the road by tall bushes. Pulling up to a closed gate, the driver turned to Gus.

"It's closed. I don't get it."

"I'm sure they probably just went to pick up our truck. You go; they'll be here soon. What do I owe ya?"

"I charge a flat fee of thirty dollars for any Mesa Verde runs, but I'll take a twenty for this here short one."

Pulling some bills from his pocket, Gus took care of the fare.
Then he got out and scanned the surroundings, while collecting
her walker from the trunk. Only then did he come to open her
door and help her out. He leaned in to the driver's window. "You
might want to get yourself out of here. You're in a bit of a
precarious spot. If the tow truck comes back and turns into the
drive without looking too well, your pretty cab might be in the
way." A few good raps on the roof, and the old man clearly took
his words to heart as the cab peeled out of the driveway.

-

"How are you doing, Peach?" Gus checked in with her, as
she tried to fight off the panic that was threatening to overwhelm
her. The back end of the cab disappeared behind the bushes and
could be heard speeding off down the road. Left only was the
occasional sound of some heavy traffic that must have been
drifting down from Highway 160. Other than that, only sounds of
nature filled the air.

Hesitant to make any more noise than necessary, she
whispered, "Kinda freaked. What now?"

"Follow me." He indicated, before turning and heading
toward a smaller, man-sized gate on the far side of the chain-link
fence. "We're checking that out."

The entire yard, from what she could see, was filled with
cars. Mostly rusted and in various states of dismantlement, but
there were some that looked in better repair off to one side. To
the far left there was a large half-open barn, with the makings of
a car shop inside, from what she could make out. Attached to that
a small, rather decrepit one-story bungalow. Other smaller
buildings were scattered among the piles of rusting car debris.
They were obviously not used for anything particularly
important, since getting to them would be virtually impossible.

The most eye-catching structure was off to their right. A large metal contraption, which looked like an old-fashioned laundry press; except it held a car in its open jaw. Not a single living soul was in sight, and the entire scenario scared the hell out of her.

"Emma, come over here. Stick close by me." Looking over, she could see Gus had managed to get through the gate and inside the fence. She was about to leave her walker by the gate and only take her cane through, but Gus shook his head no and folded her walker to maneuver through the opening. "Not leaving that behind," he stated firmly. "We are going to check the house out first. It seems the most obvious place, but also the easiest to search while staying pretty much covered." Pulling a gun from the waistband of his jeans, it suddenly hit her how real and familiar this all seemed.

"Never realized you had that on you."

"Won't leave home without it, and wasn't told to come unarmed. So yeah, I have it on me." Draping his free arm around her shoulders, he led her to the ugly looking bungalow. "For now, maybe leave your walker here by the door, and simply hang on to the back of my jeans. Can you do that? I feel better with you behind me. That way you're covered at all times."

"Yeah, sure. Just don't drop me when I stumble or make any sudden moves," she tried to joke.

"Not gonna let you fall, darlin'. Promise."

Leading the way with her clutching the back of his jeans, Gus entered the hallway, making sweeping motions with his gun, trying to cover all the doorways that came into view. When they entered the last doorway at the end of the hall, he tried to quickly back her out again. But he was too late. She had gotten a quick glimpse of a red spattered wall and a body lying in a pool of blood.

"Don't look," he growled, as he tried to press her head into his chest.

"Too late," she mumbled into the fabric of his Henley. "Just tell me it's not them."

"Not them. A man. Looks to belong here. Wearing greasy coveralls and has been dead for a bit I'm afraid. Let's get out of here."

Once outside, the shakes hit and Emma was grateful for the sense of stability her walker gave her. Feeling a little guilty for the sense of relief that it wasn't Kara or Arlene lying in that pool of blood in the kitchen, she needed to take some action.

"Do you think we should we yell their names?" she wondered.

"Sure, wouldn't hurt. Whoever is around would already know we're here, anyway. I have a feeling we are pawns in a nasty little game, and I don't know the rules yet."

With that, Gus cupped his hands around his mouth and yelled out, "Kara! Arlene!"

She followed suit, yelling out their names over and over again. They slowly made their way into the yard, along the far left side. Suddenly, Gus motioned her to stop and be silent with his finger to his lips. Waiting to see if she could pick anything up, she heard it. It was very faint. A voice, but she couldn't make out what it was saying. It appeared to be coming from the opposite end of the yard. Spurred on, Emma started yelling again and moved toward where she thought the voice had come from, when she was held up by a strong arm around her waist. "Hold up, darlin'. You can't go walking out into the middle of the yard, unprotected. You might be walking into a trap. We have no idea who or what we're dealing with. We'll go together, but let's stick to the edge and not cross over the open yard. Okay? Let's pause in between calls, so we can actually listen, as well."

Rather than say anything, Emma simply nodded her head and trusted Gus to take the lead once again.

Slowly making their way around the yard, Gus urged her to call again. This time they could faintly make out, "Mom. I'm here…" in response. It almost made her fall to her knees in relief–hearing Kara's voice–if Gus's quick reflexes hadn't kept her on her feet.

"Oh shit." Gus stared across the open space to what she realized must be a car crusher, and when she followed his gaze, and spotted what he must have seen, all the blood seemed to freeze in her veins. Hands, and what looked to be a face, were pressed to the window of the truck that was clutched in the jaws of the massive machine. A small whimper left Emma's lips.

"I see you've found my surprise."

The unknown voice behind her had Emma whipping around and backing into Gus's chest, who had turned and was frozen in place.

"You like? Almost like a real family reunion, isn't it?" the man mocked.

CHAPTER TWENTY-SIX

This was it. That small tingle of unease that had wormed around in his gut all this time was standing in living color right in front of him. The suspicion he hadn't been willing to acknowledge for too long, because it seemed too far-fetched, had been right on the fucking money. Right up to the moment he looked at the man, he had hoped the fingerprints had not been his. That there could not be any way he was here. Involved in this huge fuck up of a case. There was no mistaking the resemblance, but only on the surface. The man in front of him was hard, especially his eyes, that shone full of cold hatred directed at him. His stance appeared to be relaxed, a gun held loosely, pointing at Emma. The other hand clutched a remote device, the total picture making him look like a symbol of vengeance. Undoubtedly the image he was going for.

"You're his brother," Emma gasped in front of him. He instinctively wrapped a protective arm around her midsection and pulled her back into his body. "What have you done with my daughter and Arlene? What do you want? Is it me? You can have me if you let them go. Please!" Emma's pleading had only served to plaster a satisfied grin on the bastard's face. Determined to stay in control of his boiling emotions, he kissed Emma on her head, whispering apologies in her hair. Never once did his eyes leave those of his brother, Will.

"How very heartwarming; both the plea and my brother's protection. But I'm sorry to disappoint you. I'm afraid you hold very little interest for me now, Ms. Young. That ship has sailed."

"I don't understand...I thought Silva...you don't work for

him?"

"Oh but I do; I guess I should say 'did'," he chuckled to himself. "Since I couldn't quite abandon this job the way I was instructed. And I'm sure Bruno is less than happy about that. But you see; it was the most serendipitous event for me, this assignment. I was supposed to keep an eye on you, Ms. Young, to see if Mr. Corbin showed his cowardly face. Then I was supposed to bring him in. Next thing I know, Bruno wants me to engage in a little break-and-enter, snatching any type of electronic storage devices. Imagine my surprise, when my little duplicitous brother here showed up at the scene. Only a glimpse, mind you, but that traitorous face of his has been burned in my brain, there was no mistaking it. And just like that a menial little job had turned into a beautiful opportunity for some justice. A chance thrown in my lap to give karma a little…assistance. What are the odds?" he said, broadly smiling, making Gus sick to his stomach.

He did this. Kara and Arlene getting hurt had never been about Emma, it was about him. About something he was responsible for, and the vaguely familiar sick feeling of carrying some kind of infectious disease slowly settled in his bones again.

Obviously pleased with himself, Will punched a button on the remote in his hand, and a loud metallic grinding noise started up, startling Emma.

"No!" Realizing what had just been set in motion, she threw up her hands as if to ward off what was happening. "Please stop it. Don't hurt them…take me. It's me you want…please!"

Gus was biding his time; he knew Caleb could not be far behind. And Joe had his eyes and ears on them as well, thanks to Neil's nifty work on Emma's walker. But they had better move fast, or he was going to have to move on his own. Turning to his brother, he confronted him.

"Innocents now, Will? This is how low you've sunk? You're willing to hurt a bunch of harmless, innocent women to try and get a rise out of me? Is that the best you can do?" The slight tic on the side of his brother's mouth was his tell he was trying not to let Gus's taunts get to him. So Gus pushed a little more. "Of course they're a bit easier to control, aren't they? And we both know you always liked things easy, using the uniform to push your weight around. No brains, little brawn, and now women. You were always a pussy."

By now, the veins in Will's forehead were standing out against the fiery red of his face. All traces of his smirk had disappeared, and his eyes were squinted down to glaring slits.

"Shut the fuck up. You little lying bastard! Traitor!"

Gus let out a loud laugh, while gently pushing Emma to the side, keeping his eyes firmly locked with his brother's hateful ones. "That's rich. Traitor? Seriously? Let's see what Silva's croonies in prison have to say when their favorite bitch is back, huh? Brother dear?"

Finally Will snapped, launching himself at Gus, who managed to give Emma one final shove to get her out of the way of the oncoming mass of fury.

But Emma had been prepared. Figuring out what Gus was playing at; she was waiting for something; anything to happen. She needed to get her hands on that remote. She had kept her eyes on the crusher as soon as the roof of the car had started pressing down and the windows had popped. There was still time. As soon as Gus gave her a shove and got tangled up with Will, Emma went for it. She tried to get her bearings and looked around for the controls. Finally spotting them half underneath the pile of pounding and punching limbs and body parts belonging to Gus and Will. She had no time to concern herself with that now. One focus and one only, and that was stopping that God-awful machine crushing the car holding her daughter and likely Arlene. On hands and knees, she inched closer to where she could try and snatch it, if the two men rolled the other way. Seeing her opportunity, she dove under the two struggling bodies. While her hand was trying to grab hold of the control unit, she felt something connect with her jaw. Before she even had a chance to push the button–for the third time in as many weeks–her world went black.

CHAPTER TWENTY-SEVEN

❖ One Day Earlier ❖

Arlene

Arlene swore that man was going be the death of her. Frickin' Seb: hovering and fussing, being all up in her face about where she was going and when she would be back. She was going to trip balls all over his ass if he didn't give her some room to breathe.

Ever since he had found out she had taken off after Emma in her truck with Caleb, he had been berating her for jumping in without thinking. Risking her life without using any common sense. Well. Her common sense told her loud and clear that she didn't need another controlling arsehole up her business. And certainly not one who was on her bloody payroll. Who the hell did he think he was anyway? Fine, she might at some point have felt a bit of attraction to the dangerous looking, inked up ex-con, who walked in looking for work. And it's possible that had a little something to do with why she gave him a chance to prove himself in her kitchen. She had to admit, there had been nights, where she fantasized about all the incredible things his skilled hands might be able to do to her body. But that sure as hell didn't give him the right to try and bully his way into her life.

Pulling up to Emma's porch, she could see Gus sitting on the porch, his head in his hands, looking dejected. The perfect subject for some of Arlene's early morning special.

"What'd you do? You get kicked out?" She had to laugh, it was so much fun to try and get a rise out of the big, unflappable man.

"Ha. No, more like I escaped. Kara caught us in a...let's say, compromising position this morning and it didn't go over too well."

Oh...this was too perfect for words. She would file this away for future torture of her bestie. But finding out Kara had gotten really upset and was crying, sobered Arlene a bit. Not enough to let Gus off the hook though, so she needled him a bit more before heading in to collect Kara, who she was supposed to take to the airport this morning.

"So how are you doing, honey?" She looked over at Kara, who was still sniffling a little beside her. She had walked in on a complete meltdown earlier and had marveled at the way Emma had managed to settle her daughter. And then again when she peeked out the window when Kara went outside to talk to Gus. The man had risen a few marks in her book right then. His calm acceptance of her slightly embarrassed apology obvious, when he wrapped his big arms around the girl. She doubted she would ever have had the patience to deal with kids. But she would never have to find out now, would she?

"I'm okay, thanks, Arlene." Kara met her eyes with a little smile brightening her face. "Just a little messed up in the head is all."

A snort escaped before Arlene could suck it back.

"Sorry, babe–those have got to be the words of the century. Welcome to the club," she said with a wink to Kara. "Gus is a good guy. Your mom is a smart cookie. And when she isn't, and if he fucks up, know that I'm here to kick his behind and set her straight. I'll be looking out for her by proxy–how's that? And you can call me anytime you think she isn't being straight with you, 'cause I am nothing if not straight. All right?"

Kara giggled a bit at that and nodded.

Next thing she knew, her body jerked and her hands flew off the steering wheel. At the same time a crunching sound came from behind her. Her eyes flew to the rearview mirror as her hands were groping to regain purchase on the wheel. She could see a tow truck backing away from her tail end. Pulling on the wheel to get her off to the side of the road, she could see the other truck pulling off on the shoulder as well.

"What the fuck was that?" Turning to Kara, she scanned the girl top to bottom, to make sure she was still in one piece. "You hurt, doll?"

"I'm good. What happened?"

"Some idiot just ran up the back of my truck. Hang on, I'm gonna see what's up with my back end."

No sooner had she opened the driver's side door; it was slammed right shut again, almost pinning the foot she was about to drop down.

"Hey! What…?" Before she managed to finish the expletive that was lodged in her throat, the door was yanked open again and the big body of a man squeezed in the opening, a gun leading the way. Kara screamed in the seat beside her, but Arlene reacted and hauled back her fist, aiming for his groin. Unfortunately, without any real punch behind it and from an awkward angle, the hit missed its intended target. It did nothing more than glance over a fucking sharp belt buckle, straight into a set of pretty hard abs. The only result a grunt from him, sore knuckles and a knock over the head with the gun for her. Damn.

A pounding headache kept her from opening her eyes. Even breathing friggin' hurt, but she could hear Kara softly crying.

"Shhhh." She tried, sending a dagger through her own head. Jesus F. Christ! He'd done a number on her. Breathing in deeply she tried again. "Kara, come here."

"I can't."

"Why not."

"I'm chained to the backseat and you're in front of me, handcuffed to the steering column."

Well damn. She hadn't even noticed that. Couldn't sense anything but the intense hammering in her head. Carefully pulling open one eyelid, the fading sunlight told her it was probably late afternoon or early evening.

"Christ, how long have I been out of it?"

"Most of the day. He held me at gunpoint after knocking you out, and had me sit here behind you and shackled me down. Hooked us up in the truck on the tow and pulled us to some kind of junkyard and onto this massive contraption. He hasn't said a word, simply unhooked us from the tow truck and left us here. That was hours ago. I think." She hesitated for a moment before continuing, "This is gonna sound crazy, but Arlene, he looked just like Gus. Same build, same coloring, same eyes, except this guy's eyes are hard and angry, and the lines in his face aren't kind-looking but mean. He also looks quite a bit older. It was creepy."

With her brain not functioning too well, Arlene wasn't able to process that information to satisfaction. Looked like Gus? Father? Brother? For all she knew, he had no family, but then again, what did she really know about him? Not one to sit back and wait for things to happen, this time Arlene really had not much of a choice. She was seriously incapacitated by the knock on her head and immobilized with handcuffs. So she simply closed her eyes again and waited.

"Arlene, are you awake? Wake up!" The whispering hadn't really registered until after the kicking of her seat had woken her up.

"Awake now," was her curt reply.

"Hush, I hear something, I think he's coming back."

Sure enough, the sound of boots hitting dirt and gravel was coming closer.

"Okay, let me do the talking," she said over her shoulder, which made Kara snort. "What's so funny?"

"Like I could stop you–besides I'm about scared dumb. Just please don't piss him off, Arlene. Okay?"

"Smartass. Not gonna piss him off, I'll be as sweet as one of your momma's pies." Earning her another incredulous snort from the backseat. Well! All her outward brawn didn't take away the creepy fear that swirled in the pit of her stomach, when she finally saw the man approaching. It was dark outside now and only the watery light from a few light posts over by the gate reached this far. The rest of what she could see was pitch black. No moon in her field of vision, but it was hard to tell with the high peak of Mesa Verde right there.

"You need to make a phone call," he said, as he climbed up the machine on which her truck was sitting to door level. "Not sure which one of you should make it for maximum effect." He seemed to ponder the question for a bit, not able to make up his mind.

"You leave her alone and pick someone your own age, you miserable piece of shit," Arlene spit out, not able to hold her tongue. "Just leave her out of your little games."

She was hoping to get him riled up, so his focus would be on her and not on Kara, who had started to sniffle again in the backseat. With a knowing smirk on his face, he turned to the cowering girl, pulled open the cab door and tossed her a key, while holding the gun trained on her head.

"Here, unlock yourself and hand me back the key."

Fuck. It would've been easier for Arlene to try and fight him for the gun if Kara was left in the truck. Now it looked like she would be left behind. But he surprised her when handing Kara another key as soon as she had herself unlocked and out of the cab.

"Now you can unlock her hands, but no funny stuff, I'm keeping the gun to your head at all times. So one wrong move from either of you and you, little one, will bear the consequences."

Swallowing down her rage, Arlene sat perfectly still, while Kara fumbled with shaking hands, trying to get the much smaller key to fit the handcuffs. Finally free, she rubbed her wrists, scraped raw by the hard metal and started to climb out of the cab after Kara.

"You wait," the man instructed her. "Wait until the two of us are down, I'll tell you when you can get out. Don't forget who's gonna suffer if you fuck up." His voice was almost without emotion; just a hard biting edge intended to instil fear. Dammit, she hated to admit it did.

After a minute or two, she was told to come down. She saw him standing with one arm wrapped around Kara's throat, and the other holding his gun against her head, a knowing smirk on his face. The girl, despite her decent height, was still a good head shorter. But Arlene had a few inches on Kara yet, and a decent number of pounds too. Although nothing near to matching the behemoth of a man they were facing, she figured she had better odds than most, given her size. But first she had to make sure Kara was out of the line of fire.

On the way across the yard, she tried to get some answers.

"What is it you want from us?" Which didn't get a response. Then as they got the dirty little house, she tried again. "Why don't you let her go? You don't need both of us."

And again. Nothing. Getting frustrated, she pushed a little harder.

"Look, I don't know what sick depraved plan you have, but I

can promise I won't make it easy on you unless you set her free."

"Bitch, shut the fuck up."

Okay. That was a response. Of sorts. Not a helpful one, but a reaction, and he seemed to have loosened his grip on Kara's neck a little. Maybe if she could piss him off enough, he would point that thing at her instead of Kara. But that was too risky.

"I'll shut up if I can use the bathroom. Been shut in that truck all day, I've gotta pee like a race horse."

"No."

"Fine, I'll pee right here then, in the house, and stink up the place for ya. Jesus, let me use the bathroom, will ya? What am I gonna do? You really think I'm going to risk you harming a hair on her head? Besides, I'm sure she needs to go too."

"You need to shut your mouth or I'll do it for you."

Enraged, he let go of Kara and stalked toward her, pointing the gun at her now. Just one more little push and hopefully Kara could get away.

"Better men than you have tried, without success, I might add." Watching his approach, she focused on his gun hand. When he was almost close enough to put his hands on her, she ducked low and charged into his midsection, surprising him, but not enough for him to drop the gun. A shot went off, luckily missing her by a hair. She kept trying to muscle him backward, trying to force him to the ground, but it was no use, the man was fucking rooted like one of those big giant sequoia trees. So she yelled at Kara to run, to get out and run as fast as she could. All the while trying to fight with hands and feet, even biting wherever she could; anything to distract him long enough for Kara to get away. Last thing she remembered was one of his big hands around her throat, slamming her head repeatedly into the floor.

Someone was pulling at her, mumbling swear words. She couldn't make out much that made sense, just snippets.

"Leave me alone…" she managed to croak out. "Just don't touch me anymore..."

"Jesus, woman, I'm gonna spank your hide if you live through this, I swear to God."

Wait. What was Seb doing here? So confused.

"Grab her feet, Kara, we've got get her down before the whole roof caves in."

Kara was still here? She didn't understand any of it. So tired…

CHAPTER TWENTY-EIGHT

Gus had tried keeping half an eye on the car crusher as he was taunting Will. He knew they didn't have much time to get the women out of their precarious situation. He also couldn't lose sight of the fact that Emma was squarely in the sight of his brother's gun. With the hatred gleaming in his eyes, he had no doubt Will wouldn't hesitate to pull the trigger, just to hurt him where he must have realized it would have the most impact. What he hadn't counted on was Emma throwing herself in the fray, trying to get a hold of the controls. Stupid. He should've known that she would not be content to sit by the sidelines. She got knocked out good. Again. Jesus. Her poor body didn't deserve all the abuse.

Struggling to avoid the worst of his brother's raging punches, he focused his hold on the gun hand, making sure the barrel stayed far away from his body. Wishing with all that was holy that Caleb wouldn't wait too long to show his mug, or he might not be able to hold on much longer. All the noise was starting to blur together: the grinding of the crusher, Will's swearing and growling as his fist was pounding Gus's face to pulp, even Gus's own grunts with every hit that found its mark. He tried to twist and turn his body underneath to shield his face as best he could–holding on to the gun with both hands. Despite that, more than just a few made it through and his eyes started swelling shut.

Suddenly the weight was lifted off him, and with his one half open eye, he saw Caleb with a handful of sheriff's deputies wrestling Will to the ground and cuffing him. In the next moment, he was scrambling around on hands and knees, trying to find the controls.

"Caleb!" he tried yelling out. "The girls–they're in the crusher …"

"We've got them, Boss. Medics are en route. Lay back, we'll take it from here."

He rolled over and dragged himself to Emma, who seemed to be coming to, a red welt on her jaw where she got hit in the struggle.

"Hey, baby." Stroking her cheek, he waited for her to open her eyes. "We're quite the pair." Blinking a few times, her eyes finally focused on his face and widened in shock.

"Oh my God, Gus, your poor face." Only to be followed with; "The girls, where are they? Are they okay? Please tell me they're okay." Emma struggled to sit up, but he held her down, wanting her to take it easy.

"They're fine, they got out. I haven't seen them yet, but Caleb said they got out. Medics are on the way."

"Is it over?" Her big blue eyes are looking at him.

"Yeah, Peach. I think it's over."

The voice of her daughter had her struggling up from the stretcher, where the EMT had insisted she remain, while they examined her properly.

"Mom! I just need to see my mother, please? Mom, are you in here?"

"Yes, baby, let me see you. Come here." Pulling Kara in a tight hug, she couldn't care less what the damn EMT told her, or what anyone wanted her to do, for that matter. She needed to hug her daughter tight, and then she needed to go home. No damn hospital stay again.

Kissing her hair, she asked her girl how she was holding up.

"I was pretty much a mess, Mom, but Arlene–she rocked. She has no fear, I swear to God. She did everything she could to protect me, even got herself beaten so bad." At Emma's sharp intake of breath, Kara burst into tears. "Oh no, you didn't know?"

All moisture suddenly dried from her mouth and throat, as fear grabbed hold of her. "Know what? Tell me what happened to Arlene? Is she okay?" She couldn't help the trembling in her voice.

"She fought for me, Mom, wanted me to run, but I couldn't leave her, I…I just couldn't. He just kept slamming her head into the floor, and I started screaming at him to stop because she wasn't moving. The whole night he had me back chained into that truck, and I didn't know what happened to her. This morning he carried her out and just threw her in the front seat. She looked so bad, but I could see her chest moving."

When she took a deep shuddering breath, Emma interrupted, "Honey, you are killing me here. Is she okay? Where is she? Please…"

"Sorry. She's on her way to Cortez, she was saying some stuff when Seb pulled us out, it was all a bit jumbled, and she looks a mess. They took her right away in the ambulance with flashing lights and all."

"Seb pulled you out? I'm so out of the loop. Okay, here is the deal. Can you find Gus for me? He needs to get looked at, and then I want us to go to the hospital."

The EMT perked up at that and tried to get her to lay back down to strap her in for the ride, but she set him straight.

"No. Not riding in the back of an ambulance. I got knocked out in a scuffle, plain and simple. My reflexes are good. I know the date, month, and year and who the president currently is. I am not a bloody invalid! Now get me out of this damn truck."

She wrestled herself off the stretcher, out of the ambulance, and found herself face-to-face with a grinning Gus.

"I need my walker," she said at no one in particular, and then directly at Gus, "What are you laughing about?" When his grin turned into a chuckle.

"Not an invalid, darlin'? Here, let me find you your walker."

"Oh. Shut up." But she couldn't hold back a smile at her own ridiculous outburst. Blame it on stress, or whatever. "Wait, don't you need to get checked out?"

"Aren't we heading for the hospital in Cortez?" he asked with an eyebrow raised.

"Smartass." Was the only reasonable response she had.

CHAPTER TWENTY-NINE

Sitting on her own shower stool, with the hot water pounding down on her, for the first time in weeks, not feeling rushed, or anxious, or unsure, was blissful. The stress from the past few weeks was being pounded out of her tight muscles. The strong pulses from her deluxe showerhead, made her skin tingle and had her moan out loud.

"Sounds like I'm missing something good." Gus's deep voice came from the door opening where he was leaning, quietly observing.

"You snuck up on me." She smiled at him. "Gonna stand there and watch?"

"That an invitation?" His hands were already reaching for the hem of his shirt.

"Open invitation for you, Big Guy."

"Hmmmm, sounds good. Get ready 'cause I'm coming in hungry."

In no time flat, stripped naked, he sank on his knees in front of her and grabbed the loofah and soap. "Lean back against the wall, baby. I want to wash you."

Doing as he asked, she settled back against the tile and closed her eyes. The water was soothing and Gus lifted first one arm and then the other, using the loofah to rub soap into her skin with a firm circular motion. Neck and shoulders, then down to her chest and breasts, where he spent some time teasing. Kissing and nibbling on her, by now, very erect nipples. Sucking one between the roof of his mouth and tongue before letting it go with a plop and moving to the other side. She was in turn languid with relaxation and squirming in need. Leaving her breasts after that little appetizer, he took his loofah over the soft rolls of her belly. She had long given up trying to hide herself from him. It only seemed to aggravate him, and he really did seem to find pleasure in all aspects of her, hard and soft…so she just let herself be as she was. And he appreciated all of it, and showed her by gently cleaning her bellybutton. He then used the fingers of his hands to slip and slide between every fold her body had shaped. His fingers simply tracing every contour of her, almost reverently. From her waist he moved right down to her legs, which received the same treatment, ending with a delicious foot massage on either side. Back to languid. Very much so.

"Not done with you yet, Peach. I save the best for last." His already deep voice even lower with the contained arousal that was evident in his eyes. Well, and his almost purple, straining erection.

"Changing position for this one." With that, he pulled her up, sat down in her place, and turned her around to have her straddle his thighs.

"Perfect. My face in your luscious tits, and my hands and cock within reach of your ass and pussy. Just the way I like it."

Seeing his face up close had her flinch.

"Your face sore, babe?"

"Not too bad, and not bad enough to keep me from doing this." Planting his face right in between her breasts, licking at the moisture collecting there. His hands were busy soaping up between her butt cheeks very thoroughly. So thoroughly in fact, she was sure once or twice a finger slipped inside her anus, causing her to hiss air between her teeth at the slight burning, but oh so good sensation.

"I love having all this access from all sides. Being able to put my hands anywhere on you, opening you up further, just by moving my own legs wider. Kiss me. Let me taste you."

Wrapping her arms tighter around his neck, she sealed her lips on his and slid her tongue along the seam of his mouth, gaining entrance. All the while, he continued playing with her sex, sliding his fingers through her wetness and dragging it to her clit to tease, and her puckered hole behind, to finger her ass. Something she found she surprisingly enjoyed. Pulling his hands clear for a moment, she almost whimpered.

"Would you lean over and grab what's in the front pocket of my jeans?"

"But I'll get them all wet."

"Don't care. Just grab it."

Reaching over and sneaking her hand into his pocket, realization caused a snicker to burst free as she pulled out one of her little pink toys. This one, a long silicone bullet: good for clit stimulation and shallow penetration. She had no idea what he had in mind, but remembered the promise he made on the first night they met.

Taking the vibrator from her, he played with it through her wet folds for a bit, before sliding it in and out of her pussy a few times, making it nice and wet with her juices.

"Slide down on my cock, baby. I want you to ride me if you can. You can use the grab bar above my head for extra leverage and I'll help."

Grabbing on to the bar above his head, she pulled herself up and slowly sank down on him, until he was buried and she felt completely filled. That is, until one of his hands pulled her cheeks apart and the other slowly pushed the vibrator into her butt. She felt a brief stretching sensation before the slow buzz from the bullet pushed her in sensory overload. It immediately had her grinding her pelvis down on his dick, trying to reach a massive orgasm that she could feel building.

Incoherent and pleading, she was wild for release. And when the vibrations were turned up a notch, almost making her scream.

"I'll get you there, sweetheart. Hang on." Grabbing her hip with one hand, Gus started thrusting his hips up in tandem with Emma's grinding down. When he could feel the tightening of the walls of her pussy, he took his hand off the vibrator and slid it between them, pressing his thumb down firmly on her clit, finally sending her over. And she was taking him with her. Lost in the contractions of her body, he was unable to hold back and could feel the long strands of seed pumping from his cock.

His back against the tile, his woman draped over him, sated, his dick still inside her getting soft. He was happy. He never had known this kind of feeling before, but he was sure this had to be it. The moment in time where everything could stop, just as it was and never change, and it would be absolute perfection. This was it. Happiness. Who'd have thought?

Especially since just the day before, they probably had one of the worst days of their lives. Both of them were still exhausted, as was Kara. She opted to bunk with Dana in the motel, rather than take the couch or even sleep in the bed with Emma. She wouldn't hear of it. Luckily she had incurred no physical damage, but he was pretty sure she would do well with some counseling for the emotional trauma.

Then there was Arlene, who would be okay, physically, even

though she had had a beating worse than he had. And apparently had fought like a tiger. Both her and Emma were women to be reckoned with. Part of him was proud of them, but another part wanted to tan their hides. Although by the sounds of it, Seb had already called dibs on Arlene's hide. Yeah, physically she would heal, but something was off about her and that worried Gus. She never quite was clear on what happened overnight, claiming she was out cold for most of it. But there was a shadow in her eyes that wasn't there before. She might want to visit a shrink too, although he had a feeling she'd have to be hauled kicking and screaming. So he'd leave that up to Seb as well. One fiery independent woman was handfuls enough for him.

"Babe, what are you thinking so hard about?" Emma mumbled in his neck. "I can hear the wheels turning."

Chuckling, he said, "Just thinking about my fierce woman."

"Well, this fierce woman is starving."

Giving her a slap on her butt, he nudged her upright. "Get up then. Off with you. How about you get dressed and I'll get breakfast cooking for a change?"

Her eyebrows about in her hairline, Emma gasped, "You can cook? Get out of town!"

By the time Emma walked into the kitchen, he had a green pepper, mushroom and cheese omelet sliding onto plates. The coffee was perked and bread was popping out of the toaster. Perfect timing to make the ultimate impression, he smiled to himself.

"Well damn. You can cook. And it smells great." Emma sat down on a stool at the counter, watching him put the final touches on breakfast, when a knock at the door announced the first interruption of the day. Gus was pretty certain it wouldn't be the last.

Opening the door, he found Joe waiting on the other side, looking a little the worse for wear. "What are you doing out and about again? Haven't you had enough of us?" He teased his friend.

"Ugh...don't give me a hard time, please. Bloody Naomi has been on my case already."

"Yeah, well. Considering she's the physician who treated you for a nasty gunshot wound and also, you look like crap, you might want to take whatever she says a little more seriously." Inviting Joe to sit down with them in the kitchen, he added a third plate and divvied up the omelet between them. Then he made some extra toast and poured them all a coffee.

"This case is coming to a head, Gus, I can't not be in the midst of things right now." Joe grabbed his cup in both hands, looking at Gus with some concern. "Besides, I needed to give you the lowdown on your brother's interviews from last night. Agents from the Durango FBI field office were going to come in this morning to have a go at him because of his connections to Silva. And get this–those connections apparently go back as far as his days in the Detroit police force."

Stunned by that bit of information, Gus needed a minute to process. "You mean that little example of police corruption was at the hands of Silva?"

"Apparently so. And not only that, the FBI had their

suspicions all this time. There have been pockets like this over several larger police forces throughout the country."

"Why the hell wasn't I informed of this?" Putting both hands in his hair, he pulled in frustration. "No. Scratch that. What I'd really like to know is how it is possible to have me assigned to this task force, when the powers that be knew all along my brother was involved with the same man who was under investiga..." His eyes opening wide, he roared out in anger and slammed his fist on the counter as the twisted truth of it all hit him. "You guys fucking set me up! You used me as bait. Worse, you decided to use Emma as bait, just to be able to get a hand on one of Silva's inner circle. You bastards!" He saw blood and had Joe up by the collar against the kitchen wall, before Emma's voice broke through the raging in his ears.

"Gus–Let him go. He's trying to tell you something, you've gotta let him go."

Reluctantly loosening his grip on Joe's neck, he took a step back, put his hands on his hips and waited.

"I swear to you, I had no idea. Gus–think about it. Do you think the FBI would let a lowly chief deputy of a county sheriff's office in on the secrets of a national investigation? Think!" Walking back to the counter, he sat down heavily and took a long drink from his coffee. "I started suspecting something when the fingerprints came back from the rental truck they found. I found out the same time you did, that they belonged to your brother. At the same bloody time, Gus. You could've come to the same conclusions I did."

"Wait." Emma was holding up a hand, her eyes searching his face, anger evident in hers. "You knew about your brother's involvement before Kara and Arlene were taken?"

Fuck, fuck, fuck. How was he going to explain that he hadn't wanted her to know how soiled he had felt, how guilty, how responsible, for her life possibly being invaded and threatened by someone of his own family? He settled for a simple. "Yeah."

"Out. Get out. I can't believe this. You asked me to trust you? Even knowing what we would be walking into, you asked me to trust you? Knowing you were lying to me the whole time? Get the fuck out of my house, Gus."

Like a punch to his midsection, all the air was sucked out of his lungs, and he was left gasping for his next breath. Emma stalked off to her bedroom and slammed the door.

"Christ, I'm sorry, buddy, I had no idea you hadn't told her."

"I was so ashamed, Joe," he choked out. "Just the thought that someone related to me might be responsible for putting her through all that misery simply was too much. I was struggling with the urge to want to kill my own brother for all that was done to my woman. And damn if that wouldn't make me as miserable a bastard as he was." Sinking down on a stool, he let his head hang down, dejected. "I can't blame her for wanting me gone. Especially not after finding out I was part of an elaborate bait operation, even if I wasn't aware of it myself."

Pushing himself off, he gathered plates and cups, quickly washing them in the sink.

"Come on, let's leave her alone." He clapped his friend on the shoulder. Joe stopped him at the door.

"Gus? You're an idiot."

249

CHAPTER THIRTY

"So how long are you gonna make him suffer?" Arlene wanted to know when Emma went to visit her in the hospital with Kara, later that morning. Kara had already given her hell for sending Gus packing, telling her she was being way too harsh and not thinking things through. Now here was Arlene, the one person she had expected to back her up one-hundred-percent, questioning her as well?

"What the hell is wrong with you people? The man lied to me. About something pretty damn important, I might add. And don't start on me about how it must've all been a big shock to him. I get that that. But what you guys don't get is that he should've trusted me enough to tell me, knowing it wouldn't have made a difference."

"I get that, Ems, but aren't you cutting off your nose to spite your face? You're making your point, but does he know why it is you are really so mad at him? Did you bother to explain this to him? He isn't a mind reader either, you know," Arlene scolded her. Fuck if she didn't have a point.

"Well, shit. You know I hate it when you're being all reasonable."

Chuckling, Arlene patted her hand. "Always more sides to a point than the one you're sitting at, Bestie."

"Why don't you kiss my ass, Arlene?"

"Not planning to any time soon, but I happen to know the name of someone who would gladly," she deadpanned, sending

Kara into a fit of giggles.

"All right, you two. Enough of that. I guess I'd better see if I can find the man and have a chat."

Kara chose to keep Arlene company a bit longer and promised to hitch a ride with Seb later, who would be by after the lunch rush at the diner. So Emma was alone when she pulled into the motel parking lot, keeping an eye open for the familiar Yukon. She knew it had been retrieved from the Mesa Verde parking lot by a deputy the day before, but she didn't see it. Dana's rental was there though, so Emma got out of her Escape and knocked on the door of the unit she knew housed the team's temporary headquarters.

"Hey, it's you," Dana said, as she pulled the door open. "Come in. We're just packing up and getting ready to head back to Grand Junction. I was going to stop in to say goodbye before hitting the road, though, but you saved us a trip."

Of course, they would be heading home. Her mind hadn't even processed this far. She was going to miss them, Dana especially.

"I'm just now clueing in that you guys have a home to go to. I'm so sorry; I've been so self-absorbed, I never even stopped to consider all you left behind. I feel awful now."

"Nonsense, no one is waiting for us at home. My kids are all grown and too busy for me most of the time, and Neil is single and his family is back in Denver, right, Neil?" she said over her shoulder to the man in question, who was on his knees under a table, trying to untangle a knot of cables.

"Hey, Neil, didn't see you there."

"Emma, so happy it's over for you." Looking a bit sheepish he added, "How's Kara this morning, she doing okay after yesterday's ordeal?"

"Yes, thanks, she'll be alright, although I'm thinking the worst of is probably still going to hit, but we'll be ready. Thanks."

"No problem, erm…tell her I said hi, and it was nice meeting her, okay?" A ruddy blush was creeping up the young man's cheeks, as he was doing his best to avoid her eyes. If she wasn't mistaken, someone had a wee thing for her daughter.

"Sure thing."

"Can I get you anything?" Dana wanted to know.

"No thanks, I was actually just looking for Gus."

"Well, he's already gone. You missed him by about thirty minutes. Came in, told us to pack up and go home, and said he had to get back right away." Seeing the shock on Emma's face, she grabbed her hand. "Did he not say goodbye? That's not like him–Did something happen? Emma?"

By now big tears were rolling down Emma's face. She could not believe he up and left. Well. She did tell him to. But she only meant for him to leave her house, to give her some breathing space. Would he have heard it that way, though? Could he have thought she was cutting him off completely? She may have just fucked up big.

Decidedly uncomfortable with the drama unfolding in the motel room, Neil skipped out, claiming a sudden need for coffee, leaving Emma with a fussing Dana.

"Oh, honey, did you two fight?"

Bawling and using up the one measly, little box of tissues assigned to the room, Emma spilled everything to the older woman: from her insecurities to his patience with her, from their instant connection to their declarations of love. Concluding with their promise of honesty to his lies by omission and her subsequent reaction.

"I see." Was all Dana said.

"What do you mean, you see?" She sniffled.

"Did he tell you how he came about starting up GFI?"

"What's GFI?"

"That's the name of his investigative company, Gus Flemming Investigations. Did he tell you anything about his family?"

"Yes, he did. Everything actually, at least I think so."

"So you know that he carries a lot of guilt over putting his father and brother away, and his father dying in prison. And you also know that until his mother, whom he was very close to, fell ill with Alzheimer's, he hadn't seen her for many years because she blamed him as well. He must've mentioned his wife's abandonment when things got tough. And frankly, that's about all the experience he's had. People get mad or disappointed, they walk away. In his world, there is no turning back from that, he's never had anyone fight with him and stay. Do you get what I'm saying?

Yes, she did. She understood perfectly. She had effectively enforced his belief that love came with a myriad of strings, conditions, and restrictions. And if even one was broken, it was over. Instead of making him see that despite disagreements, arguments, and trust issues, love was always a good cause to fight for. Dammit. She really did need to fix this fast.

"I gotta go." Getting up, she gave Dana a big hug before making her way to the door, where she stopped and turned around.

"Oh, could you write me down the address for his home and office? In case he won't answer my calls?"

"Absolutely." Dana smiled, already grabbing for pen and paper.

CHAPTER THIRTY-ONE

To say Kara and Arlene were angry at her would have been an understatement, but at this point, it wasn't enough to make her reconsider. Neither of them apparently thought she should or could drive to Grand Junction on her own. She kindly, but firmly, reminded them that a scant three months ago, she drove all the way across the frickin' country by herself! Then they went on to state the obvious, like why didn't she call instead of going. Seriously? Of course she had called, but the man wasn't answering his phone. Or maybe just not calls from her. She didn't know, and didn't care anymore, at this point. All that mattered was getting to him and setting this straight, once and for all.

She hated things breaking down because of lack of proper communication. She hated it even more when she was to blame for it.

-

So here she was, on the road, just leaving Cortez behind; a small overnight bag, her medication, and a map on the passenger seat beside her with what was supposed to be the fastest route. It would take her through Utah, which made no sense to her, but whatever. She would apparently pass through Moab, which she had heard was gorgeous and hadn't had a chance to visit yet. Maybe on the way back…

An odd sense of well-being came over her. After spending the last few weeks under constant scrutiny, and for the most part, confined to her house or restricted in her movements, she felt quite liberated and free. Whizzing down the highway, by herself, chasing down the man she intended to fight for, love, and keep forever.

Disabled, my ass!

Next chance she had, she wanted to stop for some gas and a few snacks, so she could drive right through without anymore stopping. She was anxious to find Gus, battling down the occasional pang of fear that it might be too late. She was probably not too far behind him, only an hour or so. On the off chance he might stop somewhere for food, she would drive through any town slowly, checking to see if she could spot his Yukon.

Assuming he was on the same route, although it being the fastest way, that seemed likely.

=

Passing through a place named Pleasant View, she didn't really see anything, except an old grain elevator and a few outbuildings. No gas station. She really had to get filled up before long but hadn't wanted to turn east into Cortez to get it. She was heading in the opposite direction. Fuck. The gage was hitting the red zone on her dashboard. Better find something soon or her sorry ass was going to be stranded by the side of the road. And that'd be that for this rescue mission.

It wasn't much longer before she drove into a little town. She hadn't seen a sign, or maybe she missed it, but it sure looked big enough to have gas somewhere. It took her until she was almost through town to find a pump on the opposite side of the road.

Pulling in, she was pleased to see that attached to it was a small sized supermarket. Perfect. She could scoot in after she filled up and grab some food and drinks.

Gassed and paid, she pulled the car up to the market and

pulled out her walker. Inside, she popped a basket on top and grabbed some fruit, water bottles, and a box of crackers and headed to the cash register. There she also snagged a few chocolate bars, for energy.

"Excuse me," she asked the pretty young woman manning the register. "Where am I exactly? What's the name of this town?"

"Dove Creek. You're in Dove Creek." She smiled.

"Huh, such a pretty name. Fits the place. Thanks…" Taking a quick peek at her name tag, she replied, "Rena. Have a great day."

"You, too."

The bag with reinforcements perched on the seat of her walker, she pushed open the door, just as it was pulled from the outside. With the forward pressure, she went stumbling outside, and would've landed face first, if a strong arm hadn't caught her mid-fall. A strong arm that felt very familiar. And a smell that was familiar too.

"Gus," she breathed out, when her eyes finally reached his face. "I was coming after you."

Picking up her groceries and pulling her and her walker to the side of the door, he turned to her.

"Good to know, Peach, 'cause I decided I couldn't leave, so I was coming back to you. Prepared to tie you down and carry you off, if I had to."

"I'm sorry…" they both started at the same time.

"I need to go first," Emma said. "I was angry, and had reason to be angry, but I should've explained what the reason was. Instead, I let you think up your own reasons, and they were probably way worse than the truth. I didn't want you to leave for good, Gus. I just needed space to cool down. I was mad. Not done." Putting her hand up to his cheek, she claimed his full attention. "I didn't stop loving you."

He dropped his forehead against hers, not once losing eye contact.

"I'm an idiot." She snorted at that. "I know, everybody has told me so, myself included. But you kind of go with what you have been taught to expect, you know? That's not a reflection on you; it is on me. My head knows this, my heart seems to need a little time to get used to things, it's way out of practice, you see." He gave her a little wink and wrapped her in his arms, his back against the wall.

"You know, I had some time to think in the car alone, on my way to Grand Junction. By the time I got to Monticello, I knew I was making a mistake, running off the way I was. So I was coming back to fight for you. For just about the best thing ever to happen to me. And all the way here, I was thinking of a way to run my business from Cedar Tree, even part of the time. I like it there, if you don't mind me hanging around." Emma looked up at him with shiny eyes, and he took the invitation to kiss the stuffing out of her, until someone very loudly cleared their throat. When Gus looked up, an older couple was standing a few feet away, eyeing them with obvious disapproval. Huffing once more, they stalked off into the store, leaving Emma and him chuckling.

"I guess this isn't the most romantic of places for a make up, make out session, is it?" he concluded.

"Oh, I don't know, the name is pretty enough–Dove Creek–I just found that out. It has a romantic ring to it, I think."

"Either way, we should probably get out of here. Head back to Cedar Tree and put everyone's mind at rest? And my mind and certain other parts of my anatomy could use some attention as well." He smirked.

"I'll call pest control." Was Emma's retort, jumping to get out of his way when he tried to tickle her side in retribution.

"By the way, Big Guy, how come you happened to stop here?" She wanted to know.

"Was coming to grab a drink and a chocolate bar, for energy."

"Really? I've got some, I'll share."

Looking down at Emma standing beside her Escape, Gus can't help but wonder out loud.

"Three weeks ago, who'd have thought…"

Stroking her cheek with the back of his hand, he leans in to kiss her sweetly.

"What are the odds? Hey, Peach?"

EPILOGUE

"Hello?"

"Hey, you..." She heard a deep, sleepy man's voice.

"Uhm...hi? Do I know you?" she asked, grinning, knowing full well who was on the other end.

"I sure fucking hope so," he growled back at her, obviously not amused. "I have my hand full with a hard-on here, with your name on it, woman. And by all accounts, that pussy of yours should be getting wet right now by the sound of my voice–and no one else's."

"Hmmmm, gonna have to check the validity of that statement, darlin'. Oh yeah, my fingers are sliding through all these delicious juices, just waiting for your tongue." She can't hold back the little groan that leaves her lips, as her fingers encounter the hard little nub of her clit, proudly peeking out from her slick sex.

"Fuck, Emma, you're killing me here. I was just supposed to call to let you know I'll be leaving shortly. I have the U-Haul already hooked up and am ready to go, but now I have this raging hard-on to rub out."

"Payback is only fair, Big Guy. Remember, I have had my little pink toys to keep me company these last few weeks, while you've been packing up your shit. Although fun enough, they don't near measure up to the real thing. You hear me? I need you. Badly."

"Darlin', save it for me, please. I'm heading out now. No

stops. And when I get there, get the wedges ready; be naked, 'cause I'm coming straight for you. Can't fucking wait to be home, for good."

A smile on her face, Emma countered, "Can't wait for you to get here. Hurry. I love you"

"Love you, Peach. Be ready, I'm not done with you."

-

After hanging up, Emma grabbed her cane and made her way in to the kitchen. She poured herself another cup of coffee before pulling out her bag of flour and the mixing bowls. The crate of peaches Arlene just dropped off yesterday was still sitting on the porch. Baking was a good way to kill some time, and Gus would love to have a choice for dessert, she thought with a grin.

THE END

ABOUT THE AUTHOR

Freya Barker inspires with her stories about 'real' people, perhaps less than perfect, each struggling to find their own slice of happy, but just as deserving of romance, thrills and chills, and some hot, sizzling sex in their lives.

Recipient of the RomCon "Reader's Choice" Award for best first book, "Slim To None," Freya has hit the ground running. She loves nothing more than to meet and mingle with her readers, whether it be online or in person at one of the signings she attends.

Freya spins story after story with an endless supply of bruised and dented characters, vying for attention!

Freya

https://www.freyabarker.com

http://bit.ly/FreyaAmazon

https://www.goodreads.com/FreyaBarker

https://www.facebook.com/FreyaBarkerWrites

https://tsu.co/FreyaB

https://twitter.com/freya_barker

or mailto:freyabarker.writes@gmail.com

ACKNOWLEDGEMENTS

There are a great many people I owe thanks to. Many of whom I have met through the incredibly tight and welcoming world of Indie writers and bloggers.

First and foremost I have to thank my family; my hubs and all our combined kids for putting up with my cranky self when I didn't want to be disturbed and was too preoccupied to move from behind my iPad to listen to your stories or cook a decent meal.

To Gina Sorelle, who showed me that writing about 'less than perfect' people was not only possible; it could be beautiful and exquisite. Gina, you are a treasure and an example.

To Debra Kayn, without whose encouragement I wouldn't have put the first word on paper. Debra, you are a consummate professional and a dear friend.

To Brook Greene for the best line ever!! It fit Arlene perfectly! Muah!

To an amazing group of authors who have encouraged, pushed, corrected and supported when I needed it. Brook Greene, Jaci J. and Ava Manello. Ladies, having you at my back has been priceless. I would have truly been lost without you!!

To my beta-readers Linda, Deb, Bonnie, Helen, Kim and especially Catherine, I asked you to give it to me straight, since I prefer it honest and without frills, and you did. I can't tell you how much I appreciate that! You are the best!!

To Karen Hrdlicka, an amazing editor, a great friend and fantastic human being. Thank you with all my heart.

And last but most definitely not least, a very heartfelt and special thanks goes out to Dana Hook. She has become a treasured friend, a great colleague and a loved family member.

The loudest mouth - the biggest heart - the sweetest smile. I love you tons!

ALSO BY FREYA BARKER

CEDAR TREE SERIES:

SLIM TO NONE
HUNDRED TO ONE
AGAINST ME
CLEAN LINES
UPPER HAND
LIKE ARROWS
HEAD START

PORTLAND, ME, NOVELS:

FROM DUST
CRUEL WATER
THROUGH FIRE
STILL AIR

NORTHERN LIGHTS COLLECTION:

A CHANGE OF TIDE
A CHANGE OF VIEW
A CHANGE OF PACE
(Coming soon!)

ROCK POINT SERIES:

KEEPING 6
CABIN 12

(Coming soon!)

SNAPSHOT SERIES:

SHUTTER SPEED
FREEZE FRAME
IDEAL IMAGE
PICTURE PERFECT
(coming soon!)

Made in the USA
Monee, IL
28 October 2020